SOME GIRLS DROWN

CONTENT WARNING

This is an almost true story woven from heartfelt memories. The events might not unfold in the exact sequence they occurred, and some names may have been gently altered. Details have smudged over time, and not every word can be recalled with perfect accuracy. There are moments too fragile to share fully, and so, I leave them in the silence between the lines.

© 2025 Jessica Bell. All rights reserved.

No part of this book may be reproduced, stored in a retrieval system, or transmitted in any form or by any means, electronic, mechanical, photocopying, recording, or otherwise, without the prior written permission of the copyright owner.

CONTENT WARNING

This book contains explicit depictions and discussion of childhood sexual abuse, familial trauma, emotional and physical abuse, and the lasting psychological impacts of these experiences. Some scenes may be distressing or triggering for readers. Discretion is advised, and we encourage readers to prioritise their well-being and seek appropriate support if needed.

CONTENT WARNING

For my children.
I will *always* fight for you

Chapter One

AGE 7

Ayanna stood just inside the front hall of Granny's cottage, pressing herself against a wall and fiddling with the hem of her dress. She'd been so excited to come here for Christmas, Granny's house always felt more magical than anywhere else. The cottage was large but cosy, all honey-coloured stones on the outside and polished wood floors within. The gardens out back stretched deep, even in winter, with neat rows of trimmed hedges and lanterns dotting a winding path.

Despite its size and clear signs of wealth, paintings in gilded frames, plush rugs, and tall windows that let in the afternoon sun, nothing felt ostentatious or showy. Granny's touch was everywhere: fresh flowers on side tables, tasteful seasonal wreaths on the walls, and a vase of cranberries floating in water on the mantel. There was something warm and elegant about it all, like each item had a proper place and a story behind it.

At seven years old, she was already learning how to carry the unease that came with family gatherings, especially at Christmas, with so much formality and duty. She stood by the living room window, her heart fluttering like a caged bird in her chest.

She wore the scratchy green dress her mother had picked out, with a ribbon that dug into her waist every time she moved. The other girls, her cousins, all blonde and pale and perfect in their glittery cardigans, looked like they'd stepped out of a magazine. Ayanna's tights had a snag in the back and her braids were too tight. She pressed her hands to her scalp when nobody was looking, trying to soothe the sting. Her skin, a warm brown that deepened in the summer, felt loud under the ceiling lights. Everyone else seemed to match the cream furniture.

She wished she could be smaller. Less brown. Less noticeable. She wanted a cute fringe like Laura had, but the one time she'd tried to cut one in, her mother had cried and now she had to have her hair in braids until her real hair grew back. The braids pulled and itched her scalp.

Aunty Clara had called her exotic again when she walked in, like Ayanna was a packet of foreign crisps. Someone else had said she looked just like *Storm* from the *X-Men*, then gone silent like they'd realised it was a bad thing.

The grown-ups smiled too widely. Their laughs were too quick. Every question felt like a test.

Ayanna stared at the snowflakes clinging to the corners of the windowpane, pretending she was somewhere else. Somewhere soft. Somewhere she didn't have to be the only one. She could hear the clatter of forks and the low hum of conversation, the way it always started just after the Queen's speech. Someone was probably already opening the Baileys.

She wasn't sure if she felt sad or angry. It just sat there, heavy in her belly like too much pudding.

A swish of fabric drew Ayanna's attention. Granny bustled into the hall, all soft grey curls and a welcoming smile. She wore a simple but beautiful wrap dress in a deep plum shade, pearl earrings glinting under the light. "There you are, my sweet," Granny said, her voice warm as a fire on a cold day. She held out her arms, and Ayanna slipped into them, inhaling the comforting smell of roses and cinnamon that always seemed to cling to Granny's clothes.

"You look lovely, darling," Granny murmured, straightening one of Ayanna's braids with gentle fingers.
"Are you all right? You seem quiet."
Ayanna mustered a small smile. "I'm okay, Granny.

Just… lots of people here."

Granny nodded, patting Ayanna's shoulder. "That's the joy and curse of a big family, I'm afraid, plenty of company, but it does get noisy!" She leaned down conspiratorially. "Grab a biscuit from the tin in the kitchen if you get peckish. I made your favourite ginger ones."

Relief flickered across Ayanna's face. "Thanks, Granny!" She adored her grandmother. Granny never seemed rushed or preoccupied, she always had time for a quick hug or a soft word, always asked about Ayanna's day, and listened like it mattered.

Granny gave one more squeeze, then hurried off to welcome someone else. "I'll be in the sitting room if you need me," she called over her shoulder, the ends of her wrap dress swishing elegantly as she went.

The room behind her buzzed with conversation, the clink of glasses punctuating the festive chatter. Ayanna turned, her eyes seeking out her mother's familiar form. Alice stood among a cluster of relatives; a glass of wine clutched in her slender fingers. Their eyes met, and

Ayanna searched for reassurance in her mother's eyes. Instead, she found only a strained smile, the corners of Alice's mouth tightening with worry.

Ayanna's stomach knotted, she drifted to the sidelines of the room, her back against the wall as if she could disappear into the cream-colored paint.

"Ayanna, dear, why don't you join the other children?" Aunty Clara's voice cut through the room, drawing attention to Ayanna's solitary figure.

Ayanna forced a smile, "I'm okay here, thanks."

Aunty Clara's perfectly arched eyebrow lifted, a slight frown marring her porcelain features. "Nonsense, it's Christmas! Go on, have some fun."

Ayanna's eyes darted to her mother, silently pleading for intervention. Alice's eyes met hers, a flicker of understanding, before her mother turned away, engaging in animated conversation with another relative.

With leaden feet, Ayanna pushed away from the wall, her steps carrying her toward the hallway. She bore no ill will toward her cousins, she loved all of them, but Barney, Uncle

Chapter One

Arthur's son, always looked at her in a way that made it clear she was different. She knew she was a stranger here, and the knowledge of this pressed down on her, an invisible barrier separating her from the easy laughter and shared memories of her cousins. She paused at the threshold, her hand resting on the wood of the doorframe.

The sound of a car door slamming outside sent a jolt through Ayanna's body. Uncle Henry had arrived. The room fell silent as he strode in, his shiny dress shoes clicking against the hardwood floor. He exuded an air of authority, his broad frame filling the tailored suit jacket, and his steelgrey eyes surveying the gathered family members with a critical gaze. A shiver ran down Ayanna's spine as his attention landed on her, a fleeting moment of scrutiny that left her exposed.

"Merry Christmas, everyone," Henry announced, his deep voice resonating through the room. "I trust you've all been behaving yourselves?" His question was met with a chorus of laughter and affirmative responses, the tension in the room dissipating slightly.

She noticed him accept Granny's warm greeting, he patted her shoulder and said something that made Granny laugh.

Then turned taking in the rest of the room, taking note of who was nearby. She tried not to draw attention to herself, but even from where she stood, Ayanna's stomach fluttered.

He made a polite beeline for Alice, exchanging a quick pleasantry with the aunts. Alice's voice brightened, but the smile on her lips looked tight to Ayanna's eyes.

Ayanna watched as her uncle made his way through the room, shaking hands and exchanging pleasantries with the adults. His movements were precise, calculated, each gesture imbued with purpose. As he approached her mother, Ayanna noticed the way Alice's smile tightened, her body stiffening almost imperceptibly.

"Alice," Henry greeted, his thin lips curling into a smile.

"You look lovely, as always."

"Thank you, Henry," Alice replied, her voice steady despite the flicker of discomfort in her eyes. "We're so glad you could join us."

Ayanna's eyes darted between her mother and uncle, her young mind trying to decipher the currents of tension that swirled around them. She couldn't shake the idea that there was something more, a history she wasn't privy to, lurking beneath the surface of their polite exchange.

"I have someone I'd like you all to meet," Henry announced, jovially, his voice cutting through the conversation. "If you'll all follow me outside, I'd like to show you something."

A buzz of excitement filled the room as the family members began to make their way towards the front door. Ayanna hung back, her stomach knotting with a mixture of curiosity and apprehension. She glanced at her mother, seeking reassurance, but found Alice's attention focused on straightening the already immaculate living room.

As the crisp winter air hit Ayanna's face, she inhaled deeply, the cold burning her lungs. The crunch of snow beneath her feet interwoven with the excited chatter of her cousins as they gathered on the front lawn.

Ayanna craned her neck to see over the crowded bodies of her relatives. Henry emerged from his sleek black sedan; a large, wriggling bundle cradled in his arms. As he approached, the bundle let out a high-pitched bark, and Ayanna's eyes widened in understanding.

"Meet the newest member of the family," Henry declared, his voice ringing with pride as he set the squirming puppy down on the snow-covered lawn. "A purebred chocolate Labrador, the finest of its kind."

Ayanna watched as her cousins surged forward, their eager hands reaching out to pet the puppy's dark silky fur. The air filled with laughter and delighted squeals, and for a moment, Ayanna felt a pang of longing, a desperate wish to be a part of the joyous scene before her.

But as she took a step forward, her heart fluttering with a tentative hope, Uncle Henry's voice cut through the merriment, his next words sending a chill down Ayanna's spine.

"I've named her Ayanna."

A stunned silence descended upon the gathering, Henry's words hanging in the frigid air. Ayanna felt the breath catch in her throat; her body frozen in place as the implications of her uncle's statement sank in. The laughter that followed, sharp and cutting, pierced through her like shards of ice.

"*Ayanna?*" Aunty Clara snickered, her voice dripping with barely concealed amusement. "How funny you are,

Chapter One

Henry."

The cruel laughter intensified, ringing in Ayanna's ears as she stood immobilised. Her mind raced, struggling to process the dehumanising act, the casual cruelty of her uncle's choice.

Confusion and hurt battled within her, threatening to overwhelm her as she fought back the hot tears that pricked at the corners of her eyes, determined not to let them see her break.

"Come now, Ayanna," Uncle Henry chuckled, his tone patronising. "It's just a bit of fun. Don't be so sensitive."

But Ayanna could see the glint of satisfaction in his cold, grey eyes, the subtle curl of his lip as he revelled in her discomfort. The apprehension that this was no mere coincidence, but a deliberate act of humiliation, like lead in her stomach.

As her cousins crowded around the puppy, cooing and laughing, Ayanna felt a profound sense of isolation wash over her. She stood apart, a pariah in her own family, the chasm growing wider with each passing moment.

"Ayanna, come pet her!" one of her cousins called out.

But Ayanna remained frozen, her feet transfixed as if the snow had risen up and encased her. She couldn't move, couldn't speak, couldn't breathe.

Inside her, a storm of emotions raged, battering against the fragile walls of her composure. Hurt, anger, and shame swirled together in a toxic brew trying to claw its way to the surface.

But she remained silent, her small body trembling with the effort of containing the hurt within. She knew, with a certainty that belied her young age, that any reaction would only fuel their cruelty, would only serve to further alienate her from the family she so desperately longed to belong to.

So, she stood, a solitary figure among the merriment, her pain hidden behind a mask of stoic endurance. And as the cold wind whipped around her, Ayanna made a silent vow to herself, a promise born of hurt and determination.

She would not let them break her. She would not let their cruelty define her. Somehow, someday, she would rise above the pain and forge her own path, far away from the suffocating confines of this family that had never truly been her own.

Chapter One

Ayanna's mother's face was a portrait of discomfort, her lips small as she offered her daughter a weak, strained smile. She approached Ayanna, her movements hesitant, "Ayanna, sweetheart," she began, "I'm sure Uncle Henry didn't mean any harm. It's just a... a joke."

The words fell flat, even to her own ears. Ayanna looked up at her mother, her dark eyes swirling with a mixture of pain and duplicity. "But why, Mama?" she asked, her voice trembling. "Why would he name a dog after me? Am I... am I not good enough to be a person? Why did he name her after me, is it because of her colour? Because she's black? What is wrong with me?"

Her mother flinched, "Nothing, baby. You're perfect just the way you are. It's just... sometimes people make mistakes. And can't see that what they're doing can hurt."

Ayanna searched her mother's face, hoping to find the comfort and reassurance she so desperately needed. Instead, she found only a reflection of her own pain, a silent acknowledgment of the wrongdoing that had been done to her. In that moment, Ayanna realised that her mother, too, was trapped in the web of this family's dynamics, unable or unwilling to stand up for what was right.

Ayanna's hands curled into tiny fists. She remembered how Granny had once told her that Uncle Henry had a habit of making decisions quickly, without always thinking them through. She'd never minded before, but now it felt like a punch to her stomach. She stared at the dog, at the swirl of deep-brown fur dusted with snow, at the wide eyes that found everything wondrous. And she felt singled out in a way that made her cheeks burn.

As if on cue, Aunty Clara's voice cut through the tension, she spoke in a patronising manner that left no doubt of her selfassured superiority.

. "Oh, Ayanna, don't be so sensitive," she chided, her perfectly manicured hand waving dismissively in the air. "It's just a silly little joke. You really need to learn to lighten up, dear."

Ayanna felt the sting of her aunt's words, each syllable a tiny barb embedding itself in her already wounded heart. She looked to her mother once more, silently pleading for her to say something, anything, in her defence. But her mother's gaze dropped to the floor, her silence a deafening admission of defeat.

Chapter One

In that moment, Ayanna felt as if an invisible wall had sprung up between herself and the rest of her family. She was alone, an outsider, their collective indifference pressing down upon her.

She wondered, not for the first time, what it would be like to truly belong, to be seen and valued for who she was, rather than who they wanted her to be. But as the laughter and chatter of her family swelled around her once more, Ayanna realised that such acceptance might forever remain beyond her reach, a dream as elusive as the warmth of a genuine embrace in this house of cold, refined charades.

Ayanna stood, her presence as insubstantial as a ghost. The laughter and chatter swirled around her, a chorus of sound that never quite included her own voice. She watched as her cousins huddled together, whispering and giggling, their eyes darting in her direction with a knowing cruelty that made her stomach turn.

Aunty Clara glided through the room, her dress shimmering under the soft light of the chandeliers. She paused beside Ayanna, "Ayanna, dear," she said, her voice dripping with false sweetness, "why don't you go play with the others? I'm sure the puppy would love some extra attention."

Ayanna flinched, she looked up at her aunt, searching for some glimmer of remorse or understanding, but found only a cold, dismissive smile. "I... I think I'll just stay here," she mumbled, her voice almost lost in the noise of the party.

Aunty Clara's grip tightened, her nails digging into Ayanna's skin through the thin fabric of her dress. "Don't be rude, dear," she said, her tone sharpening. "After all, Uncle Henry went to such trouble to honour you with the dog's name. The least you can do is show some gratitude."

Ayanna felt the heat of shame rising in her cheeks, her eyes stinging with unshed tears. She nodded, unable to find the words to express the depths of her hurt and confusion, a physical ache deep in her bones.

Granny, who had been watching in puzzled silence, finally cleared her throat. "My goodness, it's freezing out here," she said, kindly enough, as though she believed the cold might be the real problem. "How about we all head back inside, hmm? We can warm up and talk properly." She gave Ayanna's shoulder a gentle pat, her touch comforting.

She stood alone, watching as her family celebrated a holiday that had lost all meaning for her. She felt like a stranger, a

Chapter One

shadow drifting through the halls of a life that no longer seemed to belong to her.

As the evening drew to a close, Ayanna slipped away from the buzz of conversation, finding her way up the narrow stairs at Granny's house. She didn't live here; her real home was with her mother, but this space had become hers over time. Years ago, it had been Alice's bedroom, echoing with her teenage memories. Now, from the faded lilac walls to the scattered books on the nightstand, it belonged to Ayanna whenever she came to stay. Granny had insisted on it: "You need your own corner in this house, my girl," she'd say whenever Alice had to work, and Ayanna came over.

Yet tonight, each step up those stairs felt heavier than usual, her footfalls a reminder of the distance between her and the very people who should have felt like home. By the time she reached the threshold of her room, her refuge within Granny's world, the ache of not quite belonging pressed all the more. Even here, in a room made hers by Granny's warmth and care, Ayanna couldn't shut out the lonely truth: sometimes, even family felt unbearably far away.

She closed the door behind her, leaning back against the solid wood as if it could shield her from the pain that consumed her. The laughter from downstairs was a cruel soundtrack to her own misery. Ayanna looked around at the familiar walls of her bedroom, the space that had once been her sanctuary. But now, even this private refuge felt tainted by the events of the day, the memories of her family's treachery seeping into every corner.

Ayanna sank down onto her bed, burying her face in her hands as the tears finally began to fall. She wept for the little girl who had been so eager to please, so desperate for love and acceptance. She wept for the future that stretched out before her, a landscape of uncertainty and pain. And most of all, she wept for the loss of the family she once believed she knew, the people who had proven themselves capable of such callous cruelty.

With a shaking hand, Ayanna reached for her diary, the worn leather cover a comforting presence beneath her fingertips. She flipped to a blank page, pen poised above the paper, Ayanna hesitated, her thoughts a swirling mass of emotions. How could she possibly put into words the depth of her pain, the magnitude of her sense of disloyalty?

But as the pen began to move, the words poured out of her in a torrent of unfiltered energy. She wrote of the

Chapter One

humiliation that had burned through her as her family laughed, the searing pain of being reduced to a punchline in her own home. She wrote of the confusion that had gripped her, the desperate need to understand why her own flesh and blood could treat her with such callous disregard. And she wrote of the anger that simmered beneath the surface, the fury that ate away at her from the inside out.

As the pages filled with her anguished and childish scrawls, Ayanna felt a certain catharsis, a release of the toxic emotions that had been corroding her soul.

Her pen came to a stop, and she closed the book in front of her, a deep sigh left her lips as she allowed her eyes to wonder around her room. Spotting an old, deflated balloon half hidden behind the radiator she allowed herself a smile as another memory surfaced, one untouched by pain, untainted by cruelty. A memory of warmth, of laughter, of a love that felt like safety.

She squeezed her eyes shut for a moment, willing herself to hold onto it, to let it steady her. And as she did, the anger in her chest softened just enough for her hand to move again, the ink shifting from jagged frustration to something gentler.

A soft smile appeared on her lips as she allowed herself to drift into the happy memory.

Fridays were McDonald's nights. The one day of the week that was just for the Ayanna and Alice. Ayanna lived for those nights.

She would bounce into the car the second her mother got home from work, grinning for real this time, because for a few hours, she could forget everything else.

They always ordered the same thing. A Happy Meal for Ayanna, a cheeseburger and fries for Alice. Her mother always asked for extra pickles, even though she didn't like them, because she knew Ayanna did.

"Here," Alice would say, plucking the pickles off her burger and dropping them onto Ayanna's. "Don't say I never do anything for you."

Ayanna giggled, crunching into them. "You're the best, Mama."

"I know," Alice said with a wink, stealing one of Ayanna's fries.

Chapter One

They would sit in their usual booth by the window, dipping fries into ketchup, talking about everything and nothing.

Alice would tell her about her workday, and Ayanna would listen, nodding along even though she didn't understand half of it.

And when Alice asked about school, Ayanna told her the good parts.

The parts that wouldn't make her worry.

She never told her about the bad days. Never told her about the moments when she felt like a ghost, like she was fading out of existence.

Because she didn't want to ruin this.

After dinner, they always grabbed balloons.

Alice would swipe two of the plastic-sticked balloons on the way out, grinning like a kid herself. "Ready?" she'd ask.

And Ayanna always knew what was coming.

Her mother would swing the balloon, landing a soft *thwap* against Ayanna's arm. "First hit!"

Ayanna gasped in mock outrage. "Not fair, I wasn't ready!"

"You snooze, you lose," Alice teased, running ahead.

And just like that, the chase was on.

Ayanna took off after her, swinging her balloon wildly, laughing so hard she could barely breathe.

People on the street turned to watch, smiling, shaking their heads. Two figures, a grown woman and a little girl, chasing each other down the pavement, their laughter carrying through the air.

Ayanna wrote about these memories and smiled. No matter the disconnect she felt with her extended family, she knew her mother would always be by her side.

Chapter Two

HENRY

He knew the moment it left his mouth.

"I've named her Ayanna."

It wasn't just the girl's name. It was the way it landed; too fast, too sharp, too final. Like a punchline no one had set up.

He hadn't looked at her, not right away. He kept his eyes on the dog instead, like pretending that was all he meant would somehow make it true. But he felt the air change. Laughter had followed; awkward, stilted, the kind that tries to patch over discomfort without actually addressing it. A few chuckles. Someone said, *"Oh, no you didn't,"* under their breath. It all faded into the background, like noise under water.

Because he knew.

He saw it.

Ayanna's stillness. The flicker in Alice's eyes. That silence that wrapped around the room tighter than any words. He didn't look at anyone. Didn't try to explain. The moment was already gone, too far down the line to fetch back.

Now he was back home, coat hung neatly, shoes lined up by the radiator, and that moment clung to him like damp.

He didn't bother turning on the television. No music. No distractions. Just the soft hum of the boiler and the distant sound of a neighbour's car reversing into their drive.

His house was always clean. Not sparkling, not show home sterile; just sensible. Comfortable. The hallway smelled faintly of floor polish and the lemon oil he used on the banister. Coats hung in order of season. The umbrella stand hadn't moved in thirteen years. Nothing in the house was new, but everything worked. Everything had a place. The sitting room was all brown tones and low lighting: a tweed sofa with arms gone shiny, cushions that matched the curtains, two lamps with identical brass bases. His favourite chair sat opposite the fireplace, and on the coffee table, a matching set of coasters all squared perfectly to the grain, ready to be used.

He stood in the doorway for a minute, mug in hand, letting the warmth seep into his knuckles.

Chapter Two

The tea was too strong.

He drank it anyway.

The name had come too easily. That was the problem. He hadn't planned it. It wasn't a joke, not really. It was just... something he said. Something that felt sharp enough to say aloud.

And once it was out there, once he saw Ayanna's face go still, he understood. But there was no taking it back. Not because he didn't want to. Because he couldn't. Not in front of everyone. Not with Alice there, watching him with that wounded expression like she was the one who'd been wronged.

And he immediately felt the ground shift beneath him. Not because he thought it was racist; he hadn't even made that connection until the reactions started. Until the air changed. He wasn't that man. He didn't say things to provoke. Didn't stir the pot. He made order. Maintained boundaries. He did what made sense. But sensible people didn't walk into a room full of family and name a black dog after their Black niece. Even he could see that now. And still he hadn't corrected it. Hadn't stumbled out an apology, or laughed it off, or even offered a shrug to acknowledge the discomfort. Because once he'd done it, once the name was out, to take it back would've been worse.

It would've made it real. It would've been an admission. And Henry didn't do that. He didn't backtrack. He didn't explain. That was the point of being the steady one, the voice of reason. If you started second-guessing yourself in front of people like Alice, you'd never stop.

She hadn't shouted. She never did, not anymore. That was the clever thing about Alice. She'd learned that silence carried more weight. That when she made herself small and trembled at the edges, people bent around her without quite knowing why.

He could still hear her voice, quiet, heavy, just enough quiver to draw the eye. *"You named your dog after my child?"* As if he'd done it to *her*. Like everything always circled back to her. He hadn't even thought of it that way. It wasn't about race. He hadn't made the connection. Didn't think in those terms. He just... picked a name.

Ayanna was a tidy name. A strong name. It fit the dog. That was all. But now, back in his house, his neat, ordered house, it didn't feel like "all." It felt like something worse.

Chapter Two

Not because he meant harm. Sensible men didn't mean harm. But because it was harming all the same, and now he couldn't admit it without unravelling everything he believed about himself.

He sat in his armchair and rested the mug on a coaster. The room felt suddenly cramped, like the walls had edged in while he was out. The cushions were too stiff. The lamps too yellow. He shifted, adjusted, sat still again.

Ayanna was only seven. He didn't know her. Not really. She was a timid girl, hard to read. All limbs and eyes, and that strange way kids sometimes have of seeming older than they are without actually being wise.

He wasn't sure what she thought of him. She rarely spoke to him directly. But she watched, sometimes, from behind her mother's legs. Not afraid...just assessing.

He couldn't remember if he'd ever knelt to speak to her at her level. Probably not.

He sipped his tea. It burned now, somehow hotter than before.

He'd been appalled when Alice came home that day, dropping the news like it was nothing, pregnant, unmarried, and by a Black man she barely knew. He wasn't racist, not at all. But the sheer *stupidity* of it. The thoughtlessness. The spectacle. Henry couldn't abide people who made reckless, avoidable messes and expected applause for surviving them. And now she was a single mother, acting like the world owed her softness for it.

And now, was he taking it out on Ayanna? Was he punishing a child for how he felt about her mother?

Alice had scooped the girl up without fuss, just enough movement to suggest retreat without actually leaving. She'd looked over her shoulder once, like she was waiting for someone to come after her.

Like *she'd* been hurt and wasn't sure yet whether she'd have to explain why. *"I'm sure it's just a joke,"* he'd heard her whisper to Ayanna. Soft enough that it could have been reassurance. But Henry knew Alice. Knew how her quiet could cut deeper than anyone else's noise. It wasn't comfort; it was positioning.

She *knew* he wasn't racist. She'd known him all her life.

But she'd never step forward to defend him.

Not when there was a chance to be hurt, to gather Ayanna close and say, *"see how the world treats us?"* He didn't blame the girl. How could he? She was seven. Watching.

Learning. Picking up the rules from her mother's cues. And what she'd learned today was that he'd said something wrong, and no one was going to fix it.

Henry sighed sadly.

"Come here," he murmured, barely above a whisper. The dog padded over to him, settled beside his chair, he scooped her up onto his lap and she curled on his knee.

He ran his hand slowly down the curve of her back. She let out a low, contented sigh and blinked up at him.

She didn't care what her name was. Didn't care what he'd meant by it. She just wanted his hand, his warmth, his companionship. He stroked her again. Slower this time. Gentle.

He wasn't a hateful man. He knew that much. But he was scared. Not of people like Alice. Not of the girl.

What scared him, really scared him, was that someone might one day look at him and see it. The truth. That he wasn't especially wise. Or steady. Or clever. That he wasn't cruel, but not kind enough to stop himself either. That he wasn't even sensible.

Simply scared of being seen for what he was.

Ordinary.

Chapter Three
AGE 8

The backyard was alive with the commotion of Ayanna's eighth birthday party. Children squealed as they chased balloons and darted through streams of soapy bubbles, their laughter ringing out like tiny bells in the late afternoon sun. Adults chatted in clusters, balancing plates of food and glasses of wine, their chatter creating a vocal backdrop beneath the chaos. A colourful banner reading "Happy Birthday Ayanna!" swayed in the breeze, its bright letters promising joy and celebration. To anyone watching, the scene was perfect, an idyllic family gathering to celebrate a beloved child.

But Ayanna sat apart from the activity, perched on a garden bench near the flowerbed, her small hands folded tightly in her lap. Her pale pink party dress, chosen by her mother for its delicate lace and flowing skirt, itched against her skin. She tugged at the waistband absentmindedly, her dark eyes scanning the crowd with a wary intensity. She forced a smile as a gaggle of children ran past her, shrieking with delight, but the expression didn't quite reach her eyes.

She looked over to the old oak tree at the periphery of the garden, where Barney leaned nonchalantly against the trunk, he was fourteen, nearly fifteen, caught in that liminal space where the last traces of boyhood began to give way to the unsteady promises of adolescence. He wasn't laughing or playing like the other children. Instead, he stood still, his hands shoved deep into his pockets, his eyes fixed on her. The way he looked at her sent a shiver down her spine, though she couldn't have explained why. It was an unsettling stare that made her feel small and exposed, like a bug pinned under a magnifying glass.

Ayanna's breath quickened, and she tore her gaze away, focusing instead on the paper lanterns swaying gently in the breeze. She wanted to disappear into the cheerful chaos, to blend into the blur of running children and chatting adults, but she felt rooted to the spot. The party continued around her, oblivious to her discomfort, and Ayanna's forced smile wavered.

Her mother's soft voice broke through her spiralling thoughts. "There's my birthday girl," she said, crouching down in front of Ayanna with a plate of cake in hand. Her mother's presence was like a warm blanket, wrapping her in safety, however fleeting. She leaned in, pulling Ayanna into a gentle hug that smelled of Royal Jelly and vanilla. "You're doing so well, sweetheart," her lips brushed against Ayanna's temple. "I know these big family things can be a lot. But everyone's here because they love you. You're my brightest star."

Ayanna nodded, leaning into the comfort of her mother's embrace. For a moment, the knot in her stomach loosened, and she let herself believe her mother's words. But then her eyes drifted back to the oak tree. Barney was still there, still watching. Her mother pulled back slightly, cupping Ayanna's face in her hands. "Are you okay, love?" she asked, searching for something in her daughters' eyes.

"I'm fine," Ayanna lied. She mustered another smile, but it felt brittle, like it might crack at any moment.

Her mother seemed to hesitate, her brow furrowing slightly, but then she nodded. "Good girl," she said, brushing a stray curl from Ayanna's forehead. "Now go have fun. It's your day." She kissed Ayanna's cheek before standing and rejoining the adults, her attention quickly claimed by a relative with an elaborate story to share.

Left alone again, Ayanna's smile faded. The laughter and music of the party seemed to grow distant, muffled, as if she were underwater. She glanced back at the oak tree, but Barney was gone.

Inside the house, the hallway was cool and dim, a sharp shift to from brightness outside. Ayanna had slipped away unnoticed, her small feet making no sound on the wooden floor. She lingered near the staircase, her fingers fidgeting with the hem of her dress. There was a kind of stillness that her mother often described as peaceful, but to Ayanna, it was suffocating. She strained her ears, listening for the distant sound of the party filtering in through the open windows, but it did little to calm her nerves.

The sound of footsteps made her freeze, her heart leaping into her throat. She turned her head slowly, her breath catching as Barney appeared at the far end of the hallway. He smiled, a lopsided grin that might have seemed friendly to anyone else, but to Ayanna, it felt wrong. His presence filled the space, making the hallway seem narrower, darker.

"Why aren't you outside?" Barney asked, his tone light, almost teasing, but his eyes didn't match the off-handedness of his words. Ayanna took a small step back, her heels brushing against the staircase.

"I just…needed a break," she said calmly, her voice trembling.

Barney stepped closer, his movements slow and deliberate. "A break, huh? Parties can be a bit much, can't they?" He stopped a few feet away, his hands still shoved into his pockets, his stance relaxed but his presence suffocating.

Ayanna nodded; her throat too tight to speak. She wanted to run, to bolt back to the backyard where the noise and laughter might drown out the fear curling in her stomach. But her feet felt frozen in place, as if the floor had turned to quicksand.

The air felt dense and oppressive as Barney closed the distance between them, each step deliberate and slow, the sound of his shoes reverberating in the dimly lit hallway.

Ayanna's heart pounded in her chest; the rhythm so loud it drowned out the noise of the party outside. Her breathing quickened as he drew nearer until no space remained, she felt dwarfed by his presence. She leaned into the wall, pressing herself against it, the cool plaster grounding her in the moment yet offering no protection.

Barney tilted his head slightly as if studying her. His lips curved into a small smile, but there was something off about it, something that made Ayanna's stomach roil. "Why are you hiding in here?" he asked, his tone light, conversational, like he wasn't standing too close, like this was normal. Ayanna didn't answer. She couldn't. Her throat felt tight; her voice trapped somewhere deep inside.

She glanced past him, her eyes darting toward the open doorway that led back to the kitchen. If she could just make it past him, she could run. But her legs were paralysed by a fear she didn't fully understand.

Barney took A final step closer, his breathe warm upon her, his hands in his pockets, his stance easy-going. "It's okay, you don't have to be scared," he said, his voice almost soothing. But it wasn't okay. Nothing about this felt okay.

When he reached out, his hand brushing against her arm, she flinched. The touch was light, almost gentle, but it sent a jolt of fear through her body, like static electricity snapping against her skin. She pulled her arm back instinctively, her movements quick and jerky, but Barney didn't step away. Instead, he moved closer, his hand now resting on her upper arm. His fingers lingered there, overbearing and foreign, and Ayanna felt her breath hitch in her throat.

"Relax," he said softly, the word drawing out like a command. Ayanna wanted to scream, to shove him away, but her body betrayed her. She stayed frozen, her limbs stiff and unresponsive, as if they no longer belonged to her. Her mind raced, but no clear thoughts formed. All she could focus on was the touch of his hand, the closeness of his body, and the suffocating sensation of being trapped.

The hallway seemed to shrink around her, the air thick and stale. The faint scent of Barney's bodywash, something musky and sharp, invaded her senses. She felt dizzy, her head swimming as panic surged through her.

Barney's hand moved, trailing down her arm in a way that sent a cold shiver down her spine. Ayanna clenched her fists, willing herself to speak, to yell for her mother, but the words wouldn't come. Her voice remained locked inside her, buried beneath layers of fear and confusion.

The wall was cold against her back, a polar opposite to the heat radiating off Barney's body as he leaned in closer. Ayanna turned her head away, her eyes squeezing shut as if blocking him out would make him disappear. She focused on the sounds of the party outside, the distant laughter of children, the clinking of glasses, the muffled strains of music filtering through the walls. But even those familiar noises couldn't reach her here. In this moment, she was completely alone.

Her chest tightened, each breath shallow and quick, the air barely reaching her lungs. Time seemed to slow, every second stretching into an eternity. She felt Barney's hand on her waist now, his touch lingering, and her mind screamed at her to move, to fight, to do anything. But her body refused to listen. The fear had paralysed her, leaving her helpless and vulnerable. She felt his hands move, one hand clumsy at his own waist, the clatter of his belt; the other touched upon her. The pink bow on her underwear no defence against him.

When it was over, Ayanna stood frozen, her small hands trembling at her sides. Her heart pounded so hard it felt like it might burst, her breaths coming in short, panicked gasps. She couldn't bring herself to look at him, couldn't bear to see his face.

Barney stepped back, his movements calm and unhurried, as if nothing out of the ordinary had just happened. "Better get back to the party," he said, his voice relaxed, almost cheerful.

Chapter Three

He re-buckled his belt, straightened his shirt and smoothed his hair, his demeanour completely unchanged. And then he turned and simply walked away.

Ayanna didn't move. She couldn't. Her legs felt like jelly, her knees threatening to collapse under her. Her hands still clutched at the wall, the rough texture digging into her. She stared at the spot where Barney had been, her mind a chaotic swirl of emotions, fear, shame, confusion, anger. None of it made sense. None of it felt real.

The hallway was silent now, the sounds of the party muffled and distant. Ayanna's body began to shake, a slow tremor that started in her hands and spread through her limbs. She felt cold, though she wasn't sure if it was the air or the fear that chilled her. Slowly, she slid down the wall until she was sitting on the floor, her knees pulled up to her chest. She wrapped her arms around herself, trying to make her small body even smaller.

Her breathing came in ragged gulps, her chest heaving as she fought to steady herself. Tears welled up in her eyes, but she blinked them away, refusing to let them fall. She didn't want to cry. She didn't want to feel anything. She just wanted to disappear.

Minutes passed, though it felt like hours, before Ayanna finally managed to stand. Her legs wobbled beneath her, threatening to give out, but she forced herself to take a step, then another, her movements mechanical and stiff. She couldn't stay here, couldn't risk someone finding her like this. She needed to go back to the party, to pretend like everything was normal.

Her feet carried her to the back door, where the sounds of the party grew louder. She paused, taking a deep breath and smoothing the wrinkles in her dress. She wiped her hands on her skirt, trying to erase the lingering sensation of his touch. Her face felt hot, and she placed her palms to her cheeks, willing herself to calm down.

When she stepped outside, the bright sunlight was almost blinding. The laughter and chatter of the party enveloped her, a clear disparity to the suffocating silence of the hallway. She scanned the yard, her eyes darting from one group to another, searching for Barney. But he was nowhere to be seen. For a brief moment, she felt relief. But it was quickly replaced by a heaviness in her chest, one that she feared would crush her.

Ayanna found a spot near the snack table and sat down, her hands folded tightly in her lap. She avoided looking at anyone, her eyes fixed on the ground. She felt invisible and untouchable, drifting through the party unnoticed.

Her mother approached a few minutes later, her smile warm but tinged with concern. "You okay, sweetheart?" she asked, crouching down beside Ayanna. "You've been so quiet. Are you tired?"

Speak! screamed a voice inside her *tell her!* But Ayanna did not know the words to use, didn't understand the gravity of what had happened. She didn't want it to be true, and putting the words out into the world gave them the power to engulf her.

Ayanna nodded, unable to meet her mother's eyes. "Yeah, just tired."

Her mother smoothed a hand over Ayanna's hair, her touch gentle and comforting. "It's been a big day, hasn't it?" she said softly. "Why don't you take a little break? I'll save some cake for you."

Ayanna nodded again, grateful for the excuse to retreat. Her mother kissed her forehead before standing and rejoining the other adults.

As her mother walked away, Ayanna felt a lump rise in her throat. She wanted to call her back, to tell her what had happened, but the words wouldn't come. Instead, she sat silently, her hands trembling in her lap, her heart growing heavier with each passing moment.

The months that followed were marked by a growing shadow in Ayanna's life. At school, her once-bright enthusiasm dimmed. Her grades began to slip, her mind too clouded by fear and confusion to focus on her lessons. She avoided her friends, her laughter fading into silence. Her teachers noticed the change but chalked it up to normal childhood struggles. At home, Ayanna withdrew further, her cheerful chatter replaced by a quiet voice and evasive answers.

Alice noticed the shift before Ayanna ever spoke a word. It was in the way her daughter no longer met her eyes when she spoke, in the way her shoulders curled inward as if trying to make herself smaller. The way she used to come running for a hug at the end of the day but now lingered in doorways, hesitating, like she wasn't sure if she was still welcome in her mother's embrace.

Chapter Three

At first, Alice tried to ignore it, convincing herself it was just part of growing up. Children changed, their moods fluctuated. Maybe Ayanna was just tired, maybe she was overwhelmed with school. Maybe she would come back to herself in time.

But then there were the nights.

Alice would find her daughter curled up in bed long before bedtime, a book clutched tightly in her small hands, her face blank but her grip white-knuckled. She had always been a reader, but this was different. She didn't just love stories now, she *disappeared* into them. They consumed her in a way that unsettled Alice, as though Ayanna was desperately reaching for something in those pages that real life no longer gave her.

She tried to coax her out of it.

"You used to read to me," Alice said one evening, perching on the edge of Ayanna's bed. "Do you want to read together like we used to?"

Ayanna hesitated, fingers tightening around the book. She shook her head, not quite looking at her mother. "I'm at the good part."

Alice swallowed the lump in her throat.

It hurt.

The distance between them was a slow, creeping thing, widening day by day. It was in the way Ayanna no longer clung to her hand during their walks, no longer launched into stories about her day over dinner. It was in the laughter that slowly disappeared from their home.

She missed it, God, she missed it. The McDonald's trips, the balloon fights, the easy way Ayanna had once loved her, had once *needed* her. But now there was a wall between them, and Alice didn't know how to break it down.

Didn't know how to ask why.

So instead, she tucked Ayanna in and brushed a hand over her forehead like she had always done.

"I love you," she whispered.

Ayanna replied, her voice small. "Love you too."

And Alice sat there for a moment, watching her daughter slip further and further away.

Chapter Three

Family gatherings became a source of dread even more so than before. Ayanna's every movement was calculated, her steps measured to avoid crossing paths with Barney. But he always found her, in the corner of the living room, in the garden shed, in the hallway where no one else wandered. His presence loomed over her like a storm cloud, dark and inescapable.

Each encounter chipped away at her sense of self, leaving her smaller, more broken. At night, she lay awake, staring at the ceiling as tears slid silently down her cheeks. She wanted to tell her mother, to scream the truth, but the words caught in her throat every time she tried. The fear of not being believed, of being blamed, kept her silent.

But it was more than that. It wasn't just the fear of not being believed, it was the fear of what believing her would mean.

If she told, her mother might look at her differently. Not with anger, not with blame, but with something worse, pity. A sadness that would settle in her eyes every time she looked at Ayanna, like she was something damaged, something to be handled with care, something that could never be put back together again.

She could handle being ignored. She could even handle being laughed at. But she couldn't handle that.

She couldn't handle the way her mother's love might change, even if it wasn't intentional. Couldn't stand the idea of being treated like something *fragile*. Because if Alice saw her that way, then wasn't it true? Wouldn't that make it real in a way Ayanna wasn't ready for?

If she told, everything would change.

Would her mother still take her to McDonald's for tea? Would they still have balloon fights in the street, still laugh until their stomachs hurt, still sing along to the radio on long drives like nothing else in the world mattered?

Or would those things fade, slowly at first, until one day they were just memories of a time before?

A time before Ayanna became a problem.

And what if her mother couldn't fix it?

What if she believed her, held her, told her she was sorry, and then nothing happened?

Chapter Three

What if she told and Barney still walked free, still smiled at her across the dinner table, still sat beside her at family events like nothing had ever happened?

Would she have to sit there and pretend, too? Would she have to watch her family protect him while she sat in silence, knowing none of them cared enough to stop it?

What if telling only made it worse?

What if they didn't just ignore her, but turned on her?

She could hear it already. The whispers. The *Are you sure?* The *He wouldn't do that.* The *She always was a little dramatic, wasn't she?*

What if they made her out to be the liar, the troublemaker, the one ruining things for everyone?

What if her mother had to choose, and she didn't choose Ayanna?

She could survive being hurt. She had survived it already.

But she didn't think she could survive being abandoned.

She could already see how it would play out. The muted tension. The way the family would close ranks around

Barney, like a fortress she'd never be able to breach. The way her mother would sit, hands clenched in her lap, unable to look at her.

And worst of all, the possibility that maybe, just maybe, her mother already knew.

Because hadn't Alice always been good at not seeing things? At smoothing over what was difficult, pretending away the cracks?

Hadn't she already chosen silence in so many ways?

Ayanna squeezed her eyes closed tight, as if she could push the thoughts away, as if she could shove the words back down before they made their way out.

She couldn't risk it.

She couldn't risk the only good thing she had left.

So, she swallowed the truth. Swallowed it whole, like she had every other time. She buried it down deep, where it festered inside her, growing heavier with every passing day.

And no one noticed.

No one saw.

Chapter Three

She had never felt more alone.

One night, Ayanna sat at the kitchen table, her small hands gripping her chair as she watched her mother wash dishes. "Mama," Ayanna began, her voice trembling. "I don't like being around Barney."

Her mother turned, her brow furrowing. "Why not, love?"

Ayanna hesitated, her heart pounding. "He…he makes me feel weird."

Alice frowned, setting the dish she was washing onto the drying rack. She turned off the tap, drying her hands on a dish towel before crouching beside Ayanna. "Weird how, sweetheart?"

Ayanna swallowed, her fingers coiling in the hem of her shirt. "I don't know. Just…weird."

Her mother studied her for a moment, a flicker of something passing through her expression. Concern? Doubt? She reached out, tucking a loose curl behind Ayanna's ear. "Did he say something to you? Do something that upset you?"

Ayanna's throat tightened. Yes. But she couldn't say it.

She couldn't even look at her mother anymore.

She shook her head. "No. I just," She hesitated, then forced a shrug. "I just don't like being near him."

Alice exhaled slowly, her hand resting lightly on Ayanna's knee. "You know, love, sometimes people can be awkward. Maybe he's not sure how to talk to you." She searched Ayanna's face for a reaction, but when Ayanna only stared at the floor, she sighed. "But if he's making you uncomfortable, you don't have to be around him.
You can always come to me, alright?"

Ayanna nodded, but the knot in her stomach didn't ease.

Her mother squeezed her hand. "I mean it, Ayanna. If anything happens, if he does or says anything you don't like, you tell me."

Her mother kissed her forehead, lingering for just a moment longer than usual, then stood and turned back to the dishes. "I'll talk to him. Maybe he doesn't realise he's making you uncomfortable." Ayanna's breath caught. No.

She didn't want that. She didn't want Barney to know she had said anything. She didn't want to see that smug, knowing look on his face the next time they were forced into the same room.

She forced a smile. "It's okay, Mama. You don't have to."

Alice hesitated, watching her carefully. "Are you sure?"

Ayanna nodded quickly. "Yeah. I was just being silly."

Her mother studied her for a moment longer, then sighed, turning back to the sink. "Alright. But if you change your mind, I'm always here, okay?"

Ayanna nodded again, but as her mother turned away, she felt her silence settle in her chest.

She had spoken, and yet she hadn't.

And she wasn't sure if she ever would.

Ayanna sat frozen, her chest laden with frustration and despair. She had tried to speak, but her words had failed her.

That night she wrote in her diary, the pages filling with words she couldn't say aloud. "Because he hurts me."

Chapter Four

AGE 10

As dusk settled gently beyond the window, painting the world in muted shades of violet and indigo, the living room eased into a comforting cocoon of warmth and familiarity. A single lamp cast a gentle glow across the worn carpet, illuminating a meticulously arranged battlefield of colourful Risk pieces sprawled atop the coffee table. Ayanna sat crosslegged, her posture relaxed, one hand thoughtfully turning a pen between her fingers, the other tracing paths and strategies across an open notebook beside her. Her expression was a serene mixture of contemplation and subdued amusement.

Alice leaned forward from the opposite side of the table, the soft light accentuating the determined sparkle in her eyes. She hovered her fingers playfully above a gathering of red troops, lips curled into a mischievous smile. "Now, if I move my troops here," she said, voice filled with mock seriousness, "I can flank your defences and conquer Europe before dawn!"

Chapter Four

Ayanna looked up, a flicker of amusement tempering the distant look in her eyes. She forces herself to focus on the moment, on the warmth of her mother's enthusiasm. "Ambitious," she teased,

Alice laughed, the sound reverberating through the room. "Ah, but I've got a secret weapon." She leant in conspiratorially, stage-whispering, "Brownies in the oven, set to go off when I make my move."

A genuine giggle bubbled up in Ayanna's throat, chasing away the phantom sensation of unwanted hands and whispered threats. She clings to this moment, to the comfort of her mother's playful grin and the promise of warm brownies.

They traded anecdotes as they played, recounting historical battles gone awry with increasingly absurd twists. "And then," Alice declares, barely suppressing her laughter, "the general's horse sat on the battle plans, and the whole army ended up in the wrong country!"

Ayanna's own laughter mingled with her mother's, a defence against the raw edges of her memories. But even in this pocket of joy, the tension still lurked, a tightness in her chest that made each breath feel heavier than the last.

As the clock ticks towards 3 A.M., their whispered quips take on a softer, more poignant tone. "I promise this is safer than any battle, darling," Alice's hand brushing Ayanna's knee in a feather-light touch.

Ayanna nodded, not trusting her voice. In the lamplight's gentle glow, their shared laughter felt like a fragile shield, a gossamer barrier against the darkness that threatened to seep in through the cracks. For now, in this stolen slice of night, they held fast to the game, to the stories, to each other.

But the laughter doesn't last.

Tomorrow, the spell would break.

The thought coils around her ribs, tightening with every tick of the clock. She tried to push it away, tried to stay in the moment. But the dread crept in, quiet and insidious, curling around the edges of her thoughts like smoke under a locked door.

The scent of her uncle's cologne would cling to the air, thick and suffocating. The hum of expensive conversation would form a backdrop to the constant, gnawing awareness of Barney's presence.

Chapter Four

She will have to laugh when expected.

Smile when it's polite.

Pretend she doesn't feel his eyes on her.

Her mother noticed her sudden distance. "You okay, love?" she asked carefully, Ayanna forced a nod.

Alice studied her for a moment, as if trying to decipher something just out of reach, then let it go.

These past few days had felt like a precious gift, a rare window of peace, laughter, and gentle companionship between just the two of them. They had been free to linger late into the evening, playing games and sharing stories without the intrusion of schedules or responsibilities. But tomorrow marked the end of that reprieve. The summer holidays had begun beautifully, but now reality was knocking at the door. Alice would return to her night shifts at the hospital, the demanding hours of a nurse pulling her away just when Ayanna needed her most. Ayanna would be dropped at Granny's house, her usual sanctuary. But during the holidays, Granny's home transformed into something else entirely, shadowed by the presence of Barney, and the safety Ayanna relied on would dissolve like morning mist.

* * *

The dining room stretched out like a stage, all finished mahogany and gleaming silverware, the very picture of refined elegance. Ayanna sat stiffly in her chair, the high back digging into her spine as she surveyed the assembled relatives with a wary eye. Outwardly, the scene is one of warm familial cheer - pleasant chatter and chiming laughter floating above the clink of fine china.

But beneath the veneer of joviality, Ayanna felt the undercurrents of tension, the subtle barbs woven through seemingly innocuous remarks. She picked at her food, her appetite withered by the growing sense of dread that curdled in her stomach. Even among this crowd of familiar faces, she was desolate, abandoned adrift in a sea of forced smiles and practiced niceties.

It was then that Barney glided into the seat beside her, his movements smooth and calculated. He settles in with a disquieting calm, his smile a perfect mask of charm. Ayanna's skin prickled with instinctive revulsion as he leant in, his presence overwhelming in its nearness.

She froze for a fraction of a second before lifting her head, forcing a small, polite nod.

She cannot give him more than that.

She will not.

He smirked, like he was amused, like he knew something no one else did.

Like this was a game.

Ayanna forced her spine to stay straight, her expression blank.

She wouldn't let him win.

But God, she already felt so tired.

The moment seemed to unfold in slow motion, each second stretched taut with horror. With a deliberate, almost carefree motion, Barney's hand disappeared beneath the drape of the tablecloth. Ayanna stiffened, every muscle locking in anticipation of the inevitable. She felt the brush of his fingers against her thigh, a featherlight touch that quickly turned brutal as he forced his fingers inside her.

Ayanna's entire being revolted, her mind reeling even as her body remained paralysed. She wanted to scream, to bolt, to shatter the suffocating pretence of normalcy - but the scream lodged in her throat, a silent, agonised plea that no one heard. The violation at once shocking and sickeningly familiar.

Around them, the dinner party continued, oblivious to the nightmare unfolding in their midst. Barney's face betrayed nothing, his pleasant expression firmly in place as he engaged in light conversation, his free hand gesturing animatedly.

She's trapped, pinned between the chair and the relentless force of Barney's touch, every fibre of her being crying out in silent anguish. The whispered threat in her mind, an insidious refrain: *"Who do you think they'd blame?"* It wove through her thoughts like a malignant force, intensifying the despair that threatened to consume her.

She could speak up now, his hands where they are, they'd have to believe her. But as she looked out at her family around the table, her uncle's passive and dismissive, her mother timid and afraid. The words wouldn't come.

In this room filled with light and laughter, Ayanna had never felt more alone, more violently severed from any sense of safety or belonging. She endured the assault in a now familiar blur of disassociation, her spirit retreating deep within herself even as her body remained a helpless captive to Barney's whims. The clatter of cutlery and hum of voices fade to a distant buzz, drowned out by the roaring of her own heartbeat, the silent screams that no one heard.

And so, Ayanna's life continued, the joy she felt with her mother, that safety, became something fragile, something fleeting. A flicker of warmth in an otherwise cold existence.

She clung to those moments, tucked them away like pressed flowers between the pages of a book, knowing they would have to last her through the nights when she couldn't breathe, the days when Barney's presence turned her body to stone.

Morning light spilt into the small kitchen, painting the room in a soft, buttery glow. Ayanna stood at the counter, her hands wrapped around a chipped mug of hot cocoa as she watched Alice putter about with the easy grace of familiar routine. A brief day back home, 24 hours of peace. The air filled with the comforting scent of toast and the gentle lilt of jazz from the battered radio perched on the windowsill. "Hold still, sweetie," Alice said, a playful glint in her eye as she brandishes a ballpoint pen. "I'm going to count every single one of these gorgeous freckles." She leant in, the tip of the pen hovering just above Ayanna's nose as she makes a show of squinting in concentration.

Ayanna couldn't help but giggle, the sound bubbling up from some half-forgotten place inside her. She held her breath, going cross-eyed as she tried to watch the progress of the pen. Alice making little tally marks on a scrap of paper, her tongue poking out in exaggerated focus.

"Look at that," Alice declared after a long moment, holding up the paper with a flourish. "Over two hundred beautiful stars, right there on your face." She tapped Ayanna's nose with a gentle finger, her smile warm and adoring.

Ayanna ducked her head, a shy grin tugging at her lips even as a flicker of uncertainty danced behind her eyes. The praise, so freely given, felt like a precious and fragile thing - something to be cherished and protected. She held it tight, even as some small, wounded part of her whispers that she doesn't deserve such love, such unblemished affection.

They settled at the small table by the window, the sunlight dappling the worn wood as Ayanna leant into her mother's side, savouring the solid warmth of her presence. Alice's arm came up to wrap around her shoulders, a shield against the world beyond those kitchen walls. They stayed like that, watching the dust motes dance in the slanted sunbeams.

But even in this refuge of safety, Ayanna felt the whisper of unease, the involuntary tensing of muscles when Alice's hand brushes against her hair. A fleeting thing, a shadow that flits across her face and is gone just as quickly. She hates the flinch, hates the way her body betrays her, even here in the sanctuary of her mother's embrace.

It's a constant push and pull, this dance between the girl she wants to be and the fractured, fearful creature that trauma has moulded her into. She fluctuated between leaning into Alice's touch, craving the grounding reassurance of her mother's hands, and shying away, her skin crawling with sense memory.

Still, she held fast to those moments of reprieve, those pockets of normalcy and connection. She knew, with a wisdom beyond her years, that they were precious and few. Each shared breakfast, each whispered joke and gentle hug, was a beacon against the darkness - a reminder that there was still softness in the world, still some untainted corner of her heart that knew how to laugh.

As the morning unfolded in a veil of golden light and clinking dishes, Ayanna let herself drift in this in-between space - caught between the girl she was and the woman she will become, between the wounds that marred her spirit and the tentative hope that still fluttered beneath her breastbone. She breathed in the mingled scents of honey and lemon dish soap, the taste of safety and home, and for just a heartbeat, the shadows retreated, held at bay by the fierce, unwavering love of a mother for her child.

Chapter Five
AGE 11

Ayanna woke up to the sound of birds chirping outside her window, their melody soft yet persistent, signalling the start of a new day. Sunlight streamed in through the thin white curtains, painting her bedroom in a golden glow that felt at odds with the pit in her stomach. Today was supposed to be exciting, her first day of Year 7, the first year of high school, a time when the world supposedly opened up a little more. But Ayanna couldn't muster any of the anticipation she'd imagined she might feel.

The light felt too bright, too glaring, as if it were mocking her. She lay still for a moment, her eyes fixed on the faint cracks in the ceiling above her bed, wishing she could stay wrapped in the familiar safety of her room. The thought of facing her classmates, her teachers, it all felt overwhelming.

Her school uniform hung neatly on the back of her chair, freshly ironed by her mother the night before. The white shirt, grey pleated skirt, and blue cardigan should have felt like a symbol of something new, a fresh start. Instead, it felt like armour she wasn't sure she was strong enough to wear.

"Ayanna, love, are you awake?" her mother's voice called gently from the hallway, accompanied by a soft knock on the door.

"I'm up," Ayanna replied. She forced herself to sit up, the coolness of the morning air brushing against her arms. Her braids, done the night before, fell freely over her shoulders, a reminder of her mother's careful hands working through her hair in the glow of the bedside lamp.

She lay still in her bed, the duvet pulled up to her chin, as if the fabric could shield her from the memory of yesterday. Her small body felt weighed down, each breath laboured as if she had to consciously remind herself to pull air into her lungs. Her mind replaying Barney's words, his demeanour, the way he walked away every time as though nothing had happened.

Her bedroom, usually her safe haven, felt smaller today. The soft lilac walls, dotted with drawings she had taped up over the years, seemed to close in around her.

Summer had come and gone, its long, sweltering days stretching into a haze of heat and suffocating tension. Her birthday a blur that she didn't want to remember. Every year, Barney and Arthur's visit seemed longer than the last, but

Chapter Five

this time, the six weeks at Granny's house felt endless, a slow trickle of hours piling up into an unbearable weight. Ayanna had started counting down the days to his departure the second he arrived, but that only sharpened her awareness of him, making her jump at the sound of footsteps she recognised too well.

Throughout the summer, Barney's presence was like a toxic fog that seeped into every moment, his low laughter echoing in the halls, the lazy sprawl of his body on Granny's couch while he flicked through television channels, his eyes finding Ayanna whenever he thought no one else was watching. She could sense him entering a room before she even saw him: the shift in energy, the prickling on the back of her neck, the sudden hush that settled over her thoughts. When she would catch his eye, there was often a faint smirk curling at the edge of his lips, as though daring her to speak up. She never did.

The cold sneer in his voice when he cornered her in the pantry weeks earlier, how he'd whispered, "No one will believe you," before brushing past her as though it were all just a game. Then, at night, she'd toss and turn, chasing the memory of his hand pressed firmly against her arm, the way he feigned innocence if a door opened nearby, quickly shifting into light conversation as though nothing had happened at all.

There were little humiliations each day; moments that might've looked innocent to anyone else but felt charged with menace to Ayanna. He'd lean too close as she tried to slip by him in a hallway, his breath hot on her ear as he murmured a dirty joke that turned her stomach. At dinner, across the table, he would lock eyes with her for just a second too long, then give the smallest shake of his head, as if to say, *don't you dare.* Sometimes he'd offer her a seat and pat the cushion next to him, smiling a smile no one else found suspicious. Other times he'd wait until she was clearing her plate to brush a hand against her back, so quick it almost felt imagined, except she could never forget the chill it sent through her.

He had a thousand ways of reminding her she was trapped. When the family gathered to play board games late into the night, he'd slip whispered comments into her ear that made her skin crawl. Insults disguised as friendly teasing, or references to "secrets" she'd never want exposed. Whenever her mother or Granny noticed her sudden discomfort, Barney would smoothly interject with a story or quip, redirecting attention so deftly that Ayanna felt invisible again.

Chapter Five

And still throughout all of the days of humiliation and torment. The nights were so much worse.

She didn't speak up. She never did. Sometimes, shame mingled with the fear; shame that she couldn't force her voice out, that she kept letting him get away with those lingering touches and venomous words. Other times, she felt sure he was right, that even if she did scream the truth, no one would believe it or no one would want to hear it. He had woven himself seamlessly into the family's fabric, a charming nephew, the well-liked son of Arthur. Where Ayanna saw cruelty in his eyes, others saw only easy confidence. Where she heard threats, others heard jokes. And every time the family laughed at one of his witty remarks, it chipped away at her hope that they could ever see who he really was.

By the end of the six weeks, Ayanna was more exhausted than she'd ever been. Each day had been a performance of normalcy, helping Granny cook, smiling politely, pretending her heart wasn't pounding whenever she heard Barney's footsteps on the stairs. The silence weighed on her like a second skin; she wore it constantly, even in her sleep.

When Barney and his family finally packed their car and drove away, Ayanna waited for relief to flood her chest, for the knot in her stomach to unwind. But it never came. Instead, his voice continued to echo in her dreams, those secret looks and private taunts replaying over and over, as if burned into the back of her eyelids. She hated that even in his absence, he still had power over her, that her shoulders tightened whenever the phone rang, or a shadow stretched across the corridor at dusk.

She loathed the way her mind clung to the memories of his hands, his laugh, his mocking eyes that told her she was alone in this nightmare. Every time she closed her eyes, she saw him. The dread festered like a wound, refusing to heal. She had held onto silence for so long, and now that he was gone, it felt worse, heavier. Because she realised the end of summer wasn't an escape; it was just a pause until the next time he walked into Granny's house, slipping effortlessly back into his role as the amiable relative no one could ever suspect.

And so, Ayanna carried that silence with her, day after day, biting the inside of her cheek whenever the urge to speak rose. She told herself it was self-preservation, that no one would listen anyway.

Chapter Five

The secret had festered inside her all summer, growing darker and heavier with every forced smile, every moment she avoided his gaze in the shared spaces of her Granny's home, and in the still moments between laughter and lingering family chatter, the torment endured, a relentless reminder of the pain that refused to be silenced.

Downstairs, she could hear her mother humming softly in the kitchen, the clinking of dishes as she prepared breakfast. The sound was familiar, grounding, and yet it felt distant, as though it belonged to another life, one untouched by the suffocating cloud that had hung over Ayanna for so long. Her stomach wrenched. She didn't want to leave the cocoon of her bed, but she knew she couldn't stay there forever. The first day of school was here, and even though Barney was gone, her anxiety clung to her like a second skin.

She forced herself to sit up, her arms wrapping instinctively around her knees. The movement was slow, every muscle in her body tense as if bracing for an unseen impact. Her stuffed bear, lay on the floor by the bed, his stitched smile staring back at her. She wanted to pick him up, to clutch him tightly like she had when she was younger, but something held her back. She didn't feel like she deserved the comfort.

It was as though her silence had not only stolen her voice but also her right to be soothed.

Ayanna's eyes flicked toward her school uniform, hanging neatly on the back of her chair. The crisp shirt and pleated skirt seemed to taunt her, the gnawing instinct that she would never escape this cycle.

Her bare feet touched the cold floor, and she shivered. The faint chatter of her neighbours outside, the sound of a car engine starting in the distance, all filtered through the window, grounding her just enough to take the next step. She made her way to the dresser, her fingers trembling as she pulled open the drawer to retrieve her underwear. When she caught a glimpse of herself in the mirror above the bureau, she froze.

Her reflection stared back at her, but it didn't feel like her. Her eyes were no longer warm and lively; they were dull, rimmed with exhaustion she hadn't yet earned at just eleven years old. Her hair, which her mother had styled into neat braids the evening before, was slightly undone from tossing and turning all night. She felt hollow, as though she were looking at a stranger wearing her skin.

Chapter Five

Ayanna quickly averted her eyes, pulling on her clothes without bothering to straighten the creases. She didn't want to see herself, not today. She smoothed her shirt absently, her fingers tracing the fabric as she tried to summon the courage to leave her room.

When she finally descended the stairs, the smell of buttered toast and scrambled eggs greeted her. Her mother stood by the counter, still humming as she flipped through the pages of a magazine, her coffee cup steaming by her side. The kitchen was warm, the morning sun casting soft patterns on the tiled floor, but to Ayanna, it felt stifling.

"Good morning, love!" her mother greeted cheerfully, glancing up. "Did you sleep well?"

Ayanna hesitated, then nodded, offering a faint, almost silent "Mhm."

Her mother did not notice the slight tremor in Ayanna's voice or the way she hunched defensively. Instead, she placed a plate of eggs and toast on the table, motioning for Ayanna to sit. "You look so smart" she continued, her voice bright. "You look ready to take on the world, little one." Ayanna slid into her chair, the warmth of the toast and the familiar scent of butter momentarily grounding her. She glanced up at her mother, her expression softening as she caught the genuine affection in her eyes. For a brief moment, the heaviness inside her lifted, carried away by the brightness of her mother's smile.

"I'm not little anymore, Mum," Ayanna said with a small grin, picking up her fork and poking at the eggs. "I'm in Year 7 now."

Her mother gasped playfully, one hand flying to her chest as if Ayanna had just dropped a bombshell. "Year 7? My goodness, when did my baby grow up? What happened to the little girl who used to run around here with pigtails and sticky fingers?"

Ayanna giggled, a light sound that bubbled up from somewhere deep and momentarily untouched by her hidden worries. "She's still here," she teased, "but now she's a Year 7 girl. Practically a teenager." She struck an exaggerated pose of mock sophistication, tilting her head and flipping an imaginary strand of hair.

Her mother laughed, the sound warm and full, and reached out to brush Ayanna's cheek affectionately. "A teenager already? Don't get too big for your boots now."

For that fleeting moment, the kitchen felt safe. It was a moment of love, uncomplicated and pure, between mother and daughter, a glimmer of joy that Ayanna tucked away to hold onto for the harder days ahead.

"That Barney, though," her mother added absently, sipping her coffee and thinking back to happy memories of the past 6 weeks, desperately trying to maintain the positivity she had just found with her daughter. "Such a cheeky boy. Always up to something. It was nice seeing you two spending so much time together."

Ayanna flinched at the mention of his name. Her fork clattered against the plate as her fingers slipped, the sound startling her mother enough to glance up. *Spending time together* She wished her mother knew that she had so much wanted to escape him, but every time she turned around, in every moment of peace, he was there. Ayanna wiped her face as she felt a tear try to escape from her eyes.

"Everything okay, Ayanna?" her mother asked, concern flickering in her eyes for the briefest moment.

Ayanna nodded quickly, her head bowed low as she pushed her eggs around the plate. "Yeah. I'm fine," she mumbled "I just got something in my eye."

Her mother didn't push. "Alright, then. Don't take too long with that food. You don't want to be late on your first day," she said, her tone soft but firm.

Ayanna nodded again, but she barely heard her mother's words. She finished her breakfast in silence, each bite tasteless, before excusing herself to go back upstairs for her bag and shoes. Her mother didn't stop her, chalking up Ayanna's mood to first day nerves.

Chapter Six
AGE 12

Several months had slipped softly by, and during the school term, Ayanna was spared Barney's presence entirely. Yet even though the school corridors felt like a necessary shield from his looming shadow, Ayanna discovered that no amount of distance could quiet the turmoil inside her. Every morning, she wrapped herself in the routine of classes and textbooks, grasping at any semblance of normalcy, but the relief was fragile at best.

Some days, she'd find herself pausing just inside the main entrance, noticing the stale smell of disinfectant and the sharp glare of fluorescent lights. Her heart would pound unexpectedly, as if it had been waiting for the precise moment she felt safe to remind her that safety was an illusion. The hum of a thousand conversations became a wall she couldn't break through, each voice blending into an overwhelming drone. In those moments, Ayanna's skin would prickle with the sense that the locker-lined walls were too close, that the school itself was shrinking around her, trapping her in a place she both needed and resented.

In class, she'd slip into a seat at the back, hands clammy against the edges of her desk. The clock at the front of the room ticked in slow, punishing seconds, each one pressing on her chest. Sometimes she'd catch herself counting her own heartbeats between the ticks, silently urging time to move faster so the day could end. But no matter how many times the bell rang, releasing her into the hallways, a hollow dread clung to her ribcage. She'd glance around and half expect Barney to materialise at the corner, even though she knew he was gone.

The teachers' voices often blurred into static, and she'd drift in and out of the lesson, wrestling with a surge of restlessness. If she were lucky, a friend would nudge her back to reality, but most of the time she navigated the day alone, eyes darting to the door or the nearest window. Anxiety radiated through her limbs, leaving her foot tapping ceaselessly against the floor, an urgent staccato that kept her tethered to the present. She wanted to focus on something, anything, besides the nagging fear that her sense of safety could dissolve at any second.

At lunch, she'd try to settle at a table in the far corner of the dining hall, scanning the sea of faces for any flicker of danger that only she seemed to sense. Her appetite was fickle, her stomach knotted too tightly to accept more than a few bites. Outside, the chatter and laughter painted the illusion that life was simple and bright, but inside, Ayanna felt the swirl of panic threatening to pull her under.

Despite it all, a small part of her craved these halls more than she wanted to admit. Here, at least, Barney was a memory and not a presence. Here, she could wrap herself in the day's structure, bells, classes, homework, to temporarily crowd out the darker corners of her mind. Yet the refuge never lasted long. Each time she leaned into the promise of routine, she felt that cold edge of dread waiting just beneath her skin.

When the final bell rang, Ayanna would pack her books with trembling hands, aware that the uneasy peace of school vanished as soon as she stepped off the school grounds. The relief of leaving the building mingled with the fear of heading home, back to a silence she didn't know how to fill. In that solo trek back, her thoughts tumbled over themselves, each one reminding her that while Barney's face wasn't here, the weight of what he'd done was always with her, refusing to let her truly breathe free.

Now, with Christmas approaching and the family looming like an inescapable storm cloud, her dread deepened into a constant, pulsing ache. The thought of returning to Granny's house with everybody there, where every smile and polite conversation would mask the undercurrent of pain, made her heart race.

Late one evening, as the house lay hushed under the spell of approaching winter, the burden of her secret finally became too heavy to bear. In the silence of her own heart, Ayanna's thoughts raced: *I can't keep this secret anymore. How many more days do I have to keep pretending I'm okay? If I speak up, will anyone actually listen, or will they just ignore me and tell me to smile?* Every stolen moment of terror reverberated relentlessly in her mind. At that moment, a surge of determination battled against a tide of fear. The anxiety, the shame, and the guilt wove together into a turbulent storm inside her, and she realised that silence was no longer an option. She needed to tell someone, her mother, only a single room away, yet it felt like miles between them.

Before she even fully understood what she was about to do, Ayanna stood in the narrow, dimly lit hallway outside her mother's bedroom door. The single overhead light, a flickering bulb that cast weak, wavering shadows on the faded carpet, seemed to pulse in time with her racing heart.

Chapter Six

The muted hum of the light and the soft rustle of the worn carpet beneath her feet were the only sounds in the oppressive stillness. Each step felt surreal, both muted and monumental, as if the very floor was trying to hold her back from crossing the threshold.

Her mind swirled in a frantic tempest of doubts: *What if she doesn't believe me? What if I'm too weak, too small, too broken to voice this truth?* The secret she had harboured for so long bore down on her relentlessly, making each breath shallow and desperate. Every flicker of the overhead light seemed to echo her inner turmoil, illuminating momentary reflections of her pale, anxious face in the darkened wood of the door frame.

The air in the hallway carried the faint smell of old books and dust—a constant, silent reminder of years spent burying her pain in silence. Her thoughts clashed with one another in a relentless assault; *If I say something, will I ruin everything that's still good? Am I brave enough to tell the truth, or will it break me?* The very idea of breaking her silence felt both liberating and terrifying.

She hesitated, caught between the crushing weight of the secret and the desperate need for release. The door before her seemed almost to beckon, a narrow portal between the suffocating isolation of the hallway and the unknown that lay beyond, an invitation to finally reclaim her voice. With each trembling heartbeat, the decision loomed larger, its magnitude insurmountable, yet she knew that if she did not step forward now, she might never find the courage again.

Her heart pounded in her ears as doubts and desperate hope warred within her. Yet, amid that inner mayhem, a small, insistent voice whispered: *You must speak up. You deserve to be heard. You deserve to be safe.* And so, Ayanna found herself stood outside her mother's bedroom door, her hands trembling at her sides. Almost three years of carrying Barney's actions had hollowed her out, leaving her with nothing but a growing desperation for it all to stop. Her heart pounded as she rehearsed the words she had been too afraid to speak. What if her mother didn't believe her? What if she dismissed her pain, like others had done to the small concerns she had dared to voice in the past? Still, Ayanna knew she couldn't keep silent anymore. She raised a fist, knocked quietly, and stepped inside when her mother's soft voice beckoned her in. Her mother sat on her bed, flipping through a Georgette Heyer book, her expression warm but tinged with fatigue.

Chapter Six

"What's wrong, love?" she asked, her gentle tone steadying Ayanna for just a moment. Ayanna hesitated, her feet frozen in place, the words caught in her throat. the secret she had carried for so long threatened to choke her. Her mother tilted her head, concern deepening in her eyes.

"Ayanna?"

"I... I need to tell you something," Ayanna's voice was shaking. She stepped closer, her fingers twisting nervously around the hem of her sweater. Her mother reached out to take her hand, grounding her, but it was the small squeeze of reassurance that unlocked the floodgates.

Ayanna's confession finally burst forth in a torrent of raw, jagged emotion. Her voice trembled as she began, "Mum, I...I need to tell you something." In that moment, the dam of her long-held secrets broke, and she could no longer contain the storm within. "Barney... he..." she stuttered, each syllable strangled by the tightening in her throat, as if the very sound of his name dredged up a litany of unspeakable memories. Her eyes burned with tears, blurring her vision into a desperate haze as she managed to force out the words: "He did things to me... I tried to scream; I tried to fight, but I was so scared. No matter how hard I said 'no,' it happened over and over until I felt completely empty."

Her voice cracked as each fractured phrase tumbled out, disjointed and laden with the unbearable weight of repeated violation. The painful fragments spilled over, brief, halting admissions of how, time after time, she had been trapped in that horrific moment, unable to stop him. Her hands shook uncontrollably as they clutched the edge of her sweater, desperately trying to ground her collapsing spirit. The room seemed to shrink around them, the soft glow of the lamp dimming with every halting breath she took.

Her mother's eyes widened in horror and disbelief, her grip on Ayanna's trembling hand tightening as though trying to anchor them both against the tidal wave of pain. "What… what did he do, Ayanna?" her mother managed, her voice thick with despair and disbelief. In that crushing silence, Ayanna's confession continued in broken, raw whispers, each word punctuated by a strangled sob: "I…I couldn't make it stop. Every time I said no, the words got caught in my throat, and he kept doing it…again and again. I'm so sorry… I tried so hard to fight, but I was too scared. It never ended. I'm so… so … *tired*."

Chapter Six

The power of her words, each one a jagged shard from a shattered childhood, filled the space between them with a truth so unbearable it threatened to suffocate them both.

For a moment, her mother was frozen, her hands trembling as she processed the enormity of Ayanna's revelation. Her lips moved silently, forming words that never came out. Finally, she stood, pacing the room as though the movement might help her grasp what she had just heard.

Alice's world shattered in that instant. The moment Ayanna's raw confession faded into trembling silence, Alice felt her heart clench so painfully it was as though ice had wedged itself in her chest. Her eyes widened in disbelief and horror as her daughter's fragmented words echoed in the dim room. For a long, suspended moment, time seemed to slow, each heartbeat pounding out the unbearable truth.

A tidal wave of regret and anguish crashed over her. She could barely breathe; every syllable of Ayanna's confession sliced through her. Tears, unbidden and bitter, streamed silently down her cheeks. Her mind reeled with a thousand "what ifs", *what if she had been braver, what if she had protected her daughter, what if she had spoken up sooner.* The realisation that

Ayanna had suffered over and over again, that the abuse had been a relentless, recurring nightmare, broke her in a way she could never have imagined.

Her heart felt so heavy, it was as if it might shatter completely. In that excruciating moment, Alice's body went rigid, and a silent cry, unuttered and raw, bubbled up within her. She was hurt, deeply, irreparably hurt; by the cruelty of others and by her own failure to shield the one person she loved more than life itself. The overwhelming sense of loss and guilt, of being unable to be the guardian Ayanna so desperately needed, left her utterly broken. All at once, her world had become a vortex of sorrow and remorse, and as she stared at the space where her daughter's pain hung between them, and didn't know what to do.

"Why didn't you tell me sooner?" she asked, her voice sharp with guilt and pain. "Why didn't I see it?" Ayanna stayed silent,

Alice's trembling hand fumbled with the receiver as she lifted it from the cradle of the old landline. The phone's weight in her hand felt unbearably heavy, and every digit she punched in on the rotary dial vibrated with urgency. From Ayanna's hidden vantage point by her mother's bedroom door where she had retreated, the low murmur of the conversation seeped through the air.

Alice's voice cracked as she began, "Arthur... something's happened to Ayanna" Her tone was raw, almost pleading, and each syllable seemed to echo in the silent hallway. Ayanna couldn't catch every word, but she caught snippets: "I... I knew she'd changed... I never knew why until now... it explains so much..." The words spilled out haltingly, punctuated by a choked sob that made the room feel even colder.

As Alice continued, her voice grew more desperate. "I can't keep watching her suffer. I've tried... I've tried to protect her, but I'm failing. I need your help, Arthur... He's your son!" The intensity of her plea was matched by the tremor in her tone, a sound that made Ayanna's heart pound with both dread and a strange, flickering relief.

In that moment, the overhead light in the hallway flickered intermittently, casting long, jittery shadows on the worn carpet, a visual echo of the instability that gripped Ayanna. Each pause in Alice's words left
Ayanna's mind swirling with frantic doubts: What if Arthur didn't believe her? What if this confession only opens deeper

wounds? The fragments of conversation mingled with Ayanna's own racing thoughts, left her suspended in a terrifying limbo.

Alice's words, barely more than a whisper at times, resonated with a desperate vulnerability. "I know... I know this is terrible and wrong, and I just... I can't do it alone," she said, her voice trembling, heavy with a mixture of sorrow and determination. Ayanna, hidden in the doorway, felt her body freeze as the reality of this moment, the moment when the secret would no longer be hers alone dawned on her. The secret of what Barney had done, repeated too often, was now out in the open, shared with someone who might finally help, or so she hoped.

As Alice's conversation with Arthur unfolded in disjointed, halting bursts, Ayanna's mind churned with terror and uncertainty. Was this the beginning of freedom, or the start of something even more terrifying? In that charged silence, punctuated by the frantic beeps of the phone line, Ayanna trembled, not knowing if this confession would bring justice and healing or plunge her deeper into the nightmare she had always feared.

Chapter Six

The following afternoon, as the grey light filtered weakly through the curtained windows of their quiet home, Alice gently but firmly ushered Ayanna toward her bedroom. Despite Ayanna's insistence, her soft protests and trembling pleas that she didn't need a babysitter, Alice would not relent, her voice both tender and resolute as she murmured, "I'm going to see Arthur, Ayanna. You need to stay here, okay?" With a heavy sigh that carried years of worry and unmet hopes, Alice's hand trembled as she led her daughter down the hall, each step on the muted carpet a reminder of the unyielding isolation that had become their world. Once Ayanna was alone in her room, her mother's footsteps fading into a distant echo along the carpeted hall, she sank onto the edge of her unmade bed. The familiar chaos of her room, a jumble of clothes, textbooks, and scattered personal items, felt momentarily like a sanctuary from the turbulent events of the day. She reached for the worn cover of her diary, its pages a silent witness to years of pain and hidden secrets. In the heavy silence that followed, she began to write, each word emerging as though her heart itself was trying to force the truth onto paper. Her pen scratched out fragments of fear and confusion: *"I don't understand why Mum is going to*

Arthur instead of calling the police..." The words were broken by moments when her heart pounded seemingly out of her chest and tears blurred the lines on the page. She paused, her fingers hovering uncertainly above the page, and then continued with desperate urgency, *"What if this doesn't fix anything? What if nothing changes?"* Her writing became a fevered cascade, a mix of raw hope and gnawing dread that collided with her every thought.

The dim light from a lone bedside lamp cast shifting shadows across her scribbled words, making the room feel both intimate and isolating. Every so often, the steady hum of the refrigerator and the faint rustle of the curtains in the breeze punctuated her internal monologue. In those moments, Ayanna's mind spiraled into memories of the past, snatches of laughter, moments of unguarded tenderness, and the crushing weight of isolation. The diary became her confessional, a place where she could admit her uncertainty about whether her pain would ever be understood or mended. The ink bled into the paper as she attempted to capture the swirling emotions that churned inside her: a desperate hope that her mother's visit to Arthur might be the beginning of a long-awaited rescue, contrasted with a terror that this new step would only deepen the chasm of betrayal.

She scribbled phrases that felt incomplete, as though the true story of her suffering was too vast to contain in mere words. The act of writing was both an exorcism and a torment, a momentary reprieve from the gnawing questions that haunted her:

In that vulnerable space, Ayanna's heart both ached with longing and pounded with defiance. And yet, as her pen finally slowed, she couldn't shake the lingering uncertainty that, with every confession, the storm outside only grew fiercer.

Time lost meaning as she scribbled in a rhythm both comforting and unnerving,. Two hours later, the soft click of the front door startled her from her reverie. Glancing at the clock, Ayanna's pulse quickened as she realised Alice had returned far earlier than expected. She raced down the stairs allowing herself the hope and joy of seeing her mother, knowing everything would be fixed. Alice appeared in the doorway, her once steady face now marred by deep lines of heartbreak and defeat, eyes brimming with a silence that screamed of painful secrets. Alice moved directly to the sofa, where she sat heavily. In that charged silence, Alice's broken voice whispered fragments of her visit, snatches like "How could he mean that" and "This can't be real...", though Ayanna caught only displaced echoes, unable to grasp the full conversation. The weight of sorrow pressed down on them both as Ayanna's mind raced with terror and uncertainty: *Had this meeting gone terribly wrong? Was there no rescue in sight?* The feeling of relief at having finally taken a step toward change overwhelmed by the crushing fear of what the future now held left Ayanna trembling, lost between a desperate hope for healing and a deep-seated dread of even greater pain. Ayanna dropped to the sofa beside her mother and for a long time, they sat side by side, a fragile moment of shared silence, both mother and daughter enveloped in a sorrowful, unspoken understanding that the path ahead was now irrevocably altered. As they sat in silence her mother placed a hand on her knee, a gesture that was meant to be reassuring but felt hollow. Ayanna looked up at her, searching for something, anger, defiance, even sadness, but her mother's face was a mask of conflicted resignation. She gave Ayanna a small, tight smile, one that said, we'll talk later, but Ayanna knew they wouldn't. Later would never come. That evening, she sat on her bed, staring at the walls that had witnessed her silent suffering for years. The familiar surroundings felt foreign, her reflection in the mirror unrecognisable. Her eyes searched for the girl she used to be, the one who trusted her family and felt safe in their presence. But that girl was gone. Her thoughts raced as she sat there, her emotions a hurricane of anger, sadness, and determination. She had trusted her family to protect her, but they had chosen to protect themselves instead. The deception cut deep, but as the hours passed, a new resolve began to take shape. Ayanna reached for her journal, the one place where she could pour out her thoughts without fear of judgment. Her pen moved across the page, the words unvarnished. She wrote about her pain, her anger, and her longing for justice. But most of all, she wrote about her determination to never rely on her family again. When she finished, she closed the journal with a firm hand, her decision solidified. This was the turning point. She would find her strength, even if it meant standing alone. Ayanna lay down, her heart sombre but her mind clear. She had lost her trust in her family, but she hadn't lost herself, and that was what mattered most. As she lay in her bed that night, staring at the dark ceiling. She turned onto her side, then her back, her small body restless under her thoughts. Sleep refused to come, and when it did, it brought no peace. Her dreams were intense and relentless, pulling her back into the moments she most wanted to escape. When she did sleep, she woke gasping, her sheets tangled around her legs, her forehead damp with sweat. She clutched her pillow tightly, her breaths shallow and quick, as though the air itself had turned against her. In the morning, Ayanna moved through her routine like a sleepwalker, her movements mechanical. At school when she was there, Ayanna sought refuge in the library. She sat at one of the tables, a book open in front of her, its pages untouched. Reading had once been her escape, a way to lose herself in worlds far from her own, but now even that felt out of reach. Her eyes skimmed the words, but they didn't stick. Her thoughts drifted, unfocused, as the minutes stretched into an eternity. That night again, Ayanna retreated to her room, ignoring her mother and the smell of dinner on the hob, shutting the door behind her. The lack of sound in here was a small relief, though it did little to ease the ache in her chest. She sat on the edge of her bed, staring at her reflection. The girl in the mirror looked back at her with weary eyes, her figure slumped. Ayanna searched for the girl she used to be, the one who laughed freely and dreamed big, but she was nowhere to be found. Only the ghost of her remained.

Chapter Seven
ARTHUR

Arthur's hand trembled as he set the phone down on the scarred oak desk.

A wave of dizziness surged over him, the edges of his vision briefly darkening as if he might pass out. His chest tightened painfully, his breathing suddenly shallow, laboured. A shrill ringing echoed in his ears, drowning out the steady, familiar tick of the grandfather clock behind him. *No*, he thought frantically, shaking his head in stubborn disbelief. *Alice is exaggerating. She's confused...mistaken.* Yet even as he desperately clung to denial, his gut twisted, heavy with an awful certainty he refused to acknowledge. His body recoiled, physically rejecting the truth he'd long feared but never allowed himself to face, a truth now forcing itself violently through the cracks of his resistance.

The last echo of Alice's urgent voice still vibrated in his ears, words that were meant to sound resolute yet now came across as desperate and broken. He stared at the receiver for several long moments, as if the silence that followed could somehow offer answers. In that heavy pause, his mind swirled with conflicting emotions: a nauseating mix of horror, disgust, and an almost paralysing dread for his son, Barney.

He had just learned what Barney had done to Ayanna. Not once, but repeatedly. Now, with Alice's confession echoing in his thoughts, the reality of his son's actions crashed over him like a tidal wave. He felt both a sickening revulsion and a terrifying protectiveness. How could his own flesh and blood be capable of such cruelty? And yet, in that same moment, his heart ached with a desperate, self-centred need to shield Barney from the consequences of his behaviour.

Arthur sank into the worn leather chair behind his desk. The room around him was a study in muted order: rows of meticulously shelved medical books, a few faded family photographs in ornate frames, and the comforting tick of a grandfather clock, a sound that now felt maddeningly out of step with his inner chaos.

Thin slivers of pale sunlight filtered through the closed wooden blinds, casting stark, narrow stripes across the worn carpet and creating patterns like quiet bars of a cage.

A subtle aroma of aged leather and worn paper lingered in the stillness, lending the room an oppressive weight. The silence pressed inward, interrupted only by the faint groan of the leather chair beneath Arthur's restless movements, a subtle accusation in the otherwise hushed room.

He looked over to an old photograph on the wall: Barney as a young boy, grinning with innocent charm. Arthur vividly recalled the afternoon that photograph had been captured, a breezy summer day in the garden behind their house. Barney had been chasing butterflies, laughing freely as his small feet stumbled across freshly cut grass. Arthur had watched proudly from the patio, a gentle warmth filling his chest at the sound of his son's joyful squeals. At that moment, Barney had turned, holding up cupped hands triumphantly, eyes sparkling with delight. Arthur had believed, then, that the future would always hold such bright innocence, a certainty now cruelly shattered. The memory burned painfully against the harsh truth of Barney's actions, a stark, heartbreaking reminder of how far they had both fallen from that golden, uncomplicated afternoon.

Arthur's stomach turned as he compared that smiling child with the man who now loomed as a threat, the same child who had grown up to commit unspeakable acts. He noted, with a pain that struck him to his core, that Ayanna was nearly as old as Barney had been in that picture. The realisation was a cruel reminder of lost time, of opportunities squandered, and of the heavy cost of his failure as a father.

His thoughts spun violently. *I must protect him. I must shield him from this,* he thought desperately. Yet, even as he resolved to do so, another, quieter part of him whispered that perhaps the truth deserved to be known, that maybe justice *should* be served. The idea of involving the police loomed as a dark spectre, a necessary step for society, yet one that would condemn Barney forever. Arthur's heart pounded in his chest as he tried to reconcile these conflicting impulses. *I can't lose him. I can't let the world tear my son apart. But what about Ayanna?* The thought struck him like a blow, and his lips pressed together in a grimace of anguish.

He leaned back and closed his eyes, his mind racing through memories and doubts. In the half-light of the study, he recalled another photo, a family snapshot from years ago when Barney was a happy, carefree child. The juxtaposition was unbearable. He had believed in the promise of Barney's innocent smile. Now, that promise had been shattered by Barney's relentless cruelty. Arthur's thoughts spiralled. *How many times has this happened? How many times have I ignored the warning signs?*

With painful clarity, Arthur recalled an afternoon several years earlier when he'd come home early from the clinic. He'd stepped into the living room, where Barney and Ayanna had been watching television. Barney had jerked upright from his position on the sofa as soon as Arthur entered, moving too quickly, nervously smoothing his shirt and stepping awkwardly away from Ayanna. She had remained completely still, her body rigid, her wide eyes fixed blankly on the screen as if afraid to blink. For a heartbeat, Arthur had hesitated, noticing something strained and tense hanging thickly between them. But then he'd quickly brushed it aside, rationalizing that it was merely the awkwardness of teenagers startled by an unexpected interruption. Barney was his boy, after all— Arthur had reassured himself there could be nothing sinister in such a mundane moment. Yet now, confronted with the undeniable truth, he questioned if he'd deliberately closed his eyes, willingly blind to protect himself as much as Barney.

He felt a sickening guilt, not for Ayanna's suffering, which he even now found himself dismissing as collateral, but for the failure to rein in his son. Every new detail of Barney's actions was like another dagger driving into his soul, and yet his focus, warped by self-preservation, narrowed to one overriding purpose: to protect Barney at *any* cost.

In that moment, his phone buzzed on the desk, a reminder that the conversation with Alice had not ended his responsibilities. His mind, still reeling was filled with dread for what was to come. *Will she call the police?* he wondered, his stomach twisting. *I pray she won't. I pray for Barney's sake.*

But immediately his mind raced forward, conjuring vivid, horrifying images of blue flashing lights illuminating the street, officers knocking at their front door, and Barney being handcuffed and led away in full view of the neighbours. He imagined whispers spreading through the corridors of the clinic, patients cancelling appointments, and colleagues turning their backs on him. His family's reputation, painstakingly built over years of careful respectability, would collapse overnight. Yet, beneath these fears lay a smaller, insistent voice questioning his priorities, *wasn't Ayanna's pain more important than reputation or status? Wasn't justice the only moral choice?* Arthur immediately silenced the thought; selfishness winning the internal struggle as he clung desperately to his sheltered memories of Barney. But a tiny, rational voice whispered that maybe, just maybe, it was the only way to stop this cycle of abuse. A thought Arthur immediately recoiled from.

Arthur's hands went to his forehead, and he closed his eyes tightly, as though trying to block out the weight of his decision. Every nerve in his body vibrated with a mix of fury and sorrow. He remembered Alice's trembling tone as she had pleaded on the phone, her words still ringing in his ears. That urgency, that desperation, was a call to arms, a call that he was now forced to answer. Yet the idea of confronting the reality of Barney's actions head-on, and the potential fallout from it, filled him with an unyielding terror.

The room seemed to close in around him, the walls, the desk, the photographs—all of it becoming oppressive symbols of the life he had failed to control. Arthur's thoughts became a frantic litany: *I must protect him. I must shield him from this. I must do something, anything...* His hands clutched the edge of the desk so hard that the wood seemed to creak under his grip.

In a moment of anguished clarity, Arthur realised that his choices had narrowed to a single, damning path.

He began to rationalise fiercely, grasping for any justification that could make his choice bearable. Barney was still his child, his responsibility; it was Arthur's role, *his duty* as a father to shield him from harm, even if that harm was of his own making. He began to diminish Ayanna's suffering in his mind, forcing himself to believe she was resilient enough to move past this, or even that perhaps she'd exaggerated out of teenage confusion or misunderstanding. Arthur shifted blame toward Alice, questioning bitterly why she hadn't stopped it sooner, or why she hadn't kept Ayanna away from Barney in the first place. If she had been more *vigilant*, Arthur reasoned bitterly, none of this would be his burden to bear. These twisted justifications helped him bury the gnawing guilt beneath layers of self-serving logic, numbing him to the monstrous truth of his decision.

His son's safety, Barney's safety, was now the sole focus of his existence. No matter how unjust it seemed, no matter how deeply it hurt to ignore Ayanna's pain, his duty as a father demanded that he keep Barney away from her. The thought was monstrous and repugnant, yet it filled him with a cold, determined resolve.

Arthur knew there was no turning back. He was now at a crossroads, forced to choose between the moral imperative to help the victim and the abject, selfish need to protect his son. In that tortured instant, he prayed silently for a future where he could salvage something from this ruin, even as his heart broke anew with each memory of his son's onceinnocent smile.

Arthur's eyes, red-rimmed and haunted, flickered over the silent study.

The quiet seemed suddenly amplified, the rhythmic ticking of the grandfather clock growing louder, oppressive, relentless, each tick like a judgment echoing in his mind. Shadows gathered heavily in the corners, stretching and shifting subtly as though encroaching toward him, closing him in from every side. The familiar walls of the room, once comforting, now felt suffocating, a prison of his own making. In that desolate moment, Arthur was a father in exile from his own humanity.

His resolve hardened painfully, solidifying into a brittle, merciless determination just as the doorbell chimed, echoing through the silent house. It was Alice. He inhaled deeply, steeling himself, and rose slowly from the desk. Each step toward the door felt like a betrayal of his own humanity, but his mind was set, he would do whatever it took to protect his son.

Chapter Seven

He opened the door to find Alice standing nervously on the porch, eyes swollen and red, her fingers trembling as they twisted anxiously around the strap of her handbag.

"Arthur," she began shakily, voice barely above a whisper, "Yes," he interrupted brusquely, stepping aside to allow her entry, his tone utterly devoid of compassion. "Come in."

Alice hesitated briefly before stepping inside, her shoulders drawn tight, gaze lowered as if already bracing for what was coming. Arthur shut the door firmly behind her, the sharp click reverberating through the hallway with unsettling finality.

"We'll speak in the study," he instructed curtly, turning away without waiting for her reply. Alice trailed meekly behind him, the sound of her footsteps nearly lost beneath the relentless ticking of the clock. He felt her fear like a physical weight, but he refused to soften his demeanour. He could not afford to waver.

When they reached the study, Arthur turned to face her, his expression carefully controlled, cold, and detached.

Alice spoke first, desperate and pleading, "Arthur, we can't ignore what Barney's done. Ayanna—she deserves justice. He hurt her…"

Arthur's voice cut sharply through her words, brutal in its calmness. "Ayanna will recover. She's young; children are resilient."

Alice recoiled as if struck, her eyes wide in disbelief. "You can't mean that. This isn't some scraped knee, Arthur. He violated…"

"Enough!" Arthur snapped, his voice ringing with cold authority. "I understand your concern, Alice, but think clearly. Do you want police knocking on doors, officers questioning neighbours, whispers spreading through town? And for what? A public spectacle that will scar both of them for life?"

Alice shook her head weakly, tears already slipping silently down her pale cheeks. "Arthur, please…"

"No," Arthur interrupted harshly, stepping closer until he towered over her, his shadow stretching across the floor, dark and oppressive. "We will handle this privately. Ayanna can stay away from Barney from now on. We'll protect him from any further accusations. No good can possibly come from you overreacting."

Alice stared at him, visibly stunned by his cruelty. Her voice was barely audible, trembling with defeat. "How can you say this? How can you pretend like this didn't happen?"

Arthur met her gaze with icy intensity, forcing down the nausea building in his throat. "It's decided, Alice. I'll deal with Barney. You deal with Ayanna."

She opened her mouth to protest again but seemed to collapse internally, shoulders sagging, eyes dulling with resignation. The fight drained visibly from her body. She turned away, trembling, and whispered, "I thought you were better than this."

Arthur didn't reply, standing rigid as she walked past him toward the door. The quiet sobs shaking her shoulders cut through him, yet he remained silent, immovable, anchored in his brutal decision. As the front door closed softly behind her, he leaned heavily against the desk, feeling hollowed out, empty.

The clock ticked loudly behind him, counting down to a future he no longer wanted but had chosen anyway a future where he had shielded his son at the unforgivable cost of losing his own soul.

Some Girls Drown

Chapter Eight
AGE 13

The afternoon light filtered through the tall library windows, casting long golden rectangles across the worn wooden table where Ayanna sat in the school library. She traced the edge of her textbook with one finger, feeling the slight fraying of the cover beneath her touch. Across from her, Patricia's pen moved steadily across her notebook, the scratching sound a constant rhythm that somehow both irritated and grounded Ayanna in the present moment. The library held its usual whispered quiet, a protective blanket that Ayanna had learned to disappear into when the world pressed too close. Dust danced in the sunbeams between them, tiny universes colliding and separating in slow motion. Ayanna watched them instead of the pages before her, finding more meaning in their random patterns than in the assigned reading she was supposed to be completing. The distant sound of a book cart's wheels squeaking across the floor punctuated the silence, followed by the librarian's soft footfalls as she shelved returns.

Patricia looked up, her dark eyes finding Ayanna's vacant stare. "You haven't turned a page in fifteen minutes," she whispered, her voice holding no judgment, just observation.

Ayanna's fingers stilled on the book's edge. "I'm thinking."

"About the assignment or about everything else?" Patricia set her pen down, giving Ayanna her full attention, something that still made Ayanna uncomfortable after three months of friendship. Being seen fully was both a gift and a threat.

"Both. Neither." Ayanna shrugged, a small gesture that carried the weight of all she wasn't saying. Her shoulders, always held with a tension she rarely noticed anymore, dropped a fraction under Patricia's steady gaze.

Patricia nodded as though Ayanna had given a complete answer. This was what made their time together bearable, Patricia never demanded explanations, never pushed when Ayanna retreated. Unlike the others who had claimed friendship over the years, always wanting something in return: secrets, loyalty, blind obedience, or worst of all, the performance of gratitude.

"We could take a break," Patricia suggested, closing her own book with deliberate care. "The essay isn't due until

Friday."

Ayanna glanced around the library, her eyes skimming over the scattered students, some hunched over books with desperate intensity, others pretending to study while sneaking glances at phones hidden in their laps. No one was paying attention to them, yet she felt exposed, as if her thoughts were broadcasting to anyone who cared to listen.

"I should finish," she said, though the words tasted false even as she spoke them. Finishing meant focus, and focus had slipped from her grasp somewhere between breakfast and third period.

"You're allowed to rest, you know." Patricia's words were simple but landed with revelation.

Ayanna's fingers curled into her palm. Rest had always seemed like something meant for other people, a luxury she couldn't quite achieve. From her earliest memories, vigilance had been her constant companion, Ayanna had learned to read the room before she even understood what she was looking for. Watching for the tightening of a jaw, the flicker of irritation in an eye, the shift in posture that meant she needed to shrink, to make herself smaller. Listening for the subtle changes in tone that signalled trouble. Anticipating what was expected of her before anyone had to say it. with her uncles, with her mother, with Barney.

"Tell me about your writing," Patricia said, changing tactics with the practiced ease of someone who had learned to navigate Ayanna's silences. "Did you finish that story you were working on?"

The question offered safe ground, and Ayanna felt herself step onto it gratefully. "Almost. I'm stuck on the ending."

"Happy or sad?"

"Realistic," Ayanna replied, a hint of a smile touching her lips for the first time that afternoon. "Which usually means complicated."

Patricia laughed softly, the sound warm in the cool library air. "Like real life, then."

"Sometimes I think that's why I write, to make sense of the mess." The admission slipped out before Ayanna could catch it, and she felt immediately vulnerable, as if she'd handed Patricia a key to a door she usually kept locked.

But Patricia just nodded, her eyes reflecting understanding rather than the hunger for more that Ayanna was accustomed to seeing when she revealed any part of herself.

"Art from chaos. There's something beautiful about that."

Their conversation drifted into safer waters, classes, books they'd read, a film Patricia had seen the previous weekend. Ayanna felt the familiar patterns of their friendship settle around her. In these moments, with Patricia's steady presence across from her, the voices that usually whispered caution in her ear grew softer. It wasn't trust, not fully, Ayanna wasn't sure she remembered what that felt like, but it was a reprieve from constant guardedness.

The library clock ticked past four, and more students filtered in, exam season driving them to the quiet corners and well-lit tables. A group settled at the table next to theirs, bringing with them the scent of chewing gum and the rustle of papers being unpacked.

Ayanna felt the change immediately, the air seemed thinner, the space more constricted. Her calm began to recede like a tide pulling back from shore. Patricia noticed, she always noticed, and subtly shifted her chair, positioning herself between Ayanna and the newcomers, creating a small barrier of safety.

The gesture sent an unexpected warmth through Ayanna's chest. It was these small moments of protection, offered without comment or expectation, which made Patricia different from the others who had cycled through Ayanna's life.

"My mother asked if you'd like to come for dinner this weekend," Patricia said, her voice low enough that only Ayanna could hear. "She's making that chicken you liked last time."

The invitation hung between them, heavy with meaning. Dinner meant family, meant entering a home where dynamics were unknown, where patterns of behaviour hadn't been mapped and memorised. Ayanna had been once before, a carefully orchestrated visit that had left her exhausted from the effort of appearing normal, unscathed.

"I don't know if I can," she said, the default response to any invitation. Protection through distance, safety in refusal.

Patricia didn't push, didn't try to persuade. She simply nodded and said, "Well, the invitation stands. Whenever you're ready."

Chapter Eight

Whenever you're ready. As if Patricia understood that readiness was a moving target, a state that Ayanna reached and lost a dozen times a day. As if she was willing to wait.

A sharp laugh from the neighbouring table made Ayanna flinch, her body responding to the sound before her mind could process it as harmless. She felt her defences rising again, the brief peace of their conversation beginning to fray.

"Hey." Patricia's voice drew her back. "Stay with me."

Three simple words that asked for both the impossible and the entirely achievable. Stay present. Don't retreat into the labyrinth of memory and fear. But also, stay connected, don't pull away completely.

Ayanna took a breath and nodded, focusing on the concrete details around her, the smooth surface of the table under her hands, the gentle pressure of her feet against the floor, the steady rise and fall of Patricia's shoulders as she breathed. Anchoring herself in the physical world when her mind threatened to carry her away was a skill she was still learning.

"I'm here," she said, the words truer than they had been an hour ago.

They returned to their books, the conversation ebbing into comfortable silence. Ayanna managed to read three pages before her thoughts began to drift again, but this time they wandered toward possibility rather than fear. What would it be like to accept more invitations? To allow Patricia's steady friendship to extend beyond these contained encounters in neutral territory?

The question itself felt dangerous, loaded with the potential for disappointment or worse, betrayal. Everyone wanted something eventually. The price of connection was rarely stated upfront but always collected in the end.

Yet watching Patricia, her head bent over her work, her presence a needed constancy, Ayanna felt the faintest glimmer of what might be hope. Not trust, not yet, but the possibility that trust could exist. That Patricia might be the rare person who offered friendship as a gift rather than a transaction.

As the library lights flickered on against the fading daylight, Ayanna closed her book. The decision formed quietly but completely, she would go to dinner. One more step into the unknown territory of genuine connection.
The thought both terrified and compelled her.

Chapter Eight

"Saturday?" she said, breaking the silence between them.

"Dinner on Saturday would be good."

Patricia looked up, surprise and pleasure crossing her face in quick succession. She didn't make a big moment of it, didn't celebrate Ayanna's small step as if it were a major concession. She simply smiled and nodded. "I'll tell her. She'll be happy."

In that moment, with the soft sounds of the library around them and Patricia's smile like a lifeline in uncertain waters, Ayanna felt something inside her shift, a tiny adjustment in the architecture of her defences. Not a dismantling, not even close, but perhaps the beginning of a door where before there had only been wall.

It was a delicate hope, fragile as spun glass, but Ayanna held it carefully as they gathered their books and stepped out of the library's sanctuary into the cooler air of emptying corridors.

Ayanna sat in the classroom the next day as the walls seemed to contract with each tick of the clock, the minutes stretching into hours as Ayanna stared at her notebook. The teacher's voice had become a distant hum, words flowing over and around her without penetrating the fog of her thoughts. Her pen had left angry little marks in the margins of her paper, small acts of rebellion against the suffocating pressure of expectation that hung in the stale classroom air. She glanced at her watch, fifteen minutes until the bell. Fifteen minutes too many.

Her notebook lay open before her, its ruled lines populated with disconnected phrases and abstract shapes rather than the neat rows of notes her teachers had come to expect. Today's page featured a crude drawing of a bird caught midflight, wings extended toward the edge of the paper as if seeking escape. Ayanna understood the impulse. The classroom felt like a cage constructed of others' expectations, expectations that had followed her from home to school to every space she occupied.

Mr. Harmon's chalk scraped against the blackboard, the sound sending a shiver down her spine. "Your essays will be due Monday," he reminded the class, his back still turned as he wrote out the assignment parameters. "No extensions this time."

Ayanna's eyes drifted toward the window. Outside, spring had unfurled its tentative warmth across the school grounds.

Chapter Eight

Sunlight dappled the emerging leaves of the oak tree that dominated the courtyard, its branches swaying gently in a breeze she couldn't feel through the sealed windows. Freedom waited just beyond the glass, patient and inevitable as the changing seasons.

Patricia's face flashed in her mind, those dark eyes filled with disappointment the last time Ayanna had skipped class. "You're better than this," she had said, not with judgment but with a conviction that sometimes felt like its own form of pressure. As if Patricia's belief in her created a burden Ayanna hadn't asked to carry.

Her watch ticked past the hour. Fourteen minutes now.

The decision crystallised not in her conscious mind but in her muscles, her body making the choice before her thoughts could catch up. Her fingers slid her notebook into her bag. Her hand reached for her jacket.

Mr. Harmon turned from the board, his eyes sweeping the classroom with the practiced vigilance of a veteran teacher. "The comparison between these two historical periods is essential to understanding, "

Ayanna was already moving, her chair silent against the worn carpet as she pushed it back. No dramatic exit, no stomped feet or slammed door, just a quiet slip toward the side entrance, the one least visible from the teacher's desk. Years of creating disappearing acts had taught her the value of subtlety. Not invisible, but uninteresting enough to escape notice.

The hallway air felt cooler against her skin, an immediate relief from the classroom's staleness. Her footsteps were soft on the linoleum as she navigated the empty corridor, passing rows of dented lockers and classroom doors with their small windows of reinforced glass. Through one, she caught a glimpse of Patricia bent over her work, pen moving steadily across the page, completely present in a way Ayanna had never mastered.

Outside, the spring air carried the scent of fresh-cut grass and distant rain. Ayanna took a deep breath, feeling her lungs expand fully for what seemed like the first time that day. The concrete path leading away from the school stretched before her, cracked in places where persistent weeds had forced their way through, small rebellions against the imposed order.

Chapter Eight

She walked quickly but didn't run. Running would suggest fear or urgency, emotions she refused to acknowledge even as they hummed beneath her skin. The streets surrounding the school transitioned from institutional buildings to residential streets lined with maple trees just beginning to leaf out. Her trainers scuffed against the pavement, each step carrying her further from expectations and closer to the temporary oblivion she craved.

The park emerged around a corner, its entrance marked by stone pillars and an ornate iron gate that stood perpetually open. Inside, the manicured paths gave way to wilder areas where maintenance was less rigorous, creating pockets of semi-privacy among trees and overgrown bushes. Ayanna headed for one such spot, a clearing partially hidden by a stand of evergreens that had become an unofficial gathering place for students seeking escape from school hours.

Three girls already occupied the space, sprawled across a faded blanket spread over the new spring grass. Ayanna recognised them from school corridors and shared classes, though they travelled in different social circles. Kim with her platinum hair and perpetually amused expression; Tasha, whose calm exterior masked a sharp wit; and Kayla, tall and languid, who collected detentions like others collected trading cards.

"She shows up after all," Kayla said, lifting a hand in lazy greeting. "We had a bet going on whether you'd make it."

"Who won?" Ayanna asked, dropping her bag and lowering herself to the edge of the blanket, maintaining the careful distance she kept with everyone but Patricia.

"Tasha," Kim answered, reaching into a small backpack beside her. "She said you never miss a Wednesday escape."

"Patterns make you predictable," Tasha said, her eyes meeting Ayanna's with something like understanding. "That's why I switch mine up."

Ayanna said nothing to this, unwilling to explain that her pattern, Wednesdays when Patricia had student council and couldn't notice her absence, was a calculated risk rather than laziness. Instead, she watched as Kim produced a small plastic bag and a packet of rolling papers from her backpack.

"Quality today," Kim announced, her fingers deftly breaking apart the green substance. "My cousin came back from holiday."

Chapter Eight

The ritual unfolded with practiced efficiency, paper laid flat, plant matter distributed, fingers rolling with precision. Ayanna watched, feeling the familiar anticipation building in her chest. Here, in this hidden corner of the park, the expectations of her school days and family life seemed distant, irrelevant to the moment at hand.

"So, what was it today?" Kayla asked, stretching her long legs across the blanket. "What sent you running for chemical relief?"

"Who says I'm running from anything?" Ayanna kept her tone neutral, though the question struck uncomfortably close to truth.

Kayla laughed, the sound bright against the backdrop of rustling leaves. "Everyone's running from something. That's the whole point of this little gathering."

"Speak for yourself," Tasha countered. "Some of us are just bored."

"Boredom is fear of your own company," Kayla said with mock solemnity, then broke into another laugh. "Or whatever my therapist says."

Kim finished rolling the joint and held it up with a flourish.

"Ladies, your escape vehicle is ready for boarding."

The lighter flared, a small sun cupped in Kim's palm. The first sweetish smoke drifted upward, dissipating into the canopy of branches above them. The joint made its way around their small circle, each girl inhaling with varying degrees of expertise before passing it along.

When it reached Ayanna, she took it carefully between her fingers, feeling the slight warmth of the paper. She inhaled deeply, holding the smoke in her lungs as the familiar burn spread through her chest. The first hit was always a disappointment, just discomfort without relief, but she knew what would follow.

As the joint made its second circuit, the tension in Ayanna's shoulders began to ease. The persistent knot that lived between her shoulder blades loosened its grip. Her thoughts, which usually raced in tight, anxious circles, began to spread out, becoming softer at the edges.

"Earth to Ayanna," Kim's voice broke through her reverie. "Tell us a story."

"What kind of story?" Ayanna asked, her words coming out slower than she intended.

Chapter Eight

"Something true," Tasha suggested. "Something you'd never tell anyone sober."

Ayanna considered this as she accepted the joint again. The irony wasn't lost on her, these girls, whom she barely considered friends, asking for the kind of truth she struggled to share even with Patricia. Perhaps that was precisely why the words came more easily here, in this consequence-free space.

"I used to pretend I was adopted," she said, watching the smoke curl from her lips. "That my real family was out there somewhere, looking for me."

The confession hung in the air between them. Not the whole truth, not the complexity of being the only Black child in a white family that both cherished and failed to understand her, but a piece of it, a safer piece she could share.

"Weren't we all dramatic little shits," Kayla said with a snort, but her eyes held something gentler than her words suggested.

"My mom found my diary once," Kim offered in exchange. "The one where I wrote about hating her boyfriend. She never mentioned reading it, but the boyfriend disappeared a week later."

They all laughed, the sound melting into the ambient noise of the park, distant children playing, birds calling to each other from the trees, the occasional car passing on the street beyond their hidden spot.

Ayanna lay back on the blanket, her eyes tracing patterns in the leaves above. The high had settled in fully now, wrapping around her like a familiar blanket. In this state, the past that usually pressed so close seemed to retreat to a manageable distance. The memories of arguments overheard through bedroom walls, of awkward family gatherings where she felt displayed rather than included, of her mother's perpetual anxiety that manifested as overprotection, all receded like waves pulling back from shore.

She remembered a moment from years ago, when she was perhaps nine or ten. Her mother sitting on the edge of her bed, stroking her hair with trembling fingers. "You have to be so careful, Ayanna," she had whispered. "The world isn't always kind."

Even then, Ayanna had recognised the fear that lived beneath her mother's gentle exterior. A fear that seemed to grow in proportion to Ayanna's increasing independence, as if her mother could sense the day coming when she would no longer be able to stand between her daughter and the world's harsh realities.

"My mom thinks I'm at study group right now," Ayanna said to the leaves above her. "She tries so hard to believe the best about me."

"Must be nice," Tasha mumbled. "My mom just assumes the worst and saves herself the disappointment."

The conversation drifted, becoming more fragmented as the afternoon wore on and the joint was replaced with another, smaller one. They talked about teachers they hated, boys they might love, futures they alternately dreaded and desired. The words flowed without the careful filters Ayanna usually maintained, though even in her altered state, some walls remained firmly in place.

The sunlight shifted, taking on the golden quality of late afternoon. Ayanna felt the familiar paradox of these escapes settling over her, the simultaneous sensation of freedom and confinement. Free from the immediate pressures of school and home yet bound by the knowledge that this respite was temporary, that reality waited with infinite patience for her return.

Kayla had begun a rambling story about her older brother's disastrous attempt to make homemade wine in their basement. Kim laughed at all the right moments, while Tasha occasionally interjected with sceptical questions. Ayanna listened with half her attention, the rest drifting inward to where the first seeds of familiar disquiet had begun to sprout.

This was the pattern she couldn't seem to break, the gradual transition from blissful escape to creeping dissatisfaction. As if her mind, even chemically altered, refused to grant her more than a few hours of peace before remembering all the reasons she sought escape in the first place.

She thought of Patricia, probably leaving student council now, perhaps looking for her. Patricia, whose disappointment never manifested as anger but as a steady belief that Ayanna was capable of better choices. Patricia, who somehow managed to make Ayanna believe it too, at least when they were together.

"You good over there, Ayanna?" Tasha's voice cut through her thoughts. "You went somewhere else for a minute."

"I'm good," Ayanna answered, the lie easier than explanation. She stretched her arms above her head, feeling the grass tickle her skin where her sleeve pulled back. "Just enjoying the sunshine."

And she was, in the complicated way she enjoyed most things, simultaneously present in the moment and aware of its inevitable end, holding both pleasure and disappointment in careful balance as she lay back and watched the leaves shift patterns against the deepening blue of the afternoon sky.

Chapter Nine

The school hallway stretched before Ayanna like a gauntlet, lockers lining the walls like silent sentinels witnessing her passage. She kept her eyes lowered, one shoulder brushing against the cool metal doors as she moved, making herself smaller in the flood of between class traffic. Her body felt hollow after yesterday's escape, the artificial peace long faded, the fluorescent lights overhead hummed with merciless clarity, exposing every face, every interaction to scrutiny that Ayanna felt most sharply when directed at herself.

She stopped at her locker, spinning the combination with practiced fingers. The metallic click of the lock releasing offered a small satisfaction in a day that had presented few. Inside, textbooks were stacked in rigid order, a controlled environment she could maintain when so much else felt beyond her grasp. Her reflection caught in the small magnetic mirror affixed to the door, dark circles beneath eyes that seemed to belong to someone older, someone more worn by the world than a 13year old had any right to be.

Voices rose and fell around her, the casual cruelty and affection of adolescence flowing in currents she had never fully learned to navigate. She caught snippets of conversation, weekend plans, test complaints, relationship dramas, all delivered with an earnestness that made her simultaneously envious and exhausted. The simplicity of caring so deeply about such fleeting concerns seemed like a privilege she'd never been granted.

"Did you see Ayanna yesterday?" The whispered question from somewhere behind her sent a chill across her shoulders. She didn't turn, keeping her movements measured as she exchanged one textbook for another.

"Yeah, with Kayla's crew at the park again." The response carried a smirk in its tone. "Wonder what her perfect little friend thinks about that."

Ayanna's fingers tightened around her physics book, knuckles whitening with the pressure. The judgment wasn't new, she'd lived under various forms of scrutiny her entire life, but the mention of Patricia moved something painful inside her. She closed her locker with deliberate gentleness, refusing to give the gossipers the satisfaction of a reaction.

When she turned, Patricia stood at the end of the row of lockers, a stack of books cradled against her chest like a shield. Their eyes met across the churning sea of students, and something in Ayanna's chest loosened at the sight of that familiar face, the steady calm in Patricia's gaze, the slight upward tilt of her mouth that wasn't quite a smile but held the promise of one.

Patricia moved toward her with the quiet confidence that seemed to come so naturally to her. She didn't push through the crowd or demand space; she simply moved with purpose, and somehow, the sea of students parted for her.

"Hey," Patricia said when she reached Ayanna, her voice carrying over the ambient noise without effort. "I missed you in English yesterday."

No accusation, no demand for explanation, just a simple statement of fact. Ayanna felt the familiar knot of something like shame, though not as sharp as it might have been with anyone else. With Patricia, the feeling was tempered by the absence of judgment in her eyes.

"Yeah," Ayanna replied, the single syllable inadequate but all she could manage in the moment. Their shoulders brushed as a student pushed past, and Ayanna felt the contact like a spark, brief but bright enough to illuminate the shadows of her mood.

Patricia shifted her books to one arm and reached out, her fingers light against Ayanna's wrist. "Are you coming to study with me? The library's going to be packed with the history test tomorrow, but I thought we could use an empty classroom in the science block."

The question contained more than its surface meaning, Ayanna heard the layers beneath it. Are you staying in school today? Are you choosing to be present? Are you letting me in?

She glanced down at Patricia's hand, still resting against her wrist. The contact was gentle but grounding, an anchor in the restless current of the hallway. Patricia never pushed, never demanded, but her consistent presence offered a stability that Ayanna both craved and feared. Trusting that stability meant accepting vulnerability, a trade she wasn't yet convinced was safe. "I have that makeup work for Richards," Ayanna said, neither acceptance nor refusal. Testing the waters, measuring Patricia's reaction.

"We can start with that," Patricia answered smoothly. "I have my notes from yesterday if you need them."

The offer hung between them, simple on its surface. Notes from a missed class. But Ayanna recognised it for what it truly was, an acknowledgment of her absence without condemnation, a bridge extended across the gap she'd created.

Down the hall, Ayanna caught sight of Kayla leaning against a water fountain, watching their exchange with amused interest. An invitation lived in Kayla's raised eyebrow, the slight tilt of her head toward the exit, another afternoon of escape, of temporary peace purchased at the price of tomorrow's regret.

Patricia followed her gaze, understanding dawning in her expression. Her hand dropped from Ayanna's wrist, and for a moment, Ayanna thought she might step away, might finally grow tired of offering bridges that weren't crossed.

Instead, Patricia asked, "What do you need today?"

The question was so unexpected, so direct in its simplicity, that Ayanna felt momentarily unbalanced. No one asked what she needed, they told her what she should want, what she should do, who she should be. The novel experience of being asked left her without rehearsed response.

Chapter Nine

"I don't know," she answered, the truth slipping out before she could catch it.

Patricia nodded as if this was a perfectly reasonable answer. "Then let's figure it out together."

A group of boys passed, their laughter too loud, their bodies taking up more space than necessary. One bumped Patricia's shoulder, sending her books tilting precariously in her arms. Ayanna reached out instinctively, steadying them before they could fall.

Their hands met over the stack of textbooks, and Ayanna felt that same spark, static from the dry air and something more, something that hummed with possibility.

"Thanks," Patricia said, and in that single word Ayanna heard gratitude not just for the saved books but for something larger, for showing up, for still being here despite the pull toward escape.

The warning bell rang, its shrill tone sending a ripple of increased urgency through the hallway. Students moved faster now, conversations cut short, locker doors slammed with greater force.

"Science block?" Patricia suggested again, taking a half step in that direction. "Or somewhere else?"

The choice crystallised in that moment, follow Patricia toward the quiet study space or find Kayla, follow the path toward temporary relief. Ayanna felt the importance of the decision, heavier than it should be for such a seemingly small thing. But she knew, with the bone-deep certainty that came from years of making the wrong choices and living with their consequences, that this wasn't small at all.

"Science block," she said, the words feeling like both surrender and victory.

Relief flickered across Patricia's face, quickly replaced by her usual calm. She didn't celebrate the choice or mark it as significant, another reason Ayanna found her presence bearable when so many others became intolerable. Patricia simply nodded and began walking, trusting Ayanna to follow.

They moved together through the thinning crowd, Patricia slightly ahead, creating a path that Ayanna could follow. It was a small kindness, likely unconscious on Patricia's part, but Ayanna noticed it with the heightened awareness she brought to all interactions.

Chapter Nine

As they walked, Ayanna felt students glancing their way, whispers following in their wake. The unlikely friendship between them had been a source of speculation since it began three months ago. Patricia with her perfect attendance and hushed competence; Ayanna with her sporadic presence and reputation for detachment. On paper, they made no sense. In practice, Ayanna had never felt more understood than in Patricia's steady company.

"I heard Richards is adding an essay question to the test," Patricia said as they turned the corner toward the east wing. Ordinary conversation, a lifeline of normalcy that Ayanna grasped gratefully.

"Of course he is," Ayanna responded, feeling herself ease into the rhythm of their exchange. "Probably about the ethical applications of cell division or something equally impossible."

Patricia laughed, the sound warm in the emptying hallway. "I've been making flash cards. We can go through them together."

The offer contained no demand, no expectation, just the simple sharing of resources, of time. Yet Ayanna felt the familiar caution rise within her. Accepting help created debt.

Debt demanded repayment. What would Patricia eventually ask for in return for these accumulated kindnesses?

The question had followed them throughout their entire friendship, surfacing in moments when Ayanna's defences were weakest. Patricia had never given her reason to doubt, had never leveraged their relationship for gain, yet the fear remained, a persistent shadow cast by years of conditional affection and calculated generosity from others.

They reached the classroom, empty as Patricia had promised. Sunshine spilled through windows that overlooked the eastern courtyard, painting golden rectangles across vacant desks. The room smelled of chalk dust and the faint chemical scent of whiteboard markers, ordinary and somehow comforting in its familiarity.

Patricia set her books on a desk near the window, arranging them with the same careful precision she brought to everything. Ayanna watched her, struck again by the contradiction Patricia presented, so ordered in her external life, yet so patient with the chaos Ayanna sometimes brought to hers.

"Why do you do this?" The question escaped before Ayanna could contain it.

Chapter Nine

Patricia looked up, her brow furrowed slightly. "Do what?"

"This." Ayanna gestured between them, encompassing the study space, the offered notes, the consistent presence that persisted despite her absences. "Put up with me." Something shifted in Patricia's expression, surprise followed by a softening around her eyes. "I'm not 'putting up' with you, Ayanna. I like being around you."

The simple statement should have been reassuring, but Ayanna felt the familiar scepticism rise. Everyone wanted something. The question was rarely if, only what and when.

"But why?" she pressed, needing to understand the mechanics of this friendship that defied her expectations at every turn.

Patricia considered the question with the seriousness it deserved, taking a seat and looking up at Ayanna with clear eyes. "Because you see things differently. Because you're honest, even when it's uncomfortable. Because when you're really here, not just physically but actually present, you make me see the world in ways I never would on my own."

The answer was both more and less than Ayanna had expected. No mention of helping her, fixing her, saving her, the usual motivations people had for inserting themselves into her life. Just the simple acknowledgment of value in her perspective, her presence.

"Oh," she said, inadequately.

Patricia smiled, not pushing for more response. She opened her notebook and slid it to the centre of the desk, making room for Ayanna beside her. "Ready to start?"

Ayanna felt something settle in her chest as she took the seat. With Patricia, the constant alertness that characterised her interactions with others eased slightly. Not gone, never completely gone, but diminished enough that she could breathe more freely, think more clearly.

Outside, clouds passed over the sun, momentarily dimming the golden light. In that brief shadow, Ayanna made her choice again, to stay, to be present, to accept the offered companionship without searching for hidden motives. It wouldn't last, these moments of trust never did, but for now, in this classroom with Patricia's steady presence beside her, it was enough to hold the possibility that not everyone wanted something from her.

She opened her textbook and began.

The kitchen in Patricia's house existed in a different universe from any Ayanna had known, a warm, well-lit space where copper pots hung from a ceiling rack and family photographs crowded the refrigerator door. Light streamed through curtained windows, casting soft patterns across the wooden table where Ayanna sat, her fingers tracing the grain of the wood while trying to ignore the constriction in her chest. This room smelled of cinnamon and rising dough, of coffee grounds and lemon cleaning solution, the layered scents of a home where meals were prepared with care rather than convenience, where kitchen chairs were worn smooth from years of people actually sitting in them.

Patricia sat across from her, a plate holding a generous slice of chocolate cake positioned precisely between her knife and fork. Everything about Patricia carried this same attention to detail, from the evenly spaced buttons on her cardigan to the neat alignment of her teacup with its saucer. In the controlled chaos of high school, Patricia's orderliness had first struck Ayanna as artificial, a performance of perfection. but in her natural habitat,
Ayanna understood it was simply who she was, a person who found comfort in arrangement, in patterns, in knowing where things belonged.

Patricia's mother moved about the kitchen with the fluid efficiency. She wore an apron dusted with flour over a simple blouse and trousers, her hair, the same rich brown as Patricia's, pulled back in a loose knot at the nape of her neck. While Patricia's features carried a delicate precision, her mother's face held a weathered kindness, laugh lines bracketing eyes that missed nothing.

"More tea, Ayanna?" She asked, already reaching for the teapot before Ayanna could answer.

"Yes, thank you," Ayanna replied, the politeness automatic, a reflex born from years of careful navigation through other people's homes. She lifted her cup, watching steam curl from the dark liquid as Mrs. Reyes poured with practiced steadiness.

"I'm glad you could join us today," She continued, setting the teapot on a cork mat at the centre of the table.
"Patricia talks about you all the time."

Ayanna glanced at Patricia, trying to read her expression.

Being discussed in her absence, even positively, triggered a familiar unease. What stories had been shared? Which version of herself existed in this kitchen when she wasn't present to defend it?

Patricia seemed to sense her discomfort. "Just that you're the best writer in our English class," she said, offering a small smile. "And that Mr. Harmon asked to keep your essay as an example for next year."

The clarification should have been reassuring, but Ayanna felt the familiar tightening in her shoulders. Praise created expectations. Expectations led to disappointment. The cycle was as predictable as seasons, as inescapable as gravity.

"It wasn't that good," she said softly, focusing on her plate where her own slice of cake remained largely untouched, fork having only separated a few crumbs from the whole.

Patricia's mother laughed, the sound warm and genuine. "Patricia said you'd say that. You two are quite different that way. Patricia brings home an A-minus and acts like she's failed the entire year."

"Mom," Patricia protested, though without real heat.

"It's true," her mother insisted, wiping her hands on her apron before joining them at the table. "You could stand to be a little easier on yourself, and Ayanna could perhaps, " She paused, seeming to reconsider her words.

"Take more credit?" Patricia suggested, rescuing her mother from the awkward pause.

"Among other things," her mother agreed diplomatically.

Ayanna felt herself being assessed, though not unkindly. She recognised the maternal evaluation happening behind this woman's careful smile, the weighing of influence, the protective calculation that all mothers performed when meeting their children's friends. Ayanna had seen it countless times, though usually with less warmth and more wariness.

The wall behind her displayed a gallery of family photographs, Patricia at various ages, a man who must be her father standing beside her at what looked like a science fair, the three of them posed before mountains, beaches, city skylines. The visual record of a life lived together, of memories intentionally preserved. Ayanna looked away, uncomfortable with the evidence of family cohesion so different from her own disjointed history.

"You can do better, Ayanna," Patricia said briskly, tapping her fork against her plate with gentle emphasis.

Ayanna's looked back to Patricia's face, searching for judgment and finding instead that steady concern that was becoming increasingly familiar, and increasingly difficult to dismiss.

"Better at what?" she asked, though she knew. The question was deflection, buying time while she constructed defences against the conversation she sensed coming.

Patricia held her gaze, undeceived by the evasion. "You know what I mean. Showing up. Being present. Not just in class, but in your life." She set her fork down, her movements deliberate. "I saw you leave with Kayla's group again yesterday."

The statement hung in the air, not quite an accusation but certainly a challenge. Mrs. Reyes rose, moving to the sink with exaggerated focus on rinsing a few dishes, creating the illusion of privacy while remaining within earshot, the parental compromise between supervision and respect.

Ayanna's fingers traced the rim of her teacup while she nodded slowly. The ritual acknowledgment of facts without committing to their interpretation. "I had a headache," she said, the excuse paper-thin even to her own ears.

Patricia's expression shifted slightly, not disapproval, precisely, but a gentle disappointment that somehow cut deeper than anger would have. "You're better than the choices you're making," she said, her voice low enough that her mother couldn't hear. "I don't mean that as judgment. I mean it as truth."

Ayanna felt the words like pressure against an old bruise, painful but somehow confirming what she already knew. Her jaw tightened, holding back the instinctive rejection of both criticism and compliment. Better than what? Than whom? The nebulous standard of "better" had been a weapon wielded against her since childhood, better grades, better behaviour, better control of the emotions that threatened to expose inconvenient truths.

"I'm exactly who I am," she answered finally, the defiance in her words undermined by the slight tremor in her voice. "Not better or worse."

Patricia considered this, her head tilting slightly. "Fair enough. But are you who you want to be?"

The question slipped past Ayanna's defences with surgical precision. Who did she want to be? The question assumed agency, choice, possibility, concepts that felt theoretical

Chapter Nine

rather than practical in the context of her life. Wanting required believing in the potential for having, and Ayanna had learned early that wanting too much invited disappointment.

"I don't know," she admitted, honesty easier in this warm kitchen than it had any right to be. "Sometimes just getting through each day feels like enough."

Something softened in Patricia's expression. "I understand that. I do. But you're capable of so much more than survival, Ayanna."

Behind them, Patricias mother turned on the tap, the sound of running water creating a gentle barrier of noise.

Ayanna was grateful for the small courtesy, the pretence that this conversation wasn't being monitored.

She took a bite of cake, buying time with the mechanical process of chewing, swallowing. The chocolate was rich, complex with hints of cinnamon and crushed up digestives, nothing like the overly sweet, mass-produced versions she was accustomed to. Even this cake represented the difference between their lives, attention to detail, care in preparation, tradition passed from mother to daughter. "My

English teacher in primary school said I could probably get into uni," Ayanna said finally, offering the information like a peace treaty. "If I kept my grades up, stayed focused."

Patricia nodded, unsurprised. "You could. You definitely could."

"But that's two more years of..." Ayanna gestured vaguely, encompassing the school, the town, the life that sometimes felt like a holding pattern rather than a journey.

"Of showing up," Patricia finished for her. "Of doing the work even when it feels pointless."

Ayanna felt a flicker of irritation at Patricia's persistence, at her inability to understand what it cost to continually push against the current of expectation and memory. "Easy for you to say," she muttered, immediately regretting the childish retort.

But Patricia didn't take offense. She simply nodded, acknowledging the truth in the accusation. "It is easier for me," she agreed. "I have this, " she gestured around the kitchen, at her mother by the sink, at the home that enveloped them in its stable warmth. "I don't pretend to know what it's like not to have it."

Chapter Nine

The admission disarmed Ayanna's building resentment. Patricia wasn't claiming to understand; she was simply offering what she could, perspective from a different vantage point, concern rooted in genuine care rather than judgment.

"I'm trying," Ayanna said softly, the words emerging before she could examine them for risk.

Patricia reached across the table, her fingers stopping just short of Ayanna's hand, offering connection without demanding it. "I know you are. That's why I bother to say anything at all."

Her mother turned from the sink, drying her hands on a kitchen towel. "Who's ready for seconds?" she asked with the practiced timing of a mother who knew exactly when to interrupt a heavy conversation.

"I'd like some more, please," Ayanna said, more from politeness than hunger.

As she cut another slice of cake, transferring it to Ayanna's plate with maternal precision, Ayanna thought of her own mother, her anxiety, her hesitant affection, her perpetual fear that had shaped their relationship from Ayanna's earliest memories. Her mother loved her; Ayanna never doubted that. But her love came tangled with fear, with compromise, with the history of choices made before Ayanna was old enough to understand their consequences.

"Thank you," Ayanna said. Patricias mother smiled, touching Ayanna's shoulder briefly before returning to the counter where more dough waited to be shaped. The casual physical affection, neither demanded nor expected, felt foreign, a language Ayanna recognised but couldn't quite speak.

"What about after?" Patricia asked, returning to their conversation as if there had been no interruption. "After high school, what do you want?"

The question expanded in Ayanna's mind, growing from the specific to the existential. What did she want? Freedom, certainly. Space to breathe. Distance from the familiar patterns that seemed to trap her in cycles of advance and retreat. But beyond these negations, beyond what she wanted to escape, what did she actually want to move toward?

"I used to think about journalism," she admitted, the dream so long buried that excavating it felt like archaeology. "Or maybe creative writing. Something with words."

Chapter Nine

Patricia nodded, her eyes lighting with genuine interest. "You'd be amazing at that. Your essays always make me see things differently."

The simple affirmation created a strange ache in Ayanna's chest, not pain exactly, but the shadow of it, the memory of what it felt like to believe in possibilities without the protective layer of cynicism she'd cultivated.

"Maybe," she said, unwilling to commit even to this small hope. "If I can get my act together."

She took another bite of cake, letting the rich flavour ground her in the present moment. Her past would always be there, waiting in the shadows of memory. Her future remained uncertain, a path not yet visible from where she stood. But this moment, this kitchen, this friendship, this offering of care without demand, this was real, and perhaps, just perhaps, it was enough to build upon.

"I'm not very good at letting people help," she said finally, the admission costing more than Patricia could possibly know.

Patricia smiled, understanding reflected in her eyes. "I've noticed," she said dryly. "Fortunately, I'm very patient."

Chapter Ten
AGE 14

Two years had passed since the Alice had met with Arthur's, and though time had dulled some edges, the scars remained sharp in Ayanna's heart. Her family had moved on, or so it seemed. everything continued as it always had, laughter rang out, and conversations flowed, but Ayanna had become a subdued figure in the background, as if her presence unsettled the delicate balance the family had constructed. She didn't attend trips away or larger events anymore, but her absence wasn't discussed. She was a name left off invitations, a face missing from photos, and no one seemed eager to explain why.

Now, at fourteen, Ayanna carried herself with a guarded, simmering edge. Her long, dark curly hair framed a face that had lost much of its childish roundness, her almond shaped eyes holding an intensity that could flicker between warmth and defiance in an instant. Her skin seemed to radiate an inner strength, but her figure, often hunched slightly forward, hinted at a complex mix of anger and vulnerability.

Chapter Ten

She had grown taller, her lanky frame moving with a restless energy that betrayed her inner anarchy.

Ayanna's clothing choices were becoming more deliberate, as if to signal her rebellion. She favoured oversized hoodies and ripped jeans, items that subtly broke the immaculate expectations of her family. A small silver ring now adorned her thumb, something she had saved up for and bought herself, her own private act of autonomy. She began speaking less in family settings but had developed a sharp, cutting wit that occasionally surfaced when she felt cornered, leaving others surprised by her quick, biting comebacks.

Books were still her companions, but they weren't always her escape anymore. Sometimes they were her armour, spines stacked high on her desk, their titles bold, their themes dark, reflecting her shifting worldview. She had also started testing boundaries in ways that weren't so quiet. She scrawled small, rebellious messages in the margins of her notebooks at school, skipped lesson; choosing instead to hang out in the local park and rolled her eyes at authority figures, drawing warnings from teachers who had once praised her potential.

Patricia noticed the shift before Ayanna was willing to admit it. At first, she tried to pull Ayanna back in with gentle persistence, offering to study together, passing her notes from missed classes, waiting by their usual lunch spot a few extra minutes even when Ayanna didn't show. But Ayanna met each kindness with distance, her patience thinning, her resentment growing.

She didn't want to be studied. Didn't want to be rescued.

"You're not the only one who wants to disappear, you know," Patricia had said once, frustration creeping into her voice when Ayanna ignored yet another text.

"I'm not disappearing," Ayanna had replied coolly. "I'm just done pretending."

Patricia had given her a long look then, one that seemed to search for the girl she had first befriended. "You don't have to pretend with me."

Ayanna hadn't answered. Instead, she had shrugged, pulling out a cigarette she didn't even want just to prove a point. Patricia had watched her light it, her lips pressing into a tight line, and then she had simply stopped waiting.

She didn't chase. She didn't beg. She simply didn't allow herself to be ignored by someone she cared for anymore. She put herself first.

Chapter Ten

And Ayanna told herself she was relieved.

But the absence of Patricia's steady presence in her life was another loss she didn't quite know how to mourn.

Ayanna's aggression, though subtle, was beginning to show at home, too. She'd snap at her mother when pushed too far, her voice rising in a way it hadn't before. Once, after overhearing her aunt's dismissive comment about her absence from a family event, she threw a glass in frustration, not at anyone, but at the wall of her bedroom, the sound of the breaking glass as much a release as it was a warning to herself that her anger was becoming harder to control.

Beneath the rebellion, though, Ayanna was still the same girl who longed for love and safety. The scars of her past hadn't healed; they had merely shifted shape, manifesting as the fire that now burned just beneath the surface. She was caught in the liminal space between childhood and adulthood, between the girl who had been wronged and the young woman who was beginning to question what it might take to claim her own power.

But there was one person who never let Ayanna drift too far into the shadows: her Granny. Granny was her anchor, her safe harbour in a stormy sea of silence and judgment. Every

Sunday, without fail, Ayanna and her mother would visit her small, cozy home on the fringes of town. The cottage was nothing like Arthur's imposing house with its air of wealth and authority. Granny's house was warm and cluttered, filled with the smell of baking bread and the soft hum of a radio always tuned to a classical station. It was the only place where Ayanna felt seen. Despite the horrors that had befallen her in the confines of the walls of that space, Ayanna felt as though her Granny's energy and love washed it all away in the moments when it was just the two of them alone.

"You've grown so much," Granny would say, cupping Ayanna's face with hands worn soft by years of care. "I don't know how you keep getting more beautiful every time I see you."

Ayanna's cheeks would flush with warmth, and for a moment, everything else lifted. In Granny's eyes, she wasn't a problem to be solved or a burden to be ignored. She was simply Ayanna, her beloved granddaughter.

Granny had a knack for knowing when something was wrong, but Ayanna had become skilled at deflecting. If

Chapter Ten

Granny noticed Ayanna's occasional flinches or the way her shoulders hunched slightly, she didn't press. Instead, she filled the space with affection, smothering Ayanna in hugs and showering her with small gifts, knitted scarves, homemade jam, or a packet of biscuits she'd tucked aside just for her.

One Sunday, as Ayanna sat at the kitchen table, watching Granny knead dough with practiced hands, she felt an ache in her chest. She wanted to tell her everything, to lay the truth bare and feel the comfort she knew Granny would offer. But the words refused to come.

"You're awfully quiet today, love," Granny said, glancing back at Ayanna. "What's on your mind?"

Ayanna hesitated, her fingers tracing the rim of the teacup in front of her. "Nothing, Granny," she said softly, forcing a smile. "Just thinking."

Granny studied her for a moment, her hands stilling. Then she nodded. "Well, thinking's fine, but don't get lost in your own head. Whatever it is, you can always tell me. You know that, don't you?"

Ayanna nodded quickly, but her throat tightened, making it impossible to speak. Granny's kindness only deepened the guilt that gnawed at her. If she told Granny the truth, would it wreck this safe haven? Would Granny look at her differently, her love tainted by the knowledge of what had happened? Would Granny choose Barney too?

Granny's eyes creased into a sad smile as if she were reading her granddaughter's mind. "I know, my darling. I know you want to escape. I know it's been horrible and hard in ways no child should ever know." Her thumbs brushed away Ayanna's tears with aching tenderness. "I can't take you away from it. I wish to God I could. But this, this mess? It isn't your fault, and it never was."

Ayanna sniffled, trying not to sob.

"I can't fix the world for you," Granny continued softly. "But I can love you through it. Every broken piece, every aching bit of you, I will hold. Always. Even if no one else does."

Ayanna let out a breath that sounded like a whimper and leaned forward. Granny opened her arms, and the girl collapsed into them, clinging tight.

Chapter Ten

"You're not alone, sweet girl," Granny whispered into her hair. "Not while I'm breathing. And not after, either." They stayed like that, wrapped in the promise of love that didn't ask her to be better, didn't demand she smile. Just love, steady and strong. The kind that holds, even when everything else falls away.

She stayed close as Granny moved about the kitchen, listening to her stories about her childhood or her latest attempts at gardening. Granny's voice was constant and soothing.

Later that afternoon, they sat together on the sofa, Granny's arm around Ayanna as they flipped through a photo album. Ayanna found herself laughing softly at the sight of her mother as a child, her hair in uneven pigtails and a gaptoothed grin on her face.

"She was always getting into mischief," Granny said fondly. "Climbing trees, chasing after the boys. You'd never guess it now, would you?"

Ayanna shook her head and smiled. For a moment, she felt like a normal teenager, just a girl sitting with her Granny, soaking in the love and warmth she'd been starved of elsewhere.

As the afternoon light faded and it was time to leave, Granny pulled Ayanna into a tight hug, pressing a kiss to her forehead. "You're my shining star, Ayanna, don't let anyone dim your light."

Those words stayed with Ayanna long after they left. Sitting in the backseat of her mother's car, she replayed them over and over in her mind, clutching them like a lifeline. The family might have pushed her to the margins, but with Granny, she had a place. With Granny, she was loved. It wasn't everything, but it was enough to keep her going.

Days passed, then weeks, and the words remained, tucked into the corners of her mind, a refuge when the world felt too sharp.

And then, one afternoon, she was there again.

The air smelled of cinnamon and old books, the familiar scent wrapping around her like a hug.

The hallway was dimly lit, the late afternoon light filtering through the lace curtains in Granny's house. Ayanna's bare feet made no sound on the plush carpet as she padded softly toward the kitchen. She was supposed to be in bed resting and recovering from a cough that had lasted just a little too

Chapter Ten

long, her mother had had to work, and her Granny had happily offered to look after her for the day. Granny was doing a puzzle in the lounge and Ayanna, not wanting to disturb her had climbed out of bed to fetch a glass of water. Ayanna loved the quiet of her Granny's house, the way it always seemed to embrace her, offering a small corner of the world that felt safe.

Ayanna poured herself a glass of cool water, the gentle clink of ice cubes echoing softly against the glass. She sipped slowly, leaning against the counter, savouring the quiet. The distant sound of Granny humming to herself drifted in from the lounge, the melody gentle and familiar. She closed her eyes for a moment, letting it wrap around her like a soft blanket.

Setting her glass down carefully, Ayanna padded quietly towards the lounge, drawn by the comforting hum. Peering around the doorframe, she watched Granny hunched slightly over a puzzle, her fingers deftly fitting pieces together, eyebrows furrowed in quiet concentration. A faint smile played on Granny's lips, her wrinkled hands moving with practiced ease.

"You'll catch your death, wandering around barefoot like that," Granny said softly, without turning around. Ayanna smiled faintly and stepped inside, sinking onto the faded floral sofa. Its worn fabric, warmed by the afternoon sunlight, felt like a familiar embrace.

"Sorry," she murmured, tucking her feet beneath her, suddenly conscious of how chilly her toes had become against the old carpet.

Granny turned slowly, her expression tender. Her eyes crinkled at the corners, conveying warmth without words. "Nothing to be sorry about. Come here and help me. These sky bits always give me trouble."

Ayanna slid down beside Granny, scanning the scattered puzzle pieces spread across the coffee table. Hundreds of tiny fragments lay before them, a disorganised mosaic of colour and confusion. They worked in silence initially, punctuated only by the soft click of pieces fitting neatly into place. It was a peaceful rhythm, a comforting routine they had shared countless times before.

After several minutes, Ayanna's mind began to drift, the repetitive act of fitting puzzle pieces allowing her thoughts to wander freely. The quiet between them was soothing, but beneath it lay a faint tension she could never fully escape. She felt it each time her family dismissed her, each time a remark stung more deeply than she admitted. A sigh escaped her lips, louder than intended.

Granny looked up gently, her expression carefully neutral.

"Something troubling you, love?"

Ayanna hesitated, running her finger lightly over the smooth edge of a puzzle piece. Her chest felt heavy, the pressure of unspoken words building until she feared they might escape in a torrent of tears. Yet something inside her yearned desperately for release, for the chance to share her burdens with someone who might truly listen.

"Granny," she began cautiously, her voice barely above a whisper, "did you ever feel… like you weren't enough?"

Granny paused, her fingers hovering over the puzzle, the piece she was holding suspended mid-air. She took a slow breath, as though carefully choosing her words. When she spoke, her voice was gentle but filled with a quiet strength. "More times than I could ever count, sweetheart. Sometimes I still do."

Surprise flickered across Ayanna's face. Granny always seemed so certain, so solid in a world that felt endlessly shifting beneath Ayanna's feet. "Really?" she asked softly, the word slipping out before she could contain it.

Granny nodded slowly, setting the puzzle piece down with deliberate care. "I think everyone does, at some point. But feeling something doesn't always make it true, Ayanna. Feelings aren't facts."

Ayanna felt her throat tighten, her voice coming out smaller than she intended. "But what if people treat you like it's true?"

Granny reached over, gently squeezing Ayanna's hand, her skin warm and reassuringly soft against Ayanna's colder fingers. "People will treat you all sorts of ways, love, and very little of that has anything to do with who you really are. Most times, it's about their own fears, their own weaknesses. You can't control their actions, but you can decide what to believe about yourself."

The words hung in the air powerfully. Ayanna stared down at their intertwined hands, fighting back tears that threatened to spill. Her voice trembled slightly when she spoke again. "It's hard to remember that sometimes."

Granny nodded knowingly. "It is, dear girl. But remember, hard things teach us who we truly are. You carry more strength than you know."

Ayanna felt a lump forming in her throat. "Sometimes I'm not sure that's true."

Granny gently placed a finger beneath Ayanna's chin, lifting her face to meet her tender eyes. Her expression radiated kindness and unwavering belief. "Then let me hold onto that certainty for you, until you can find it for yourself again. You don't have to be certain right now; you just need to hold on."

A deep breath escaped Ayanna, releasing tension she hadn't even realised she'd been carrying. The sincerity and strength behind Granny's words felt like an anchor in turbulent waters. She swallowed hard, emotion swelling within her chest.

"Thank you, Granny," Ayanna whispered, aware how inadequate her words were for the depth of gratitude she felt.

Granny smiled softly, patting Ayanna's hand affectionately. "Always, Ayanna. Always."

They returned to their puzzle quietly, shoulders lightly touching, their breathing gently synchronised. The puzzle took shape slowly beneath their fingers, each piece placed a testament to patience, understanding, and silent love. Ayanna found comfort in the steady rhythm of their shared task, each completed fragment subtly reinforcing her connection to Granny.

As the afternoon wore on, the room gradually dimmed, the soft golden sunlight fading into cooler shades of early evening. Granny rose eventually, switching on a small lamp that cast a gentle glow across the cosy room. Ayanna stretched slightly, realising her limbs felt stiff from sitting so still.

"Tea?" Granny offered, smiling warmly as she moved towards the kitchen.

"Yes, please," Ayanna replied, grateful for the brief pause to compose herself.

She listened as Granny pottered around the kitchen, the familiar sounds of the kettle boiling, the clinking of china cups, and Granny's soft humming creating an atmosphere of comfort. Within minutes, Granny returned, carefully balancing two steaming mugs on a small tray.

Chapter Ten

"Drink up," Granny encouraged gently, handing Ayanna her mug. "It'll warm you."

Ayanna sipped her tea, the warmth spreading soothingly through her body. They chatted about simple things: Granny's garden, Ayanna's recent schoolwork, and a funny anecdote Granny shared about a neighbour's mischievous cat. With each passing moment, Ayanna felt more at peace, her worries pushed gently aside by Granny's steady presence.

Eventually, Ayanna settled back against the cushions, drowsy from comfort rather than exhaustion. Granny gently draped a knitted blanket over her shoulders, her touch tender and protective.

"Rest, sweetheart," Granny murmured softly. "I'm here."

Ayanna closed her eyes, comforted by the assurance. She knew, deep within her heart, that no matter how difficult things became, Granny's love would remain constant and unwavering.

Chapter Eleven
ALICE

Alice sat motionless in the living room; her fingers wrapped around the tepid ceramic mug. The tea had long gone cold, but she barely noticed, her eyes fixed on the framed photograph perched on the mantelpiece. The smiling faces of her family stared back at her, a cruel contrast to the strife swirling within her mind.

"I can't keep doing this," she chided herself so quietly that her voice was almost lost in the stillness of the room. "For Ayanna's sake, for my own...I have to find my voice."

With a shaking hand, she lifted the mug to her lips, the cold tea a bitter reminder of the choices that lay before her. In the stillness of the living room, Alice grappled with the unfolding truth that her silence, once a shield, had become a weapon turned inward, slowly suffocating the truth that longed to be spoken.

The sound of footsteps jolted Alice from her reverie.

Ayanna entered the room, her presence filling the space with a soft intensity. Alice instinctively straightened, a smile

Chapter Eleven

automatically forming on her lips. "Ayanna, sweetheart. How was your day?" The words felt hollow, a rehearsed script that barely concealed the upheaval beneath.

Ayanna's eyes met her mother's, a flicker of uncertainty passing between them. "It was fine, Mom. Just the usual." She hesitated, as if sensing the tension. "Are you okay?"

Alice's smile faltered, her hands tightening around the cold mug. "Of course, dear. Just lost in thought, I suppose." She studied her daughter's face, the lines of weariness that seemed to etch themselves deeper with each passing day. The guilt that had become her constant companion surged forward, mingling with a helplessness that wanted to engulf her.

As Ayanna began to recount the details of her day, Alice found herself only half-listening, her mind eroded by thoughts of her own inadequacy. How could she, a mother who had stood silently by while her daughter suffered, ever truly understand the depths of Ayanna's pain? The thought was a stone in her chest.

"Mum? Did you hear what I said?" Ayanna's voice broke through Alice's thoughts, a note of concern colouring her words.

Alice blinked, forcing herself back to the present. "I'm sorry, sweetheart. I was just...thinking about something else." The admission tasted bitter on her tongue, a reminder of the distance that had grown between them.

Ayanna's softened, a flicker of understanding passing across her features. "It's okay, Mum. I know you've got a lot on your mind." She reached out, her hand resting gently on Alice's arm. The touch was a lifeline, a momentary bridge across the chasm that separated them. But Ayanna withdrew her hand abruptly, a sudden darkness clouding her eyes. "Actually, no, it's not okay," she said, her voice brittle and sharp.

Alice's breath hitched in her throat. She turned to face her daughter, panic rising. "Ayanna..."

Ayanna stood up swiftly, her book forgotten. "Every single time, Mum. Every single time, you drift away. I'm right here, begging you to see me, and you just... disappear."

Alice felt her chest tighten painfully. "Sweetheart, I'm here, I've always..."

"No, you haven't," Ayanna cut her off sharply. Her eyes glistened with tears of rage and pain, her fists clenched tightly by her sides. "You've never stood up for me...not

Chapter Eleven

once. You just watch, you sit there, pretending everything is okay, while I'm drowning!"

Alice recoiled, the truth in Ayanna's words stabbing deep. "I didn't...I couldn't..."

"Couldn't, or wouldn't?" Ayanna's voice shook with anger, her pain erupting from years of silence. "You chose them over me. Every time. Your silence wasn't protection, Mum. It was betrayal."

Alice reached out, desperation clouding her voice.

"Ayanna, please, listen..."

"No," Ayanna backed away, her eyes cold, detached, haunted. "I'm done listening to empty promises. I'm done pretending that things can change."

Alice watched her daughter's shoulders sag under the weight of exhaustion, her fury giving way to resignation.

A deep sorrow took hold of Alice, mixing violently with guilt. "I wanted to protect you. I was trying..."

Ayanna laughed bitterly, the sound harsh and hollow. "Protect me? You've never understood. You can't even protect yourself. You're so terrified they'll turn on you, you'd sacrifice anything...even me. Especially me."

Alice felt her world fragmenting, the image of the family she'd clung to shattering before her. Fear surged inside her, the terrifying prospect of isolation looming. Her voice was barely audible, choked by shame. "I don't know how to fight them."

Ayanna stared at her mother, her eyes brimming with tears she refused to shed. "Then you've already lost me."

She turned and left, her footsteps heavy with finality. Alice sank back onto the sofa, feeling hollowed out, the silence settling around her thicker and colder than ever before.

In that instant, Alice felt the full force of her love for her daughter, a love that was tinged with the ache of regret and the desperate desire to make things right. But even as the words formed on her lips, the familiar fear rose up to meet them, choking back the apologies and explanations that longed to be spoken.

"I'm here for you, Ayanna. Always." The words echoed into the now empty room landing flat and inadequate, a pale reflection of the emotions that swirled within her. But they were all she could offer, a fragile promise in the face of the silence that had defined their lives for so long.

The sizzle of the pan resonated through the room as Alice mechanically stirred the simmering sauce, her eyes fixed on the swirling red liquid. The rhythmic motion of her hand belied the frenzy within, her thoughts drifting to the complex web of family dynamics that had shaped her life.

"Maybe if I had spoken up sooner," she mused to herself, as she reached for the spice rack, her hand trembled slightly, a physical manifestation of the fear that gripped her heart. The fear of confrontation, of ruining the delicate balance that held her family together. It was a fear that had been instilled in her from a young age, a learned response to the volatile temperaments that surrounded her. *Family is everything.*

The table was set, each plate and utensil placed with meticulous care, as if the perfect arrangement could somehow compensate for the imperfections that lurked beneath the surface. Alice moved through the motions, her hands steady even as her mind raced with fears and regrets.

In the living room, Ayanna sat curled on the couch, her gaze fixed on the pages of a book. But Alice could see the tension in her daughter, the way her fingers held the pages just a little too tightly. The chasm between them seemed to grow with each passing moment, a gulf of unacknowledged pain.

Alice paused, a dish towel clutched in her hands, as she watched her daughter from the doorway. The urge to reach out, to bridge the gap between them, was almost overwhelming. But the words stuck in her throat, trapped by years of silence and the fear of saying the wrong thing.

Alice knew, deep down, that she had failed her daughter in countless ways, that her silence had only widened the rift between them.

But even as the realisation washed over her, Alice found herself unable to speak., of unleashing the torrent of emotions that simmered just beneath the surface, held her captive.

And so, she remained, a silent witness to her daughter's pain, as the evening stretched on, and the shadows lengthened across the kitchen floor. The dishes were washed, the leftovers stored away, but the bitter taste of their silence lingered long after the last light had been extinguished.

In the darkness of her bedroom, Alice lay awake, her mind replaying the memories of Ayanna's conversation, the guilt of her own complicity. And as the night wore on, all that remained unsaid fell over her like a suffocating blanket.

Alice stood before the mirror, her reflection a startling contrast to the woman she had once been. In the harsh light of the bedroom, she could no longer hide from the truth that had been staring her in the face for years.

Her fingers touched the contours of her face, as if trying to map out the decisions that had led her to this moment.

Each wrinkle, each shadow, seemed to accusations of complicity, of a silence that had allowed the wounds to fester and grow.

Alice's mind wandered to Ayanna, to the pain she heard in her daughter's voice. The recognition that her own inaction had contributed to that pain was a bitter pill to swallow, but one she could no longer avoid.

As she began her nightly routine, the motions automatic and familiar, Alice's thoughts raced with the possibilities of what confronting her family might mean.

"What if they turn on me?" she mused to her reflection, her voice trembling. "What if I lose them, too?"

The fear of fracturing the already strained family ties weighed heavily on her, a burden she had carried for so long that it had become a part of her very being. The thought of losing the only family she had ever known, no matter how dysfunctional, was a terrifying prospect.

But as she stared at her reflection, Alice realised that the price of silence was even higher. The guilt, the shame, the knowledge that she had failed her daughter in the most fundamental way - those were burdens she could no longer bear.

With a sigh, Alice turned away from the mirror, her decision still unmade. The path forward was unclear, the risks and rewards in constant battle within her mind. But one thing was certain - her silence had become too much to carry, and something had to change.

As she climbed into bed, the darkness of the room mirroring the turbulence within, Alice knew that sleep would be elusive. Thoughts of her past and the uncertainty of her future would keep her company through the long, lonely hours of the night, a fitting penance for the choices she had made and the ones she had yet to face.

* * *

Chapter Eleven

Alice's hand hovered over the phone, her fingers trembling as they brushed against the cool plastic. Years of silence and complicity threatening to crush her resolve. She could feel her heart pounding in her chest, a frantic rhythm that mirrored the chaos of her thoughts.

She pictured Arthur's face, the lines of disapproval etched into his features. The thought of confronting him, of laying bare the anger that lurked beneath the surface sent a shiver down her spine.

"I can't," she cried silently, "I can't do this."

But even as the words left her lips, Alice knew that she had to. For Ayanna, for herself, for the future they both deserved. She had spent too long in the shadows, too long allowing fear to dictate her actions. She had to confront him, stand up for her daughter. Give her the voice she needed so long ago.

With a deep breath, Alice lifted the receiver, her fingers poised to dial. But as she stared at the numbers, the gravity of her decision crashed over her once more. The potential for fallout loomed large in her mind.

Slowly, reluctantly, she placed the phone back on the cradle, the click of the receiver a deafening sound in the quiet room. Alice closed her eyes, a single tear sliding down her cheek.

She lay back on the bed, the darkness enveloping her like a shroud. The unresolved conflict within her heart mirrored the shadows that danced across the walls, a testament to the battles she had yet to fight.

Alice turned onto her side, curling into herself, her arms wrapping around the emptiness beside her. The phone sat inches away, silent and waiting.

As Alice stared into the void, the spectre of regret crept into her consciousness, a lingering reminder of the actions left untaken. She knew that this moment would be a turning point, a crossroads that would define the course of her future.

But for now, in the stillness of the night, Alice allowed herself to be engulfed by the darkness, her mind a flurry of fear, guilt, and the desperate hope for a brighter tomorrow.

She told herself she would call him tomorrow. But she never would.

Chapter Twelve
AGE 14

The racket of slamming lockers and adolescent chatter crashed over Ayanna like a tidal wave as she stepped into the crowded hallway. Her heart hammered against her ribcage; each beat a reminder of her otherness in this sea of pinkish peach faces. She clutched her books tighter to her chest, a flimsy shield against the onslaught of sensations.

"Watch it!" A lanky boy bumped into her, barely sparing a glance as he barrelled past.

Ayanna flinched, her carefully constructed mask of indifference slipping for a moment. She tucked a coil of hair behind her ear, her fingers lingering on the familiar texture, an anchor in the chaos. The smell of cheap body spray and stale sweat assaulted her nostrils as she wove through the throng, her eyes fixed on the bathroom door ahead.

"Just keep moving. You're almost there."

The fluorescent lights of the bathroom flickered as Ayanna stumbled inside, the relative quiet a relief. She leaned against the cool tile wall, allowing herself a moment to breathe.

With trembling hands, she locked herself in a stall, fumbling in her pocket for the small plastic bag. The pills rattled softly as she withdrew them, each tiny capsule a promise of temporary reprieve. Ayanna stared at them; her reflection distorted in the metallic surface of the stall door.

"Is this really who I am now?" she thought, tracing the contours of her face with her eyes. The girl looking back at her seemed a stranger, lost and searching not a fourteenyear-old girl who once had such a bright future.

The bathroom door creaked open, voices drifting in from the hallway. Ayanna's fingers tightened around the bag, her pulse quickening. She closed her eyes, torn between the allure of escape and the nagging voice of conscience.

"Just this once." She lied to herself, "Just to get through the day."

As she tipped a pill into her hand, Ayanna knew that she was crossing a line, one that might prove impossible to uncross. But in that moment, with the chaos of the world pressing in from all sides, it felt like the only choice she had left.

Chapter Twelve

Ayanna swallowed the pill dry, her throat constricting around it. For a moment, nothing changed. Then, like a wave washing over her, a warmth spread through her body.

She stumbled out of the stall, gripping the sink for support. Her reflection rippled, a slow smile spreading across her face. The constant hum of anxiety that had become her companion faded to near silence.

"Is this what peace feels like?" she wondered, her thoughts drifting like clouds.

As she meandered into the hallway, the clamour of voices seemed distant, muffled. Ayanna floated through the crowd, untouchable, detached from the pressures that had been suffocating her.

But beneath the artificial calm, a seed of guilt took root. "What would they think if they knew?" The thought flickered briefly before dissolving into the dissonance.

Suddenly, a sharp voice cut through her reverie. "Watch where you're going, freak!"

Ayanna blinked, focusing on the angry face of Tara, a girl from her English class. She hadn't even realised she'd bumped into her.

"Sorry, I didn't..." Ayanna began, her words slow and thick.

Tara's eyes narrowed. "What's wrong with you? Are you high or something?"

The accusation, too close to the truth, ignited something in Ayanna. The detachment vanished, replaced by a surge of defensive anger.

"Back off," Ayanna growled, her fists clenching.

Tara stepped closer, sneering. "Or what? You gonna cry to your mommy?"

The taunt hit Ayanna like a physical blow. Before she could think, her body reacted. Her open palm connected with Tara's cheek, the sharp crack echoing in the swiftly silent hallway.

Time seemed to slow as Tara lunged at her, fingers clawing. Ayanna's drug-addled mind struggled to keep up as they grappled, tumbling to the floor in a tangle of limbs and fury.

Adrenaline surged through Ayanna's veins, amplified by the lingering effects of the pill. She barely felt the sting of Tara's

Chapter Twelve

nails raking across her arm, her own fists connecting with soft flesh.

"Fight! Fight!" The chant rose around them, the crowd pressing in, hungry for violence.

As they tumbled across the linoleum, Ayanna briefly saw her distorted reflection in a nearby window. The stranger staring back at her, wild-eyed and snarling, sent a shock of recognition through her system.

"What am I doing?" she thought, even as her body continued to struggle against Tara's assault. The guilt she'd suppressed earlier came rushing back, mingling with shame and fear.

Ayanna stumbled away from the dispersing crowd. She found herself in a secluded corner of the school's courtyard, collapsing onto a worn wooden bench hidden behind overgrown shrubs. Her knuckles throbbed, angry red welts already forming across her brown skin.

She stared at her hands, trembling fingers splayed against her thighs. "What have I become?".

The rage that had fuelled her during the fight still simmered beneath the surface, but now it twisted inward. Ayanna's mind raced, replaying not just the altercation, but every slight, every moment of exclusion she'd endured.

"Why?" she muttered, clenching her fists despite the pain. "Why did you bring me into this world if you couldn't protect me?"

The image of her mother, rose unbidden in her mind. Ayanna could picture her perfectly: those soft, worried eyes, the way she'd wring her hands when confronted with anything unpleasant. The very thought made Ayanna's jaw clench.

"You saw what was happening," Ayanna hissed, her voice thick with unshed tears. "You knew, and you did nothing."

She leaned back, staring unseeing at the patches of sky visible through the leaves above. The memory of a particular night surfaced, Ayanna, barely seven, creeping to her mother's room after a nightmare. She'd found her mother awake, crying silently.

"What's wrong, Mummy?" she'd asked.

Alice had gathered her close, "Nothing, baby.

Everything's fine."

Chapter Twelve

"You lied to me," Ayanna said now, her voice breaking.

"You chose them over me, every single time."

The bell rang in the distance, but Ayanna made no move to leave her sanctuary. The anger was giving way to a deep, aching sadness. She longed for a mother who would fight for her, who would stand up to the world that seemed determined to break her down.

"I needed you," a single tear finally escaping to trace a path down her cheek. "I still need you. But how can I trust you when you couldn't even trust yourself?"

The harsh fluorescent lights of the headteacher's office cast an unflattering glow on Ayanna's bruised knuckles as she sat rigidly in the uncomfortable plastic chair. Mr. Watkins' voice droned on, a monotonous background to the tumult in her mind.

"Ayanna, this behaviour is completely unacceptable.

Fighting on school grounds is a serious offense," Mr.

Watkins said, his brow furrowed in disapproval.

Ayanna's focus remained fixed on a point just past his left ear, her jaw clenched. She could feel his disappointment, but it paled in comparison to the burden she'd been carrying for years.

"Are you even listening to me?" Mr. Watkins' voice rose slightly, tinged with frustration.

Ayanna's eyes snapped to meet his. "Yes, I hear you," she replied, her voice low and controlled. "But do you hear me? Does anyone actually hear me?"

He leaned back, momentarily taken aback by her intensity. "Ayanna, I understand you might be going through a difficult time, but- "

"No, you don't understand," Ayanna interrupted, her carefully constructed walls beginning to crumble. "You have no idea what it's like to feel invisible in your own life, to be suffocating under secrets and silence."

As the words left her mouth, a strange sense of calm washed over Ayanna. In that moment, she knew. She couldn't stay here, trapped in this cycle of anger and pain.

"I'm done," she said quietly, more to herself than to him.

"Excuse me?" Mr. Watkins asked, confusion evident in his tone.

Ayanna stood, her movements deliberate and controlled.

Chapter Twelve

"I'm out. This isn't the place for me anymore."

The gravity of her decision, a mix of fear and exhilaration. As she turned to leave, ignoring the headteacher's protests, Ayanna's mind raced. What would come next?

Where would she go? The uncertainty was terrifying.

That afternoon Ayanna pushed open the front door, her body tense as a coiled spring. The house was still, save for the muffled sound of the television from the living room.

She paused, taking a deep breath to steady herself.

"Mum?" she called out, her voice carrying a tremor she couldn't quite disguise.

Alice appeared in the doorway; concern etched on her face. "Ayanna? What's wrong? I just got off the phone with school?!"

Ayanna's carefully constructed facade crumbled. "What's wrong? Everything's wrong, Mum. It's always been wrong." She stepped closer, her eyes locked on her mother's.

"Why didn't you ever say anything? About... about him?

About what they did to us?"

Alice's face paled, her hand gripping the doorframe.

"Ayanna, I... I did everything I could".

"Don't lie to me!" Ayanna's voice rose, raw with emotion. "You knew. You knew what they were doing."

Alice's eyes darted away, unable to meet her daughter's eyes. "It wasn't... it wasn't that simple, Ayanna."

"Simple?" Ayanna laughed bitterly. "No, it wasn't simple. It was hell. And you let it happen."

Alice stiffened, a defensive edge creeping into her voice.

"You don't understand. I was trying to protect you."
"Protect me?" Ayanna's words dripped with disbelief. "By staying silent? By pretending everything was fine?"

She could feel the anger building, a tidal wave threatening to engulf them both. But beneath it lay a desperate need, a need for acknowledgment, for validation of the pain she'd carried for so long.

Chapter Twelve

"I needed you to fight for me," Ayanna said, her voice breaking. "To stand up to them, to all of them. But you never did."

Alice's eyes welled with tears. "I did the best I could, Ayanna. You have no idea how hard it was..."

"Hard for you?" Ayanna interrupted, her hands clenching into fists. "What about me? What about the nightmares, the fear, the knowledge that I was never safe, even in my own home?"

Ayanna's chest heaved, her breath coming in short, sharp bursts. The silence that followed her outburst was deafening, filled with unresolved trauma and fractured trust. She couldn't bear to look at her mother's face any longer, couldn't stand the mixture of guilt and helplessness etched into every line.

Without another word, Ayanna spun on her heel and stormed out of the room. She slammed her bedroom door shut, the force of it rattling the framed photos on her walls. Childhood memories frozen in time, forced smiles and hidden bruises. Ayanna's gaze swept across the room, taking in the remnants of her youth. The bookshelf filled with wellworn novels, each one a temporary escape. The journal on her desk, its pages filled with dreams of a different life. Sinking onto her bed, Ayanna buried her face in her hands. "What am I supposed to do now?" she asked herself, her mind racing. The longing to run, to leave everything behind, was overwhelming. But fear coiled in her stomach, fear of the unknown, of being truly alone.

Chapter Thirteen
AGE 15

Ayanna stared at herself, dark eyes hollow, faded bruises peeking beneath her crop top. She tugged at the hem, covering her slim frame. *Fifteen going on broken,* she thought bitterly.

"Ayanna! You coming or what?" Tasha's voice carried up the stairs.

Ayanna applied another coat of mascara. "Yeah, just a sec!" she called back, her voice steadier than she felt.

She studied her reflection once more. The girl looking back was beautiful, yes, but there was a hardness there now; a wall built brick by brick with every disappointment, every silent judgment. Kindness still lived behind that wall, but lately, Ayanna found it harder to access.

Grabbing her phone, she bounded down the stairs, forcing a grin as she met Tasha's impatient stare. "Finally," Tasha said, rolling her eyes. "Thought you were gonna bail."

"Never," Ayanna replied, the lie tasting sour on her tongue. She'd considered it; curling up in bed instead, but the thought of another night alone with her thoughts was unbearable.

The bass from the party hit them before they even rounded the corner. Ayanna's heart raced, a mix of anticipation and dread coursing through her veins. The house loomed before them, windows throbbing with coloured lights, silhouettes writhing behind curtains.

"Ready to forget everything?" Tasha grinned, squeezing Ayanna's hand.

Ayanna nodded. "That's the plan."

They pushed through the front door, assaulted by a wall of sound and the heady mix of smoke and spilled beer. Ayanna's eyes darted around the crowded living room, recognising familiar faces through the haze.

"Look who decided to grace us with her presence!" Jamal shouted, weaving through the crowd with two clear plastic cups. He handed one to Ayanna, winking.

"Thought you might need this."

Ayanna took the cup, her fingers brushing his. "Thanks," she smiled, bringing it to her lips. The first sip burned, but the second went down smoother. She could already feel her anxiety beginning to soften.

As Tasha dragged her further into the throng, Ayanna caught snippets of conversation, her name a recurring utterance.

"...heard she got suspended again..."

"...always causing drama..."

"...acting out for attention..."

Ayanna's grip tightened on the cup, her jaw clenching. If only they knew, she thought. If only they could see past her, to the lost girl underneath, desperate for connection, for understanding. But it was easier to be the person they expected her to be, wild, reckless Ayanna, always good for a laugh, always down for anything.

She threw her head back, draining the rest of her drink in one long swallow. The music swelled around her, and for a moment, Ayanna let herself believe that here, in this chaos, she could escape.

Ayanna's laughter rang out, sharp and brittle, as she twirled in the centre of the room. The music thrummed through her body, each beat matching the erratic rhythm of her heart. Sweat beaded on her forehead, mingling with the glitter Tasha had insisted on dusting across her cheekbones.

"Another round?" she called out over the pounding music. Without waiting for a response, she pushed her way to the makeshift bar, snagging a bottle of something clear and potent.

As she poured, her hand trembled slightly. *Stop it,* she chided herself. *You're fine. This is fun. This is what normal teenagers do.*

The lights strobed, casting eerie shadows across faces both familiar and strange. For a moment, Ayanna felt utterly alone in the crowd, a sensation so achingly familiar it threatened to overwhelm her.

She blinked hard, forcing the thought away. That's when she saw him.

Across the room, leaning against the wall with unconstrained grace, stood a boy she'd never seen before. His eyes, dark

Chapter Thirteen

and intense, met hers, and Ayanna felt a jolt of electricity run through her.

He raised an eyebrow, a half-smile playing at the corners of his mouth. Ayanna found herself moving towards him, drawn by an invisible force she couldn't quite explain.

Ayanna shifted on her feet, swaying slightly as the alcohol buzzed through her veins, she liked the way he looked at her, not with pity, not with judgment. Just interest. Just want.

"You're Jamal's friend, right?" she asked, her words slurring at the edges, but she didn't care.

Zack grinned, tipping his beer toward her in a lazy salute. "Our parents are friends. I'm just here for the week while they catch up."

Ayanna laughed, the sound loose and light. "And you figured you'd spend it corrupting us youth?" She waved her halfempty cup toward the bottles stacked on the table behind him.

Zack smirked. "Just making sure the party doesn't run dry. No complaints so far."

She took a slow sip, letting the burn settle in her chest before answering. "None from me."

Flirting felt easy. Easier than thinking about how she'd ended up here, easier than remembering the fight with her mother, easier than the gnawing pit of self-destruction she had been feeding all night.

She tilted her head back, draining the last of the drink in her cup before dropping it carelessly on the table behind her.

"Well," she said, stepping closer, the room tilting ever so slightly beneath her feet. "Welcome to the chaos."

Zack's fingers tightened around hers, a silent invitation.

She could leave, or she could let this happen.

She chose.

Her heart pounded as he led her through the tangle of bodies, past the sticky floors littered with crumpled beer cans and forgotten conversations. His grip was steady, reassuring. He turned, his blue eyes catching hers. "Let's take this upstairs".

She didn't hesitate.

Chapter Thirteen

The bedroom door clicked shut behind them, muffling the music that still throbbed through the walls. The room was dark except for the glow of a single lamp in the corner, beckoning them towards the unmade bed.

Ayanna swayed slightly, the room spinning just enough to make her stomach dip. She closed her eyes, focused on the feeling of Zack's hands on her waist.

She needed this.

Needed the distraction.

Needed to feel something that wasn't anger or sadness or the crushing pressure of everything that came before this moment.

His hands slid up her arms, slow, careful.

"Is this okay?" he whispered, his breath warm against her ear.

A shiver ran down her spine.

She nodded. "Yeah." Her voice caught slightly, her lips feeling sluggish around the words.

She wasn't thinking. That was the point.

No thinking. No remembering. Just this.

His lips found hers, urgent and insistent, tasting like cheap beer and something sweet she couldn't place.

Ayanna melted into it, let herself be pulled under.

Her fingers tangled in his hair, gripping him like he was something solid in a world that kept shifting beneath her.

Clothes fell away, piece by piece, hitting the floor in careless piles.

The texture of the bedspread smoothed against her bare skin, grounding her and yet making her feel like she was floating.

"That was..." Zack started, but Ayanna was already moving, gathering her scattered clothes.

"It was great," she said quickly, not meeting his eyes. "I should get back out there."

Stepping back into the party felt like entering another world. Ayanna's legs were unsteady, her mind reeling. She made her way to the drinks table, pouring herself a generous measure of vodka.

Ayanna tossed back the drink, wincing at the burn.

"Having fun?" someone called out.

She plastered on a smile, raising her empty cup in a mock toast. "Best night ever!" she declared, her voice carrying a bravado she didn't quite feel. As she reached for the bottle to pour another, she told herself that if she just kept moving, kept drinking, kept smiling, she could outrun the hollowness that immersed her.

Ayanna weaved through the crowded living room, she heard her name in conversation as she passed,

"Did you see Ayanna earlier? Girl's wild tonight." "I heard she hooked up with that guy in the spare room." "She's been out of control lately".

Ayanna's steps faltered, her grip tightening on her drink. She felt a flicker of shame, quickly doused by a surge of defiance. *Let them talk.* She tossed her head, letting out a bark of laughter that sounded harsh even to her own ears.

"Sounds like someone's jealous!" she called out, her voice dripping with false sweetness. The chatter died down, replaced by awkward shuffling. Ayanna revelled in their discomfort, even as a part of her ached for genuine connection.

Hours later, she stumbled through her front door, the world tilting dangerously.

"Ayanna! do you have any idea what time it is?" Her mother's voice was sudden and imposing. Ayanna squinted at the fuzzy image of her mother, noting the worry lines etched deep around her eyes. "Time for bed?" she quipped, attempting to brush past.

Her mother's hand shot out, gripping her arm. "This isn't funny, Ayanna. I've been worried sick. Where were you?"

"Out," Ayanna snapped, jerking away. "With friends.

Living my life. You should try it sometime."

"Don't take that tone with me," her mother's voice sharpened. "I'm your mother, and I deserve…"

"Deserve what?" Ayanna interrupted, anger rising up. "Respect? For what? Standing by while everyone treated me like an outsider? For never speaking up?"

Chapter Thirteen

Her mother flinched as if slapped. "That's not fair. I've always loved you, always tried to protect you."

Ayanna laughed bitterly. "Protect me? By pretending everything was fine? By teaching me to swallow my pain and smile?"

"I did the best I could," her mother cried, tears welling in her eyes.

For a moment, Ayanna felt a pang of guilt. But the alcohol, the night's events, years of pent-up frustration, it all came crashing down. "Well, your best wasn't good enough," she spat.

As soon as the words left her mouth, Ayanna regretted them. She saw the hurt bloom in her mother's eyes, watched as she seemed to physically shrink. But pride and anger kept her from taking it back.

"I'm going to bed." Ayanna muttered, pushing past her mother.

As she climbed the stairs, she heard a soft sob behind her.

Ayanna paused, one hand on the railing. She wanted to turn back, to apologise, to seek comfort in her mother's arms like she had as a child. But the gulf between them felt too wide, too deep.

She continued up the stairs, each step heavier than the last. Ayanna slammed her bedroom door, the sound reverberating through the silent house. She leaned against it, her heart pounding, and slid to the floor. Through the thin walls, she could hear her mother's muffled sobs, each one a dagger of guilt twisting in her chest.

She buried her face in her hands, her own tears threatening to spill over. *"Why can't she understand?"* she wept to herself, her voice cracking.

A soft ping from her phone broke the silence. A text from her friend Jasmine: "Party at Mike's. You in?"

Ayanna stared at the screen, already half drunk, her thumb hovering over the reply button. She thought of her mother downstairs, of the argument, of the pain in her eyes. Then she thought of the resonating beats, the numbing drinks, the escape.

"I'll be there." she typed back, her decision made.

Chapter Thirteen

Ayanna slumped against the bathroom sink, gripping the cool porcelain like it was the only thing tethering her to reality.

Her head was spinning, a dull, nauseating swirl of alcohol and exhaustion, but she needed to get a grip. She had already decided, she was going.

Her reflection in the mirror was a blur at first, but when she blinked, hard, her face sharpened into focus. Her eyeliner was smudged, a dark shadow under her eyes, making her look as wretched as she felt. She turned on the tap, splashing cold water onto her face, the shock of it sending a jolt through her system.

It wasn't enough.

She leaned over the toilet, pressing her fingers into the back of her throat until she gagged. If forcing it out could rid her of the nausea and the heaviness in her mind, she was willing to try. Tears prickled at the corners of her eyes as she finally retched, her stomach heaving in painful waves.

She returned herself to the sink, leaning down and filling her cupped hands, drinking deeply. The water was metallic, lukewarm, not nearly as cleansing as she wanted it to be.

She straightened, gripping the edge of the counter.

Breathe.

She needed to breathe.

Her stomach lurched as the night replayed in her mind, the fight with her mother, Alice's voice cracking with something between anger and desperation. Ayanna had seen it in her eyes, the way she wanted to reach for her, to pull her back from whatever edge she was teetering on.

But Ayanna didn't want to be pulled back.

She wanted to disappear.

She fumbled for her makeup bag, fixing what needed fixing. Concealer under her eyes, a fresh swipe of mascara. She wouldn't let them see how broken she was.

She wouldn't let anyone think she wasn't in control.

Her hands were still shaking.

More water. More deep breaths.

She pulled off her dress, stepping out of the fabric like she was shedding a skin she didn't want to be in anymore.

Chapter Thirteen

Start again. That was the trick.

A new outfit, a short skirt, a different top, a spritz of perfume to drown out the lingering smell of alcohol.

She ran her fingers through her hair, willing herself to be someone else. Someone light and reckless and fun.

Her phone buzzed on the counter.

Jasmine: Hurry up. You'll miss the good stuff.

She glanced at the clock.

Her fingers hovered over her phone screen.

Then, before she could think too much, she grabbed her jacket and climbed out the window, landing softly in the damp grass.

The air was sharp and cold, sobering in a way water could never be.

She started walking, her heartbeat syncing with the rhythm of her steps.

And then she picked up speed.

By the time she reached the end of the street, she was practically running.

The party was in full swing when she arrived, music thumping through the walls. Ayanna pushed her way inside, immediately grabbing a cup from a nearby table.

"Ayanna! You made it!" Jasmine yelled over the music, pulling her into a hug.

Ayanna forced a smile, downing half her drink in one go. "Wouldn't miss it," she replied, already reaching for another cup.

As the night wore on, Ayanna found herself at the centre of the crowd of bodies that seemed to imply that this area was the designated dance floor, her body moving in sync with the pounding rhythm. She'd lost count of how many drinks she'd had, each one numbing her pain a little more.

"You okay?" someone shouted in her ear. She turned to see a concerned face, but it swam in and out of focus.

"I'm fine," Ayanna slurred, waving them off. "Never better!"

Chapter Thirteen

She spun away, nearly losing her balance. The room tilted dangerously, but she laughed, throwing her arms up in defiance of gravity itself.

In that moment, suspended between the flashing lights and the throbbing bass, Ayanna felt invincible. She was untouchable here, far from the arguments, the disappointment, the expectations.

But even as she twirled and laughed, a small voice in the back of her mind whispered a warning. She ignored it, reaching for another drink, determined to drown out everything but the music and the moment.

The world lurched violently. Ayanna's vision swam, the lights and faces around her melting into a kaleidoscope of colour. Her legs buckled beneath her, and she felt herself falling, falling, falling...

"Ayanna!" A panicked voice cut through the room. "Oh my God, someone help!"

The music screeched to a halt, replaced by a commotion of worried voices. Ayanna tried to speak, to reassure them she was fine, but her words were lost and unresponsive in her mouth. She could only watch, detached, as faces swam in and out of focus above her.

"Call an ambulance!" someone shouted. "She's not moving!" Ayanna wanted to protest, to tell them she just needed a minute, but the darkness at the boundaries of her vision was creeping in, consuming everything. The last thing she heard before consciousness slipped away was the wail of approaching sirens.

When Ayanna finally clawed her way back to awareness, it was to the steady beep of a heart monitor and the antiseptic sting of a hospital room.

Everything felt heavy. Her limbs, her eyelids, the thick ache settling deep in her skull. Her mouth was dry, her throat burning as if she had swallowed fire.

The bright lights above her buzzed too loudly, she tried to shift, but even that was too much. Her body didn't feel like hers anymore.

Something tugged at her arm.

Chapter Thirteen

She blinked blearily and looked downward. An I.V line. A thin plastic tube snaking out from a needle buried in the crook of her elbow.

Her heart stumbled over itself in her chest.

"Where...?" she croaked, the sound barely escaping.

Memories crashed down on her in broken flashes.

The party. The shots lined up on the table. Someone shouting her name. The taste of something sweet.

Hands on her shoulders, holding her up, or holding her down?

A black hole where everything else should be.

Panic clawed at her ribs.

Before she could say anything else, a nurse appeared at her bedside, her face etched with a mixture of relief and concern.

"You're in the hospital, Ayanna. You had alcohol poisoning. Do you remember what happened?" Her stomach twisted. She didn't. Not all of it.

She turned her head, wincing as the movement sent a fresh wave of nausea rolling through her.

And then she saw her mother.

Alice sat hunched in the chair by the window, her face pale, her hands clasped together so tightly her knuckles had turned white.

Her mother's eyes were red-rimmed and hollow, as if she had spent hours fighting back tears.

Their eyes met.

And the weight in Ayanna's chest was so much heavier.

Ayanna closed her eyes, bits of the night before flashing through her mind. The party, the drinks, the ...spinning out of control... She swallowed hard, shame burning in her chest.

"I... I messed up," she muttered, more to herself than to the nurse.

The nurse's expression softened. "The important thing is you're safe now. We've been monitoring you closely."

Ayanna nodded, unable to meet the woman's eyes. She stared instead at the I.V in her arm, at the crisp white sheets covering her body. Everything felt too bright, too clean, a jarring contrast to the chaos of the night before.

Chapter Thirteen

"What happens now?" Ayanna asked, her voice small and uncertain.

The nurse patted her hand gently. "For now, you rest. The doctor will be in soon to check on you, and we'll need to run a few more tests before we can send you home."

As the nurse bustled about, adjusting monitors and checking vitals, Ayanna let her gaze drift to the window. The world outside seemed impossibly far away, separated from her by more than just glass and she felt truly alone, stripped of the defences she'd so carefully constructed.

As the nurse left the room Ayanna heard her mother stand up from her seat "Ayanna," Alice breathed, her voice trembling. She approached the bed hesitantly, as if afraid her daughter might disappear. "Oh, baby girl, what have you done to yourself?"

Ayanna flinched at the question, shame coursing through her veins. She turned her face away, unable to bear her mother's forlorn look. "I'm sorry," she mumbled, the words woefully inadequate.

The tension in the room stretched between them like a taut wire. Ayanna could feel her mother's worry radiating off her in waves, clashing with her own deep-seated shame.

"I didn't mean for this to happen," Ayanna said. She risked a glance at her mother, seeing the hurt and fear swimming in her eyes. "I just wanted to forget for a while."

Alice sighed, sinking into the chair beside the bed. "Forget what, sweetheart? What's so terrible that you'd risk your life to escape it?"

Ayanna turned her eyes to the ceiling, blinking back tears. How could she explain the constant ache of not belonging, the desperate need to prove herself, to feel something, anything, other than the emptiness that had taken root in her heart? Even Alice seemed too have forgotten over the years what Barney did.

As the silence stretched between them, Ayanna realised with startling clarity how far she'd drifted from her mother, from herself. The realisation hit her like a physical blow, leaving her breathless.

"I don't know who I am anymore, Mum," Ayanna cried.

"I'm lost, and I don't know how to find my way back." Alice leaned forward, tentatively taking Ayanna's hand in hers. "Oh, my sweet girl," her eyes glistened with unshed tears. "We'll find you together, okay? You're not alone in this."

As Ayanna lay there, her mother's hand warm in hers, she felt a flicker of something she hadn't experienced in a long time: hope. The path ahead was uncertain, fraught with challenges she couldn't yet fathom, but for the first time in months, she felt a spark of determination ignite within her.

Chapter Fourteen
AGE 16

Ayanna had spent the past several months carefully piecing her life back together, each sober day a testament to her willpower. Early mornings replaced bleary eyes and headaches; her nights, once chaotic and distorted with alcohol, grew steadily quieter. But the change wasn't just external, it was a subtle shift in how she saw herself. Learning to face the world without the chemical fog had left her raw, yet oddly proud of her clarity. Still, old habits cast long shadows. While Ayanna no longer found solace at the bottom of a bottle or in the thrum of a thrashing crowd, she couldn't deny the distant siren call of that carefree abandon. Her mind often drifted to the high she used to chase, the sounds that once drowned out her loneliness. Yet each time the urge welled up, she reminded herself of the wreckage those nights had left behind.

Tonight, though, she found herself at a crossroads. It was Tasha's birthday, an event she didn't want to miss. The party was at the house of one of Tasha's college friends, a girl Ayanna had met once or twice in passing but had no real connection to. The place was impressive in the way that always made her feel slightly out of place, high ceilings, sleek modern furniture, and walls adorned with expensive art that no one actually seemed to appreciate. The kind of house where people partied hard but still expected everything to be pristine by morning, as if chaos could be contained within designated hours.

Steadying her nerves, she resolved to keep things in check; she'd drop by to celebrate, maybe dance a little, and leave before the old temptations could sink their claws into her.

The wave of sound and heat that met her as she opened the door was a physical force, and for a moment she paused, her breath hitching with a cocktail of trepidation and thrill. *This is my night*, she told herself, attempting to cast away the shadows of doubt that clung stubbornly to her mind. *No looking back. Just for tonight.*

She stepped over the threshold, her eyes adjusting to the strobing lights that painted the room in splashes of colour. The smell of sweat and sweet perfumes was intoxicating. With each pulse of the music, it felt like the floor itself was alive, vibrating under her feet.

A blur of movement, then an arm wrapped around her shoulder. "You made it!" Tasha slurred the words, already halfway to wasted, her grin loose and uninhibited. She already smelled of vodka and something fruity as she swayed slightly, steadying herself against Ayanna.

Ayanna forced a smile. "Wouldn't miss it."

Tasha grabbed her hand, pulling her deeper into the party. "Come on, it's packed. I need another drink."

Ayanna let herself be dragged forward, weaving through bodies pressed too close together, past the makeshift bar where someone was pouring shots with an unsteady hand. Laughter and shouting blended into the clamour, a sensory overload that made her pulse quicken.

But just as quickly as she had appeared, Tasha was gone, peeling away toward a different room, toward another group Ayanna didn't recognize.

She glanced around, searching for a familiar face, but none appeared. The bodies surrounding her melting into an indistinct mass. Not one of them knew her and she realised that here, among the strangers, she could be anyone, or no one at all. She wanted the anonymity, the chance to shed her history like a second skin. Her past, marked by jagged memories and fractured trust, seemed relentless in its pursuit of her peace. But not here. Not now.

Swaying slightly to the rhythm, she wove through clusters of laughing partygoers, their faces illuminated intermittently by the flickering lights. She felt the eyes of others skimming over her, just another face in the crowd, and relished it. It was both a cloak and a canvas, and she wrapped it around herself eagerly.

"Hey, want a drink?" A voice broke through to her, a voice attached to an outstretched hand holding a plastic cup. The liquid inside sloshed invitingly, a darker silhouette against the glow sticks and phone screens that dotted the space. Ayanna hesitated for a fraction of a second before her fingers curled around the cup.

"Thanks," she said, though she wasn't sure if the word reached the stranger or was swallowed by the music. She took a sip, the coolness of the drink contrasting sharply with the warmth of the room, and let it guide her further into the throng. Just one more face, one more soul searching for solace in the night.

Ayanna's throat welcomed the cool liquid, each sip like a gentle wave lapping at the shore of her anxiety. The alcohol blended with the heat of the room, a soothing cure to the raw edges of her apprehension. She found herself leaning into the conversations orbiting around her, their words vibrant. Laughter bubbled from her lips, unbidden yet sincere, as she caught snippets of jokes and stories, weaving herself into the fabric of shared experience.

"Cheers to the freaking weekend," someone shouted, raising a glass in a toast to the collective want for escape.

"Cheers," Ayanna replied, her voice steadier than she felt. Her cup met another's in clumsy camaraderie. She was becoming part of something here; seen not for the shadows she carried but for the flickering light she could still muster.

The room morphed around her with each subsequent drink. Her steps swayed, an unintentional dance to the music that enveloped her. With every tilt of her cup, her laughter grew louder, a sound uncaged, as if it had been waiting just beneath her skin for permission to emerge.

"Are you having fun?" a voice pierced the murky air, its owner's face wearing a smile that seemed to reflect her own. "Absolutely," Ayanna said, her words trailing a touch too long, the syllables playing catch-up with her thoughts. An arm reached out, steadying her as she wobbled slightly, gratitude mixing with a ripple of unease that she quickly drowned with another gulp.

The world tilted precariously with her next step, the crowd pressing in like a living, breathing entity. Colours swirled, the spinning lights painting everyone in surreal hues. Ayanna laughed again, the sound loud in her ears, as she fought to keep her balance.

"Careful there," a nearby partygoer chuckled, eyes twinkling with shared understanding.

"I'm good," Ayanna assured them, though the room spun defiantly in response. Her feet felt disconnected, her movements more guesswork than intention. But the disorientation was oddly freeing, untethering her from the night. For now, she danced on the threshold of control, her inhibitions dissolving into the pulsating heartbeat of the party.

A familiar hand gripped her wrist, grounding her for a brief moment.

"Ayanna!" Tasha's voice cut through the layers of music and conversation, a buoy in the chaos. She was grinning, her dark curls wild from dancing, a sheen of sweat catching the light. "You're still here! I was looking everywhere for you!"

Ayanna forced a smile, hoping it masked the discomfort winding its way through her chest. "Of course I am!"

Tasha beamed, leaning in to press a quick kiss to Ayanna's cheek, the scent of vodka and coconut perfume lingering in her wake. "I'm gonna get us some drinks!" She twirled once, caught up in the momentum of her own joy, then gestured vaguely toward the packed living room.
"Drink, dance, make a bad decision, just have fun!"

Ayanna laughed, but the sound felt lighter than it should, like it wasn't quite tethered to her body. "I'll do my best."
"Good!" Tasha winked, then was gone, swallowed up by the sea of bodies, her laughter trailing after her like a comet's tail.

Ayanna exhaled, shoulders dropping slightly now that the moment had passed. The warmth of Tasha's presence lingered, but the air around her still felt heavy, pressing in. She rolled her shoulders, willing herself to relax, to melt into the energy of the room the way Tasha so effortlessly did.

Chapter Fourteen

The music pulsed against Ayanna's skin, a living thing that resonated with her own heartbeat. She swayed to the rhythm, caught in a current of revellers when he appeared, a silhouette materialising from the strobe-lit mist. His smile was warm and inviting.

"Mind if I join you?" he asked, voice barely rising above the music.

Ayanna hesitated, her buzzed brain stumbling over caution and curiosity. A rogue thought warned of the strangeness in his unexpected proximity, but it was quickly brushed aside. "Sure," she said, more a reflex than a decision, the word surfacing from her longing for connection.

He sidled closer, matching her movements with an ease that suggested he was no stranger to the dance floor's call. His name was lost amid the crescendo of a new track, but Ayanna found she didn't mind. Names were anchors, and tonight she burned for the drift.

"Great party, huh?" he shouted over the music, leaning in so close she could feel the warmth of his breath.

"Best one yet," Ayanna replied, her tongue thick and clumsy, tripping over the words as they tumbled out. The drink in her hand was a lifeline, and she clung to it, letting the liquid courage fuel her bravado.

Time became a fluid thing, hours compressing into moments, minutes stretching into eternities. With each passing song, Ayanna's sense of self grew fuzzier, like a photograph smudged by too many fingerprints. She laughed at his jokes, though the punchlines arrived muffled and distorted through the music.

"Wait, what did you say?" she asked, squinting up at him, trying to piece together his sentence. Her head felt stuffed with cotton, every nod sending ripples through her vision.

"Just asking if you're holding up okay. You seem a bit..." He trailed off, an eyebrow cocked in mock concern.

"Fine," Ayanna insisted. "I'm fine." But the room spun a silent disagreement, tilting on its axis as she fought to keep pace with both the music and his banter.

"Maybe we can find somewhere quieter for you?" he suggested, his hand brushing against hers, a gesture featherlight yet laden with intention.

"Quieter sounds good," she agreed, her voice betraying a tremor she hadn't detected until it was set free. The prospect of stillness beckoned, a chance to catch her breath and chase away the fog that seemed to be wrapping tighter around her thoughts.

He led the way with a confident stride, and Ayanna followed, her steps faltering, her mind adrift on a sea of doubt and dizziness.

The moment they stepped through a side door, the atmosphere shifted. The cool air of the secondary living room wrapped around her like a shock to her overheated skin, the sudden stillness settling over her. It was a different world from the chaos they had left behind, no vibrating booming music, no drunken bodies pressing in too close. The room was dimly lit, untouched by the party, its furniture neat and undisturbed, the air holding only the faintest trace of cologne and polished wood.

Away from the noise, the stranger's hand rested lightly at the small of her back, guiding her toward a leather sofa near the fireplace. No one wandered in, no voices carried through, just silence, thick and absolute.

"Here," he said, his voice now clear and precise, "you can take a moment."

"Thank you." Ayanna's words felt heavy, like they were dredged up from deep water. The world was swaying gently, a ship finding its rhythm on a nocturnal ocean. She sank into an overstuffed couch, the fabric cool against her skin. A sigh escaped her lips as she closed her eyes, grateful for the respite.

"Better?" His concern sounded genuine, and through the fog in her mind, Ayanna nodded, offering him a wan smile. There was comfort in the idea that someone might actually care, even if it was a stranger whose name she realised she hadn't caught.

"Much," she slurred thankfully.

It started with the brush of his fingers across her cheek, an intrusion that brought her eyes snapping open. Confusion clouded her as his face loomed closer, his breath mingling with hers. The boundaries between personal space and intimacy were lost in that moment, and Ayanna tried to piece together the shift in atmosphere, her pulse quickening in alarm.

"Wait, " Her protest lost in the shuffle as his body pressed her down into the cushions. The room spun faster, the ground beneath her seeming to fall away.

Chapter Fourteen

Ayanna's senses were assaulted by the scent of him, sharp against the muggy air of the party. His touch was insistent, hands roaming where they had no right to be, each movement a brand upon her skin. Her heart hammered in her chest, a trapped bird flinging itself against the bars of a cage.

"Please," she choked out, the plea tangled in her throat. Her mind screamed for her body to react, to push, to fight, but her limbs were uncooperative with both drink and shock.

Panic surged as reality splintered, sharp pieces of comprehension stabbing at her consciousness. The violation was a shadow play behind her eyelids, too horrific to fully witness yet impossible to ignore. She was caught in the nightmare logic of a fever dream, where time stretched and compressed, leaving her disoriented and gasping.

"Stop," she finally managed. But the stranger, continued his assault, a smile curving his lips as though they shared a secret joke.

Ayanna's mind screamed a litany of warnings, each one lost in the thumping sound of hear heartbeat racing, her breath coming in short, shallow gasps as she struggled to free herself from the man's grip. She forced her eyes to focus, looking for an escape, for someone to help, but the room was empty save for them.

"Please," she tried again, voice hoarse with terror and desperation. But now there was anger too, a fire kindled within her that burned away the cloud of alcohol. "Get off me."

His grip tightened in response, fingers digging into her wrists as he pressed her back against the cold leather of the sofa. His body pinned her down, the scent of liquor and stale breath making her stomach churn. She twisted beneath him, but he was stronger, his body a wall blocking every attempt at freedom.

A low chuckle escaped him, dark amusement laced in the sound. "Relax," he breathed, dragging his lips over the side of her face. "Don't make this difficult."

Ayanna bucked against him, panic clawing up her throat. The silence of the room was stifling. She tried to scream, but the sound barely made it past her lips he forced his mouth against hers to silence her, using one hand to hold her arms in place above her head. She felt him grab at himself with his other hand and force himself inside her as terror stole her breath.

Chapter Fourteen

She kicked wildly, her heel connecting with his shin. He grunted, just enough of a shift for her to wrench one arm free, clawing at his face, her nails raking down his cheek. His snarl was immediate, the sharp sting of his palm slapping across her face in response. Stars burst behind her eyes, but the pain barely registered beneath the tidal wave of fear.

She had been here before, not in this room, not with this man, but in this same helpless, suffocating moment. The weight. The force. The sick, familiar inevitability of it.

But no. Not again.

Adrenaline surged through her veins, stronger than the alcohol, stronger than the fear. She reached blindly, her fingers finding the edge of a glass ashtray on the side table. Without thinking, she swung it with every ounce of strength she had left, the impact against his head a sickening crack.

He cursed, jerking away, his hand flying to his temple where blood began to bead against his skin.

Ayanna didn't wait to see how badly he was hurt. She shoved him off, scrambling to her feet, her breath ragged, hands shaking violently as she stumbled toward the door.

She yanked the door open, the blast of noise from the party beyond hitting her like a wave. The music, the laughter, the obliviousness of the world outside this room the music swallowed their movements, and for a moment she hoped it would shield her from his retaliation.

But he followed, his eyes blazing with something dangerous. She could feel his approach before she saw him, adrenaline surging through her veins. With one final burst of energy, Ayanna ducked under his grasp and sprinted for the exit. Her legs pumped like pistons against the rush of panic as she navigated the crowd, disorienting him long enough to disappear into the night air.

There were shouts behind her, calls of alarm and confusion that fuelled her flight. She stumbled once on the pavement outside but kept running until she reached a safe distance, collapsing against a wall to catch her breath.

Tears streamed down her cheeks as she clutched at her shirt where his hands had left bruises across her chest.

Ayanna sat on the floor, still, her breathing shallow, eyes fixed on a stain on the concrete. Her thoughts were scattered leaves in a gusting wind, each one a brief touch of horror before being swept away into the dark expanse of the night.

Ayanna's limbs felt distant, unresponsive as she tried to rise from the cold floor. The world swayed gently, mocking her attempt at steadiness. Her heartbeat thumped in her ears, a dull reminder that time hadn't stopped, even though part of her wished it would. She drew in a deep breath, only to find it laced with the metallic tang of fear.

"Focus," she whispered to herself, trying to gather the scattered remains of memory. But the images were slippery, elusive, like trying to hold onto water. There was the stranger's face, shrouded in darkness, his voice smooth as silk and just as suffocating. Then came the pressure, the invasion, the turning of her own body against her. A tear trailed down her cheek, unnoticed in the numbness.

"Should I tell someone?" The question surfaced through the fog. *"Would anyone believe me this time? Would they do anything?"* Each syllable was filled with doubt. Ayanna's past unfurled before her mind's eye, moments of being diminished, brushed aside, told she was overreacting. The familiar sting of worthlessness crept up, wrapping around her like a second skin.

"I should have known better," she chastised herself, her voice faint in the empty space. *"I shouldn't have drunk so much, been so*

trusting." Guilt gnawed at her, a ravenous creature feasting on her already frayed sense of self.

"*Is it my fault?*". Ayanna knew silence; it was an old companion, one that promised safety but delivered only more shadows. Yet the thought of speaking out, of confronting disbelieving stares and doubts yet again, clawed at her insides with icy fingers.

Her hands trembled as she pulled herself to sit against the wall, the texture of the brick rough under her fingertips, grounding her. "*Reporting it... it could help, couldn't it?*" But the words were a mere wisp of hope, quickly snuffed out by the gale of her anxiety. "*Or it could just make everything worse.*"

Ayanna hugged her knees tightly to her chest, as if she could somehow hold together the pieces of the night. The decision lay before her, a chasm that seemed too vast to cross. And yet, she knew she couldn't stay there, on the floor, forever.

Her phone vibrated against her thigh, the sharp buzz cutting through the fog in her mind. For a moment, she didn't move. She wasn't sure she could, but the light from the screen was relentless, illuminating the fractured night in sharp, sterile contrast.

Tasha.

Chapter Fourteen

Ayanna swallowed hard and forced herself to unlock the phone, her fingers unsteady as she tapped the message open.

What the hell, Ayanna? What did you do?

The words struck like a slap. Cold. Accusatory. She read them once, then again, hoping she had misinterpreted, that somewhere in the jagged edges of her understanding there was another meaning she hadn't grasped. But there was no mistaking it.

Her breath shuddered out of her.

The world tipped sideways. Tasha didn't know. Ayanna doubted anyone did. But even in ignorance, the blame had already found its way to her. It always did.

Ayanna tried to picture Tasha somewhere inside that house, probably standing with a drink in her hand, eyebrows furrowed, waiting for an explanation that Ayanna could never give.

Her grip tightened around the phone, her pulse a dull roar in her ears. A thousand replies surfaced, *you don't understand, I needed to leave, He* …..but each word felt pathetic. Small. Weak.

She inhaled sharply, blinking back the sting in her eyes, and did the only thing that made sense.

She deleted the message.

She blocked the number.

And then she turned off her phone.

Ayanna and Tasha would never speak again.

Ayanna's footsteps were automatic. She walked through the night, the cool air brushing past her skin, unnoticed. Her world had shrunk to a tunnel of numbness, where even the vibrant streetlights seemed dim and the laughter of strangers passing by felt like it came from another universe.

The solitude clung to her. The city was both deafening and silent in its indifference to her pain.

Upon reaching home, Ayanna moved through the hallway like a ghost, her steps soundless, her presence unnoticed, except by her mother.

"Ayanna," her mother's voice drifted from the living room, heavy with exhaustion, but still laced with something softer. Hope, maybe. Or worry. "You're home late."

Chapter Fourteen

Ayanna didn't respond. She couldn't She kept walking.

Her mother shifted in her seat. "Are you hungry? I saved you some dinner." The offer was familiar, a ritual they had danced through a hundred times before, an attempt to reach her, to draw her back from wherever she always disappeared to.

But Ayanna had nothing to give.

Not now. Not ever, maybe.

She ignored the invitation, ignored the way her mother's voice wavered just slightly, ignored the years of failures between them, the moments when she could have asked for help but hadn't, the moments when her mother could have seen through her silence but didn't.

Instead, she climbed the stairs, her fingers trailing along the banister as if grounding herself, proof that she was still here, still tangible.

Her mother sighed, the sound barely more than a whisper. "Goodnight, love."

Ayanna reached her door and paused.

She wanted to turn back. Wanted to say something. But what would she even say?

That she was drowning? That she had been drowning for years?

No.

She swallowed the words before they could rise, shoving them down with the rest.

She closed the door to her bedroom with a soft click that reverberated through the empty space. Her room greeted her with shadows that seemed eager to swallow her whole. Her movements were devoid of purpose as she sank onto her bed, the darkness enveloping her.

Staring into the void, Ayanna wrapped her arms around herself, the chill of solitude seeping into her bones. The violation, the clouded memories, and that old question all swirled together in a dance of despair. "*Why is it always me?*" she asked the silence, her voice breaking. The darkness didn't answer, but it seemed to press down harder, amplifying her sense of culpability.

"Should've known better." she muttered aloud, her focus fixed on the patterns of her bedroom wall. Each shadow seemed to mock her, reinforcing the idea that she invited trouble, that somehow, she was an architect of her own misery. Ayanna's mind replayed the night's events in snippets, each piece punctuated by an internal accusation that this, this was her doing.

"Maybe I'm just broken," she thought.

All alone Ayanna confronted the abyss of self-doubt, wrestling with the unfairness of blame that should have belonged to someone else, yet felt irrevocably hers.

As the night deepened, so did her introspection, even in the solitude of her room, Ayanna couldn't escape the shadows of guilt that clung to her, the belief etched deeply into her being that she was the common denominator in the bad things that befell her.

And there, in the stillness of her darkened refuge, Ayanna grappled with the harrowing thought: If she were somehow different, would fate treat her kindly? Or was she destined to be caught in this cycle of hurt, a prisoner of her own past?

The next morning after a night of tangled and broken sleep Ayanna felt those questions still swirling in her mind "*Enough!*" Ayanna chided herself. It was time to dismantle the walls brick by brick, to reveal the foundation of her truth beneath. Perhaps it would crumble; perhaps it

would stand firm. But this cycle of self-destruction had no place in the life she dared to envision, a life where stability was the cornerstone, not an afterthought.

"Courage," she reminded herself, "isn't the absence of fear. It's facing it head-on." With each heartbeat, determination threaded itself through her doubt, stitching together a newfound resolve. For too long, she had been adrift in the turbulent sea of her past mistakes, but now, the choice to swim towards the shoreline of healing beckoned with undeniable clarity.

She straightened herself, pulling away from the safety of shadows.

"Mum," she whispered as she knocked on her mother's bedroom door, her knuckles barely making a sound against the wood. "Are you awake? Can we talk?" Each syllable felt like a careful step on untrodden ground, fragile yet deliberate.

The pause stretched too long, and for a moment, Ayanna feared there would be no answer, that maybe, once again, silence would be her only response.

Chapter Fourteen

But then the door creaked open, and Alice stood there, bathed in the dim glow of her bedside lamp, her face lined with exhaustion, with worry. With something else, too, something Ayanna couldn't name but had been searching for all her life.

Without hesitation, Alice reached for her, pulling her into a tight embrace. The warmth, the familiarity of it, nearly crushed Ayanna's resolve. For a moment, she let herself sink into it, into the safety she had spent so long convincing herself didn't exist.

Ayanna clutched at her mother's sleeve, her breath coming out in uneven bursts. "Things have been… tough," she admitted, the words catching on the edges of something raw. "Really tough."

Alice pulled back just enough to look at her, her hands still resting on Ayanna's shoulders. "I know, love," her voice was thick with emotion. "I know."

Ayanna swallowed, forcing herself to meet her mother's gaze, forcing herself not to retreat now that she had finally stepped forward.

"I guess what I'm trying to say is…" She hesitated, her fingers curling into the fabric of Alice's nightshirt, her heart hammering. "I could really use some help."

She exhaled, barely realising she had been holding her breath.

Alice's face softened, and without a second thought, she pulled Ayanna back into her arms, her grip even tighter this time.

"Of course, baby," she whispered, pressing a kiss to the top of Ayanna's head. "Of course."

The words hung between them, delicate and fraught with the frenzy of hope and trepidation.

Ayanna's heart pounded like a drumbeat in her chest. "I've been trying to handle things on my own, but it's not working. I don't want to keep spiralling down, you know?"

There was a soft sigh, a sound that traversed the years, wrapping around Ayanna like a tentative embrace. "I understand, honey. It's a lot to manage by yourself." "Can we talk? Like, really talk?" Ayanna pressed,

"We can talk, Ayanna. We can start there," her mother replied, each word a cautious step forward on the bridge Ayanna had dared to construct.

Chapter Fourteen

"Okay," Ayanna breathed out, relief mingling with the fear of what lay ahead. Ayanna allowed herself a fragile smile, a candle flickering in the dark. This small conversation, this hesitant exchange, was the first fragile step toward mending bridges long thought beyond repair.

Alice smoothed a hand over Ayanna's hair, something she hadn't done in years, at least not like this, not with intention, not as a gesture of comfort. "Why don't we spend Saturday together?" she suggested. "Just us. No work, no distractions."

Ayanna blinked, surprised at the offer, at the ease with which it was made.

"We could go to the market in town," Alice continued, her voice light, testing the idea like she wasn't sure if Ayanna would accept. "Look at all the stalls, maybe grab some lunch somewhere nice. Just... be together for the day."

Something in Ayanna's chest ached at the suggestion, the kind of ache that came from remembering something good, something she thought had been lost. The market had been their thing once, back when life had been simpler. When holding her mother's hand as they weaved through bustling crowds had been a promise of safety. "Yeah," Ayanna said, nodding. "That sounds good." Alice smiled then, a small, hesitant thing, but it warmed Ayanna in a way she hadn't expected.

"Alright," her mother said softly. "Saturday, just us." Ayanna lingered for a second longer, taking in the way her mother was looking at her, not with expectation, not with worry, but with something like understanding. She turned and slipped away, back down the hallway, back into the solitude of her own space.

For the first time in a long time, she didn't feel like she was carrying everything alone.

Sliding under the covers, Ayanna let out a slow breath.

The shadows in her room seemed softer, less suffocating.

The knots in her chest had loosened, just a little. She closed her eyes, the promise of Saturday settling in her mind like an ember, small but steady.

For the first time in years, she let herself believe, just a little, that maybe things could change. That maybe, just maybe, she wasn't entirely lost.

Ayanna woke that morning to the drip of last night's rain sliding down her window, the soft patter that felt somehow heavier than her usual soundtrack. It was Saturday, the day her mother had promised her. The beacon that had guided her through the past days, hope of what today would bring.

She lingered in bed longer than she intended, replaying the memory of the party. The pounding bass was still in her chest, echoing in her bones. She could see the swirl of coloured lights in her mind if she closed her eyes long enough. And then, in the same instant, she his face, twisted and distorted, barely human, screaming in her nightmares.

By mid-morning, Alice was already up. She'd taken the day off and seemed to be forging ahead with forced optimism. She knocked on Ayanna's door, voice hesitant.

"Ayanna? I'm… I've made pancakes."

The old her, would have bolted out of bed for the promise of something warm and sweet. But at sixteen, all she felt was that familiar, hollow tension in her chest. She dragged herself up, slipped on a sweater, and padded into the kitchen.

Alice offered a wobbly smile. "I know you like them with extra syrup," she said, gesturing at the sticky bottle on the counter.

"Thanks," Ayanna murmured. She poured the syrup over a pancake she didn't quite want, picking at the edges with her fork. A wave of exhaustion rolled through her, not from lack of sleep, but from a deeper weariness she carried everywhere.

They ate in near silence. Alice tried a few times, commenting on the greyness of the sky, the route they could walk through town, an old film that had come on TV last night. Ayanna listened but responded with only nods or monosyllables. She wanted to say, *I almost told you about the party. I almost came home and spilled everything, how I nearly lost myself again, how I woke up with shame coiled in my stomach.* But she didn't. Because she knew how it would end. It would end in tears or half apologies or vacant promises, and she couldn't handle another gentle heartbreak.

Eventually, Alice sighed, setting her fork down with a tiny clink against the plate. She glanced at her daughter, and in her eyes, Ayanna saw the cracks, an exhaustion that ran parallel to her own. "We could, maybe we could walk down to the park today," she offered. "If you want."

Ayanna swallowed a lump in her throat. Her first instinct was to say no. But she remembered the shadow of hope in her mother's eyes, the memory of "Saturday, I'm yours," and she couldn't bear the thought of dousing that small, quivering spark. She needed her mother, but she just couldn't find the words anymore.

"Okay," she said softly. "Sure."

They ended up in the small, tired park that had once been the source of so many memories. The grass was still damp from the night's rain, and the sky threatened more. Yet, there was something about the looming grey clouds that suited them, mother and daughter, standing side by side, not saying much.

Alice looked around, visibly relieved that Ayanna had come with her, though unsure how to bridge the gap between them. A pair of joggers passed, laughing with an ease that made the silence feel heavier.

"Let's sit," Alice said finally, nodding toward a green bench near the old bandstand. Ayanna followed, heart clenching at the sight of their initials scratched into the wood, tiny lines from years ago. Back then, Ayanna believed in forever.

They settled, each on their own half of the bench, though the unspoken distance felt greater. Ayanna stared down at her sneakers, focusing on the muddy grass clumped at the soles.

She wanted to speak about the party, about how she felt lost all over again, about the ache she carried. But the words died in her throat.

"You mentioned a while back that new film," Alice ventured after several long beats of quiet. "The one with the…you know, the robots or something? I thought maybe we could…"

"I'm not really in the mood," Ayanna said, her voice soft but firm.

"Oh." Alice's disappointment was tangible.

They lapsed into silence again, interrupted only by the breeze rustling the last leaves that clung to the trees. The wind carried a chill, reminding Ayanna of how exposed she felt in her mother's company. Once, this woman had been everything, a fortress, a refuge. Now, Ayanna sensed the fortress had cracks. She saw it every time she looked at Alice's trembling fingers, every time her mother spoke with guilt coating every syllable. In her mother's eyes was an apology too big to speak out loud.

Alice tried again, turning toward her daughter. "I really wanted us to have a nice day."

Chapter Fourteen

Ayanna lifted her head, meeting her mother's eyes for the first time since they'd left the house. A complicated warmth filled her, love and sorrow mingling. "I know," she replied. Then, almost to herself: "I want that too."

Alice took a shaky breath, her shoulders trembling under her jacket. "It feels like we're... like we're strangers now. And I... I know I messed up. I tried, Ayanna. I tried, but..."

"You tried," Ayanna echoed sadly. "But it wasn't enough." And there it was; raw honesty that felt as if it could crack the world between them. Their eyes locked, both sets of eyes brimming with the grief of everything said and unsaid.

"Ayanna... I was doing it all alone," Alice began, voice hollow. "You know that. It was just me, and I wasn't strong enough. I got tired. I let bad people in. I, I didn't see it until it was too late."

Ayanna's jaw clenched. She remembered every instance she'd tried to speak up, every warning sign she had thrown out in desperation, only to be told, *"Maybe it's not as bad as you think,"* or *"We just have to keep the peace."* Or the worst one, *"Family is everything."*

"You let me down when I needed you," Ayanna said, not angrily, but with a weariness that pierced the air. "Over and over. And I kept hoping you'd get it. That one day you'd look at me and realize I wasn't safe, that I needed you to be...be stronger. But you just... you never were." Alice's face crumpled, tears pooling in her eyes. "I know," she whispered. "I know. I have so many regrets, Ayanna. But everything I did, every time I looked away, I was... I was too scared to face the truth. I thought I'd hold us together somehow."

Ayanna looked away from her mother, blinking back her own tears. The sadness was deeper than anger now, a reluctant acceptance. "You aren't evil," she said, voice low. "You're not a monster. You're not even *bad*. You're just... you were never strong enough to protect me the way I needed. And for a long time, I hated you for that."

Alice exhaled shakily, tears sliding down her cheeks. "Do you still?"

Ayanna shrugged, a tiny movement that carried the weight of years. "I don't know. Maybe part of me does. But the bigger part... I'm just tired. Tired of waiting for you to change into someone you aren't. Tired of being disappointed. Tired of hoping for something you can't give. But I do love you, despite everything. I don't think that will ever change".

"Ayanna," Alice choked out. "I love you. I've always loved you. I'd do anything,"

"I know," Ayanna interrupted, meeting her mother's eyes again. "And I believe that, in your way, you did. You do. But... sometimes love isn't enough to fix what's broken."

Alice's hands trembled in her lap. "So, what does that mean for us?"

"It means..." Ayanna hesitated, swallowing hard. She thought of the party she'd snuck out to, the darkness she fought every night. The secrets she couldn't burden her mother with because she knew, at last, that her mother didn't have the strength to handle them. "It means I won't tell you everything," she said slowly, each word a decision. "Because I know you can't... you can't hold it all. And that's not me punishing you. It's me understanding who you are."

Alice wiped at her tears, silent acceptance etched into her features. "I wish I could be more."

"Me too," Ayanna said, voice trembling. "But it doesn't mean I don't love you too. I guess I just... I accept that this is who we are."

A hush fell between them. It wasn't forgiveness; there was too much rawness, too many old scars. But it was an understanding, a meeting place in the space between them. Ayanna realised that maybe, just maybe, this was a step toward peace, even if it wasn't the kind of peace she'd once craved.

After a moment, Alice reached for Ayanna's hand, her touch tentative. Ayanna didn't pull away. They sat like that for a long while, two women in a silent park, the chilly breeze raking through the trees. The moment felt fragile and precious, like a glass ornament that might shatter under too much weight.

"I'm sorry," Alice breathed again, so softly Ayanna almost missed it.

Ayanna squeezed her mother's hand, tears gathering in her own eyes. "I know," she whispered. "Me too."

And they stayed like that, hand in hand, tears slipping quietly, the wind carrying away words they didn't speak. It wasn't a grand redemption or a complete reconciliation. But in that moment, they chose to share a slender thread of love, unspoken yet tangible.

Chapter Fourteen

In the distance, a dog barked, chasing a flock of birds that scattered into the grey sky. Ayanna watched them rise, dark silhouettes against a pallid sun. She felt her mother's grip tighten gently and let herself lean closer, just a fraction, letting her own head rest against Alice's shoulder. Not because she believed her mother could shield her from every wound, but because for now, this moment, the closeness was enough.

Tomorrow, Ayanna would still keep her secrets. She wouldn't mention the party or talk about Barney or the past. She wouldn't ask her mother to fight battles she was too frail to win. But she would stay in this space, neither clinging to illusions nor severing the bond entirely.

They were both broken in their own ways, but for the first time in a long while, Ayanna felt something that wasn't just anger or hurt, it was the grace of acceptance. Their family might never be whole in the way she once believed it could be, but perhaps they could still share a life. A gentler life, built on small steps and softer truths.

And so, they sat, beneath a sky that threatened rain but held back, two hearts still bruised but beating in time, finally able to breathe in the fragile love they had left.

Some Girls Drown

Chapter Fifteen
AGE 19

Time had stretched and shifted, reshaping Ayanna into someone she scarcely recognised. It was strange to think it had been three years since she'd softly closed her mother's door, carefully turning the latch with soft determination. She hadn't stormed out or slammed it shut in anger; there had been no drama, no final bitter words. Only a gentle acceptance that if she was ever going to find peace, she needed space to become herself.

Her flat was small, scattered with mismatched furniture, dogeared books, and half-filled journals spilling from every surface. It wasn't neat, nor was it organised; it was a physical reflection of her mind; untidy, raw, and restless. The walls, marked with impulsively pinned photos and scribbled quotes, told stories of late nights and early mornings, joy and regret, freedom and loneliness.

Ayanna hadn't entirely left her mother behind. In fact, their relationship had gradually softened into something quiet, cautious, but comforting. She understood now that Alice was imperfect, just as she herself was. They met regularly at their favourite coffee shop, trading cautious truths and careful laughter. Ayanna had learned to let go of resentment, choosing instead to accept her mother exactly as she was, flaws and all. The warmth they shared was fragile but precious, built carefully around the edges of their shared history.

Yet beneath the growing stability Ayanna presented, a wilder, unsettled part of her still clawed at the edges of her carefully built routine. Her loneliness was persistent, an ache she sometimes struggled to ignore. And when it became too intense, she craved the harsh neon lights of clubs, the relentless beat of music loud enough to silence her thoughts. On those nights, she was reckless and fearless, chasing oblivion in a blur of vodka shots and laughter she barely recognised as her own.

She danced with strangers whose names vanished by sunrise, lost herself briefly in stolen kisses and embraces that meant nothing more than a few hours of distraction. She sought danger, not out of despair but from a need to feel vividly alive, to prove she could still burn bright enough to outrun the shadows that lingered.

Chapter Fifteen

These nights were always followed by mornings thick with regret, but Ayanna accepted them as part of her cycle—knowing herself just well enough to understand that chaos would always have its place in her heart. Still, the aftermath always found her back at the refuge of her journals, pen scratching quickly, fiercely, capturing every thought before it faded:

Why do I keep chasing these moments that leave me empty? What am I looking for that I can't name?

Despite her reckless moments, Ayanna had grown. Drinking was no longer a constant craving, nor was numbness the primary goal. Instead, she found she could now enjoy a drink without spiralling into desperation, even if sometimes she deliberately chose otherwise. It was a subtle strength, a quiet victory in the midst of lingering turmoil.

Her conversations with Alice remained gentle but guarded. Ayanna chose carefully what she revealed, sheltering her mother from the more chaotic parts of her life. She spoke openly about work at the bookstore, the latest novel she'd loved, or even the small victories of independence, a fixed radiator, a home-cooked meal, managing to keep her plants alive. But she kept the wild nights and the restless ache to herself, unwilling to risk the fragile peace they'd painstakingly built.

One chilly afternoon, Alice sat across from her, hands clasped around a steaming cup of tea, her eyes cautious but warm.

"You're doing well, Ayanna. I'm proud of you," Alice said, her voice wavering slightly with tenderness and relief.

Ayanna smiled softly, warmth flickering briefly in her chest. "Thanks, Mum."

She knew Alice couldn't see beneath the careful smiles, couldn't know the storm that still stirred just beneath her surface. Ayanna accepted that her mother, though earnest in her love, wasn't someone she could burden with every truth. There were still places inside herself she guarded fiercely, territories too wild, too raw, for anyone to tread.

After their meetings, Ayanna would return home, restlessness often following her like an old companion. Her heart yearned for connection, for someone to see through her carefully constructed layers of calm to the raw chaos underneath, someone brave enough to face her storm headon.

Chapter Fifteen

Her writing, fiercely honest and unfiltered, held every truth she couldn't speak aloud. Pages upon pages documented her tangled thoughts, emotions she barely understood, desires she was afraid to admit even to herself. Journaling was her refuge, a constant amid the ebb and flow of calm and chaos, growth and regression.

In moments of solitude, Ayanna found herself wondering how long she could continue navigating these contradictions: healing and hurting, careful and reckless, lonely yet fiercely protective of her solitude. But as complicated and conflicted as she remained, she was learning to embrace her complexities rather than deny them.

Ayanna was still wild, still raw, still fragile. But she was also resilient, hopeful beneath it all, determined to find a balance between the calm she craved and the chaos she still carried.

She wasn't there yet—but she was on her way.

She visited her mother often, Sunday afternoons spent drinking tea at the worn kitchen table, conversations slowly shedding their old tension. The past still lingered between them, a presence neither could erase, but the resentment had eased. Ayanna no longer needed her mother to answer for the silence of the past, nor did she expect an apology that would never come. Alice had failed her in ways she couldn't forget, but she had also loved her in ways that were undeniable. That love, in its imperfect, fragile form, was enough to keep them connected. Enough for Ayanna to forgive, if not forget.

The rest of her family was nothing more than a distant memory, ghosts she had no desire to chase. She didn't have to endure their judgmental stares or forced pleasantries at family gatherings. She was free of them now, free in a way she hadn't believed possible.

Her Granny, though, remained an anchor. Twice a week, without fail, Ayanna called her. Their conversations were a mix of warmth and gentle nagging, Granny asking if she was eating properly, if she was taking care of herself, if she was happy. And Ayanna, in the safety of that familiar voice, found herself answering more honestly than she

did with anyone else. Granny never pried, never asked about the things Ayanna wasn't willing to discuss, but she listened when Ayanna needed to talk. That, more than anything, made the difference.

Life still felt like a balancing act, the past never fully gone.

Chapter Fifteen

But in the gentler moments, the scent of tea in her mother's kitchen, the laughter in Granny's voice, the satisfaction of building a life on her own terms, Ayanna allowed herself to believe that she was moving forward.

Ayanna had settled into a routine that felt almost, almost, like ordinary life. Her days began with the gentle chime of her phone alarm chirping through her small apartment. She'd roll out of bed, often alone but not always, and make her way to the kitchen for a pot of tea. If there was a companion in her bedroom, still stretched out on the king-size bed, she'd politely offer a mug, throw in a vague "Take your time" before retreating to the lounge. Usually, she'd never see them again. And honestly, she preferred it that way.

She often told herself this pattern of one-night stands was a phase: a way to fill the emptiness creeping in since she'd moved away. But each fleeting connection dissolved by morning, leaving no real imprint except an occasional pang of guilt and a subtle sense of desperation she tried hard to ignore. Yet there was an odd solace in these encounters, an ability to be touched without letting anyone get close.

Afternoons had their own rhythm. She might slip into a local café for a sandwich, laptop tucked under her arm. Then came the methodical scanning of job boards; she thought something part-time might help pay for better groceries, or maybe just new books. But the search typically ended in frustration. She'd sigh, close the tabs, and return to her reading or check her phone for messages. A few times a week, a name she barely recognised might flash on the screen, someone from a weekend fling or a friend of a friend. Most times she simply ignored the calls, reluctant to transform a passing acquaintance into something more.

Evening shadows found Ayanna scanning poems or halfheartedly texting with classmates about upcoming study groups. She never joined them, some invisible barrier always held her back. Instead, she'd find herself going through Tinder a restless flicker of curiosity urging her to keep searching for something she couldn't define. Occasionally, that search led to another night out, another face she'd meet for drinks, another morning picking up tea for two but drinking it alone in the end.

And so it continued: the tug-of-war between wanting something meaningful and preferring the safety of distance. It wasn't that she didn't want love or friendship. She just felt too fragile to risk being hurt again. So she let her nights

Chapter Fifteen

unravel in shallow embraces that never quite reached her heart.

Her phone pinged one late afternoon. An old friend, Naomi, who lived only a few streets away, had sent a text:

"Hey, it's been ages. Wanna grab a drink tonight? Thinking we could hit that new bar on Crescent Ave. My treat if you show up before 9!"

Ayanna tilted her head, considering the invitation. She and Naomi had known each other for years, though they never got close enough to share secrets, not the deeply buried ones, anyway. Still, Naomi was easy company: warm, chatty, and brimming with good humour. It would be a change from the typical noncommittal meetups she'd grown accustomed to. No pressure, no corner-of-the-bar pickup scenario. Maybe she'd enjoy a conversation that stretched beyond small talk.

There was a strange flutter of hopefulness at the idea of going out, just her and a real friend, no half-dressed stranger to usher home in the morning.

"Sure," she typed back, her fingers tapping more eagerly than she expected. *"I'll be there around 8."*

The moment she hit send, a subtle twinge of anxiety twisted in her stomach. She couldn't shake the habit of expecting disappointment or drama whenever she tried stepping out of her solitary bubble. But still, Naomi was a comfortable sort of presence: safe, but with enough sparkle to keep things interesting.

Setting her phone aside, Ayanna closed her eyes for a moment. She recalled lines from a poem she'd read earlier that day, something about how the heart thirsts for connection but dreads the storms intimacy can bring. It felt like the story of her life: always hovering at the threshold between isolation and desire.

She drew a long breath and looked around her apartment. It might not be perfect, but it was hers. The battered couch, the leaning bookshelf, the mismatched curtains, it was a refuge even if she didn't always feel calm inside it. Outside her window, the sun had started its descent, painting the horizon with streaks of orange and crimson that glowed against the buildings across the street.

With an abrupt wave of resolve, she snapped her textbooks shut. Enough reading for one day. Tonight, she'd trade her solitary dwellings for music, chatter, and maybe the gentle hum of city life after dark. Her heart wasn't healed, she doubted it ever would be, not fully, but maybe it didn't have to be. Maybe she could still find those small glimmers of warmth in a friend's smile, a conversation that went deeper than idle flirting, or even the distant promise of something more.

She stood, stretching her arms above her head, and let out a slow exhale. She knew the emptiness wouldn't vanish after a single night at a bar. Yet she felt a fragile sense of hope that maybe, just maybe, these small steps away from her usual patterns might crack the walls she'd built around herself. And for now, that flicker of possibility was enough.

There would be music, and conversation, and laughter. She could almost taste it, the normalcy she craved, the faint optimism that came with being genuinely seen by someone who cared. And that, for tonight at least, might fill her loneliness better than any fleeting stranger could.

Ayanna's fingers curled around the strap of her purse, a silent anchor as she stepped through the door of the bar. The dim lighting played tricks on her eyes, coaxing them into an anxious dance across the sea of bobbing heads and waving hands. Her friend, a beacon of confidence, led the way with an ease Ayanna envied.

A break in the crowd revealed a man standing somewhat apart from the hive of activity. Ayanna's friend caught sight of him and gestured emphatically, her hand slicing through the smoky air like a lighthouse signalling a ship to safe harbour.

"Simon!" her friend called out, her voice a lifeline thrown into the tumult.

He turned, his movements unhurried, and Ayanna found herself holding her breath. Simon's eyes met hers, and in them, she read a tranquil depth that seemed oddly out of place in the surrounding chaos. His smile was not the broad, over-eager grin of someone looking to impress; instead, it was a subtle curve of understanding, a wordless welcome that seemed to speak directly to Ayanna's hesitant heart.

He stood by the bar with an easy, grounded confidence, his stature modest but balanced perfectly by an effortless charm. His neatly styled, dark blonde hair held a hint of playful disarray, suggesting a personality warmer than his polished appearance implied. Eyes that seemed to smile even before his lips did were deep and inviting, their rich darkness accented by the gentle glow of bar lights. Though not tall, he possessed an understated strength, evident in the confident way he moved towards them. His posture was relaxed yet purposeful, creating an impression of calm assurance that drew attention, completing an image that was subtly captivating.

As he approached, Ayanna noted the quiet assurance in his gait, he carried himself with effortless ease, his jeans and plain t-shirt a quiet defiance against the flashy posturing that filled places like this.

"Hi," Simon said, his voice soothing against the raucous backdrop. "I'm really glad you could make it."

Ayanna smiled widely as her eyes lit up at the sight of him, for a moment she was completely unfiltered before she caught herself and forced her wide smile away. Simon noticed the shift almost immediately "I like it when somebody gets excited about something. It's nice."

In that moment, Ayanna felt the reluctant armour she had donned begin to soften, her uncertainties lessened by the genuine warmth radiating from the man before her. Simon seemed like a person who listened more than he spoke, who watched more than he showed, and in that initial exchange, Ayanna sensed an unexpected kinship, a promise of connection that both intrigued and unnerved her.

"Isn't it a bit early for 'The Catcher in the Rye' references?" Ayanna teased, playfully nudging the coaster back and forth between her fingers as they all settled into a corner booth.

Simon chuckled, his eyes lighting up with amusement. "I suppose it is, but when you find someone who appreciates Salinger's work as much as I do, it's never too early."

Their conversation meandered through the labyrinths of literature, touching upon the existential musings of Dostoevsky and the whimsical worlds of Terry Pratchett. Ayanna's wit shone through each time she offered a playful jab at a protagonist's expense or recounted a tale of her own misadventures in book clubs. She found herself volleying Simon's thoughtful insights with an ease that surprised her, considering the loud buzz of energy in the bar.

As their conversation veered toward music, Ayanna described her fondness for electric swing, mellow jazz, and the comforting scent of old musty books. "There's a special warmth in those older melodies," she mused, eyes bright with a nostalgic gleam, "like you're stepping into a different era for just a little while." she declared, her voice rising above the crescendo of conversations around them. They were so

Chapter Fifteen

lost in their own world that they barely even noticed Naomi's rushed goodbyes and knowing smiles.

The bar was alive with a symphony of sounds: laughter and the clink of ice against glass; the bartender's shaker performing a rhythmical dance; the intermittent cheer as a group toasted to some unseen victory. The dim glow of Edison bulbs cast a warm honey hue over the patrons, the light flickering off glasses and bottles like stars winking into existence.

Ayanna smiled, realising that her guarded exterior was peeling away, note by note, word by word.

The clatter of the bar faded away as Ayanna drifted deeper into the conversation, relaxing under Simon's intent gaze. His eyes, a deep-set hazel, held an earnestness that beckoned Ayanna's thoughts out into the open, a rare invitation she found herself accepting with burgeoning intrigue.

As the hours wove themselves into the night, the initial stiffness that had accompanied Ayanna's entrance into the bar now seemed a distant memory. Her laughter once contained, now cascaded freely, punctuating their exchange with a brightness that rivalled the intermittent sparkle of the dimmed lights above.

"So, you want to be an author, huh?" Simon's question hung between them, simple yet potent with implication.

Ayanna's smile turned reflective as she reached for her dream, cradling it in her hands for him to see. "Yes, an author. To create worlds with words, characters that breathe, stories that linger long after the last page is turned, that's the dream." The passion in her voice rose, a clarion call revealing the fervour of her ambition.

"Sounds like you'd write something I couldn't put down," he replied, the admiration in his tone blending seamlessly with the sounds around them.

The night air grew with the fusion of their aspirations, the shared language of dreams knitting an invisible thread between their two souls. And in that crowded bar, amongst the strangers, Ayanna found a kindred spirit, a listener, a dreamer, a beacon in the static of the world.

Ayanna leaned in closer to Simon, their knees brushing under the table. The warmth from the drinks that had slid down her throat now coursed through her veins, emboldening her in ways the sober light of day never could. She tilted her head, her eyes holding his in a silent question, her hand finding its way to his arm.

Chapter Fifteen

"Simon," she whispered, her voice a mixture of courage and trepidation, "I want..."

He turned towards her, his presence a steady anchor in the sea of intoxicating possibilities. Their faces were mere inches apart now, the air charged with an energy that beckoned her forward. In this moment of shared vulnerability, Ayanna's fingertips lingered along the line of Simon's jaw, a tentative exploration of uncharted waters.

Simon regarded her with a softness that swelled within the confines of the dimly lit space. As her hand lingered, he reached up, taking it with his own. His touch was gentle, yet his grasp firm, communicating boundaries without uttering a word.

"Ayanna," he began, his voice the softest melody above the bar's hum, "you're amazing, and I feel there's something special here." He paused, searching her eyes for understanding. "But I think we should take our time, get to know each other outside of this night."

His words fell like a feather, light but resolute. In his refusal was a quiet strength, a respect for her and the nascent connection they had discovered. It wasn't a rejection, but a promise of patience, a recognition of the potential depth of what was unfolding between them.

Ayanna withdrew her hand slowly, not out of embarrassment, but in acknowledgment of the care he had taken in preserving their budding rapport. She sat back, her heart aflutter, not with disappointment, but with the realisation that respect could be a form of intimacy she had never known before.

She thought back to the tangled knots of her past relationships, those hastily formed connections shaped more by fleeting desires than genuine understanding. Each time, the spark of physical attraction had burned brightly at first, blinding her to deeper needs. Yet once that initial glow faded, she found herself alone, drifting in a limbo of unmet emotional needs and hollow reassurances. These were men who had seized at her vulnerabilities rather than safeguarding them, mistaking dominance for closeness and possession for love.

The recollection made her stomach tighten; she remembered how quickly those affections had turned brittle. Whispered promises that initially sounded like devotion later became tools of guilt or control. She had often been left wondering if something inherent in her was broken, why she kept entangling herself with people who thrived on her insecurities instead of cherishing her strengths. Night after night, she'd stare at her reflection in the mirror, trying to piece together what had gone wrong, inevitably placing the blame on her own shoulders.

Now, confronted with the quiet gentleness in front of her, those old memories seemed even more hollow. The patience and respect she was finally experiencing felt like a revelation, a warmth that had nothing to prove and no hidden barbs. In that contrast, she recognised just how starved she'd been for genuine care, an intimacy that chose understanding over conquest. And as this insight swept over her, the past grew mercifully dim, overshadowed by a cautious but welcome sense of hope.

Ayanna's mind spun with a delicate whirlwind of emotions as she processed Simon's gentle refusal. The bar's sounds dulled, as if the volume of the world had been turned down to allow her contemplation. Puzzlement knit her brow, an ephemeral frown gracing her lips, not from rejection but from the novelty of the respect she was being shown. It felt like a foreign language that she understood instinctively yet had never heard spoken aloud.

Her eyes, reflecting a constellation of dim lights, flickered with the sparks of intrigue. She marvelled at how his words carved out a space where dignity and passion coexisted, a place where her soul could breathe without the taint of urgency. In this corner of her heart, Ayanna found herself cradling a fragile seed of admiration for Simon.

As the last call rang through the bar, signalling the end of the night's revelry, Ayanna and Simon shared a glance that stitched the final threads of their evening together. They rose from their seats, their movements synchronised in an understanding. The air between them was charged with the electricity of a connection neither had anticipated when the night began.

Stepping through the throng of lingering patrons, Ayanna felt Simon's presence beside her. Their farewell was a soft exchange of smiles, a silent conversation where promises of future laughter hung in the balance. His hand lifted in a subtle wave, a gesture that seemed to trace the arc of the moon outside.

She watched him retreat into the night. There was no bitterness, no sting of unrequited advances, only the warmth of a bond that had been gently knit by genuine affinity. In the quiet aftermath, Ayanna stood there, a sentinel of the threshold they had crossed together, marking the map of an unexpected journey with a waypoint of mutual respect.

The chill of the night wrapped around her, the cobblestone path beneath her feet rhythmic and expectant with each step she took away from the comfort of what had become an unforgettable evening.

Streetlights cast a golden hue over her path, their glow a soft counterpoint to the clarity crystallising within her. The cool air welcome against her flushed cheeks, soothing the emotional high that had carried her through the night. She pulled her coat tighter around her, not solely for warmth but as an embrace to the woman who emerged more whole, more seen, than she had entered that bar.

She paused at a crossing, the traffic light blinking its cyclical warning, red to green and back again. Ayanna found herself on the precipice of introspection, looking back at the night not with regret but with a growing sense of self. Simon's presence had introduced a spectrum of colour to her world, one where the greys of uncertainty blended into a palette rich with the hues of potential.

The key turned in the lock of her apartment door, and the familiar scent of home welcomed her back to solitude. In the stillness of her living room, Ayanna sank onto her couch, a soft sigh escaping her lips as she reached across to her bookcase, walking a finger along the spines of books neatly arranged on the shelf, each title a memory, a world she had immersed herself in, a solace in times of solitude. Tonight, though, the stories felt different; promises of reality mingling with fiction, where characters like Simon stepped off the pages and into her life.

She withdrew a novel, one she had discussed with him earlier, and held it close, breathing in the scent of paper and ink, a tangible reminder of their shared bond over literature.

Casting a glance at the city lights winking through her window, Ayanna felt a flutter in her chest, the wings of possibility stirring. There was a world beyond these four walls, one that held the promise of genuine connection.

Chapter Sixteen

AGE 20

Ayanna slipped into a corner booth at The Grindhouse, the scent of roasted coffee beans settling over her like a warm embrace. The low chatter of other patrons mixed with the occasional hiss of the espresso machine, creating a rhythm that felt familiar and unintrusive. She reached for her phone as it vibrated against the polished wood of the table, a message from Simon flashing across the screen: *See you in five.*

She exhaled slowly, adjusting her seat as she tucked a stray lock of hair behind her ear. The anticipation was subtle but present, an awareness that their meetings had begun to take on a comfortable regularity. It had been Simon's idea to meet today, his invitation casual yet intentional.
Ayanna hadn't hesitated before agreeing.

The door swung open, letting in a crisp breath of morning air before it fell shut again. Simon walked in with easy confidence, a scarf draped loosely around his neck, hair slightly tousled from the wind outside. He spotted her immediately, lifting a hand in greeting before weaving between tables with the unhurried ease of someone who never seemed rushed by the world.

As he reached the booth, he smiled towards the waitress who hurried over with a friendly smile to take their orders.

"Hey," he said to Ayanna, offering her a small smile. "Thanks for meeting me."

"Of course," Ayanna replied, resting her forearms on the table. "I was already looking for an excuse to get out of the apartment."

Simon chuckled, reaching for his cup with a smile and a nod to the waitress. "I hope this place still meets your absurdly high and obscure tea standards."

Ayanna raised a brow in mock offense. "Absurdly high? I just think bad tea is a crime. There's a difference."

"Right. My mistake." He lifted his cup in a mock toast. "To your impeccable taste, then."

Ayanna clinked her cup against his before taking a sip. The warmth seeped through her fingertips, grounding her.

Chapter Sixteen

Simon leaned back slightly, a thoughtful expression crossing his face. "I loved that book you mentioned last week, by the way. I finished it in two nights."

Her lips parted in surprise before curving upward. "Seriously? I thought you said you were a slow reader."

"I *am*," he admitted, "but it was too good to put down. The way the author layers the story, subtle but deliberate. The way the relationships unfold, how the small moments say just as much as the big ones. It reminded me of..." He trailed off for a second before shaking his head. "Never mind. I'm rambling."

"No, go on," she encouraged. "I like hearing your take."

Their conversation unfolded effortlessly, drifting between topics. Ayanna found herself leaning forward slightly, elbows resting against the wood as Simon mirrored her without thinking. Every so often, their hands would brush the table's surface in an unconscious rhythm, neither acknowledging the small gestures but neither pulling away, either.

Simon tapped his fingers lightly against his cup, glancing toward the café speakers. "You know this?"

Ayanna listened for a moment before nodding. "Yeah. I love this song."

"It's got that quiet build-up, the kind that sneaks up on you," he mused, tapping out the soft beat against the tabletop. "The lyrics are simple, but they *feel* like something." "Like they belong to a moment," she agreed.

Simon's lips quirked up slightly. "Exactly."

A beat passed between them, something easy yet filled with meaning. Ayanna let herself enjoy it, let herself settle into the warmth of their conversation.

The café door opened and shut again, a rush of movement as new patrons arrived, their laughter mixing into the atmosphere. Ayanna barely noticed, her focus held in the space they had created between them.

Simon lifted his cup again, his fingers curled around the ceramic. "So, what's next on your list? Because if I'm going to keep up with your literary recommendations, I need time to mentally prepare."

Ayanna huffed a quiet laugh. "I'll go easy on you. Maybe something less emotionally destructive this time."

Chapter Sixteen

"Appreciated," he said with mock solemnity. "Though, to be fair, I did survive the last one."

"That's true," she conceded. "Alright. I'll text you a title later. Consider it a challenge."

He nodded once, as if sealing the agreement. "Looking forward to it."

Their conversation continued, the world outside the café fading to the periphery. It was in moments like this, unrushed, undemanding, that Ayanna realised just how much she valued these times. The familiarity. The absence of pressure to be anything other than herself.

She wasn't sure when she had last allowed herself something like this.

As their cups emptied and the morning stretched into early afternoon, neither made a move to leave just yet. The conversation meandered, circling back on inside jokes, revisiting past discussions, laying the groundwork for the next time they'd inevitably sit across from each other in another café, another booth, another moment like this.

For now, there was nothing else she needed.

As Ayanna and Simon stepped out of the coffee shop, the warmth of the late afternoon sun settled on their shoulders, filtering through the trees that lined the street.

The pavement stretched before them in winding loops, each turn offering a moment of quiet before the city's hum returned in the distance. Birds flitted through the branches above, their calls high and sharp. Children's laughter bubbled from a playground across the lawn, but here, along this path, the world seemed softer, measured in the crunch of footsteps against gravel and the gentle sway of trees shifting in the breeze.

Simon walked with his usual steadiness, hands tucked into the pockets of his jacket, his stride unhurried. Ayanna lingered half a step behind, her fingers brushing against the fabric of her sweater, rolling the edge between her thumb and forefinger. The words she needed to say pressed at the edges of her mind, but she wasn't sure how to let them go.

She stole a glance at Simon, catching the way his features remained open, relaxed, his focus trained on the path ahead rather than on her hesitation. It was a quiet kindness, giving her space without withdrawing entirely. It made it easier, and somehow harder, to speak.

Near the stone fountain at the heart of the park, she slowed, her steps faltering. The water spilled over carved stone, catching the light in delicate arcs before vanishing into the pool below. Ayanna traced the movement with her eyes, willing herself to take in the simplicity of it. If only letting go of memories was as easy as water meeting stone.

"I think there's something I want to tell you about."

Simon stopped beside her. He didn't try to fill the silence. He just waited.

Ayanna swallowed against the dryness in her throat, her fingers still gripping the hem of her sweater. She wasn't sure how long she stood there, staring into the rippling water, the words forming and fracturing before they could be spoken.

Finally, she exhaled. "I don't talk about this. Ever."

Simon nodded, the movement slow, almost imperceptible. "Whatever it is, it's okay. Whenever you're ready," he said.

The air felt cooler now, despite the sun filtering through the canopy above. "It started when I was eight," she began, each syllable brittle, as if saying it aloud might break something irreparable inside her.

She had expected hesitation, a stumble over the first sentence, but instead, the memories came like a flood, overwhelming, unstoppable.

"I had a life that never felt like it belonged to me. Like I was borrowing it. A placeholder for someone else. It all just felt...wrong." She could hear her own breath coming quicker, her pulse pounding in her ears.

"There was a cupboard in the corner of my room, one of those old ones that creaked when it opened. I hated it. I used to imagine something lived inside it, something waiting. But it wasn't monsters I should've been afraid of."

Her hands clenched at her sides, nails pressing into her palms. The air in her lungs felt tight, as if she were back there, trapped in a space too small to breathe in. "At first, I thought I was just in trouble all the time. That I had done something wrong. Kids believe things like that, you know? You make sense of the world however you can. If you're punished, it's because you deserve it."

Simon didn't speak, but his stillness was its own kind of presence. His silence didn't stretch with discomfort, nor did it demand more from her than she could give. He was simply there, solid in a way that made it possible for her to keep going.

"It wasn't just words," she continued, her voice shaking now. "It wasn't just being ignored when I cried or told to 'be good' when I was terrified. It was hands that shouldn't have touched me. Voices that made my name feel like something dirty."

Her stomach churned, nausea rolling through her as the memories thickened. "I learned to disappear without leaving. I learned how to make myself so small that I almost convinced myself I wasn't real. And when I finally got away, when I finally grew up and left, I thought that meant it was over." A bitter laugh slipped out, brittle as dry leaves. "But it doesn't end, does it? It stays in you, like ink that never fades."

Ayanna forced herself to inhale deeply, her chest rising and falling in measured breaths. The words had emptied out of her, but they left behind an ache she wasn't sure she'd ever be rid of.

For the first time since she started speaking, she lifted her eyes to Simon, bracing for whatever she might find there.

Pity. Horror. Discomfort. She had seen them all before, in the rare instances she had let even the smallest pieces of her past slip through.

But Simon's face held none of those things. His expression was steady, filled with something quiet and immeasurable. Not pity. Not even sympathy. Just understanding, deep and unwavering.

He didn't try to fix it. He didn't tell her she was strong, or that she'd survived, or that none of it defined her. Maybe he knew those were things she already told herself on the days she needed to keep going. Instead, he reached out, his hand open, waiting for her to decide whether to take it.

Ayanna hesitated. Then, with a slow, deliberate motion, she placed her hand in his.

His fingers closed around hers, not tight, not as if to hold her together, but simply to remind her that she wasn't alone in this moment.

They stood like that for a long time, the world moving around them, but the space between them untouched by it. The sun had begun to set, shadows stretching long shadows across the path, but Ayanna's chest felt a little lighter, as if

Chapter Sixteen

speaking it aloud had finally let some of it slip through her fingers.

She didn't thank him, not yet. That would come later. Instead, she just breathed, her hand still resting in his, and let herself be here. For once, she didn't pull away.

The scent of freshly brewed tea wrapped around Ayanna the moment she stepped into Simon's apartment, a familiar welcome against the cool bite of the evening air she had just escaped. She shrugged off her coat, fingers brushing against the fabric as she hung it on the hook by the door, taking in the quiet hum of the space that had grown so familiar over the past year.

The apartment, much like Simon himself, had an effortless warmth. Books lined the shelves in no particular order, board games were stacked in uneven towers near the coffee table, and a few lingering mugs from past late nights sat waiting to be cleared. It was lived in, comfortable, the kind of place that felt more like an extension of the person than just somewhere he occupied.

Simon appeared from the kitchen, two steaming mugs in hand, his face relaxed in the kind of way that came with familiarity.

"I'd challenge you to a game, but I'm still recovering from my tragic loss last time," he said, nodding toward the still setup board game on the table.

Ayanna smirked, toeing off her shoes as she stepped further inside. "Tragic loss? Pretty sure you were a single move away from winning."

"Almost isn't enough," Simon countered, settling into his usual spot on the couch and passing her a mug. "Okay fine, you've convinced me! We're having a rematch tonight."

She sank into the space beside him, curling her fingers around the warm ceramic. "Confident, are we?"

Simon tilted his head, amusement flickering across his expression. "Let's just say I've had time to analyse your tactics."

Ayanna huffed a laugh, shaking her head. Their board game nights had started as casual fun, but somewhere along the way, they had become something more, a ritual, a constant in the rhythm of their evolving relationship.

It had been a year of small moments like this, each one layering over the last. Late-night conversations stretched across the couch, afternoons spent walking through shifting seasons, and shared meals, there was something so effortless in how they had fallen into each other's lives, how time had shaped their bond without the need for grand gestures or heavy conversations.

Ayanna picked up the first card from the deck, letting the familiarity of the game settle between them. They played in comfortable banter, teasing remarks punctuated by the occasional sound of cards being shuffled or pieces moving across the board. She didn't even realise how easily her body leaned toward his until his hand brushed hers.

Neither of them moved away.

"You play so well," Simon winked at her, fingers slipping between hers with an ease that sent a soft pulse of warmth through her chest. "It's impressive."

The air shifted. It was subtle, but Ayanna felt it settle in her bones.

Her heart tapped out an uneven beat, her fingers tightening slightly around his. She met his eyes, and the world outside this room, outside this moment, faded.

There was no rush, no urgency, no demand. Just Simon, steady, patient, always waiting for her to take the next step.

And for once, she did.

She leaned forward, closing the space between them, and pressed her lips to his.

It wasn't tentative, nor hesitant. It was quiet in its certainty, in the way their bodies gravitated toward each other like it had always been inevitable. His lips were warm, familiar in a way that sent a deep ache through her chest, not one of pain, but of something else, something she hadn't yet named.

When they finally pulled apart, neither of them moved away entirely. Their breaths mixed in the inches between them, his hand still resting over hers, her fingers curled lightly against his wrist.

Simon exhaled a slow breath, his forehead nearly touching hers. "That's been a long time coming."

Ayanna swallowed, her lips tingling, the words catching in her throat. "Yeah."

Neither of them filled the quiet that followed. They didn't need to.

Chapter Sixteen

Simon tilted his head slightly, an easy smile tugging at the corner of his mouth. "You know, you basically live here anyway."

A laugh bubbled out of Ayanna before she could stop it. "Is that your way of suggesting I move in?"

Simon didn't hesitate. "I'm just saying… at this point, your books are on my shelves, how you like your tea is memorised, and my closet has mysteriously made space for your sweaters."

Her smile faltered, just slightly, just enough for Simon to notice. Not because she didn't want this, but because the idea of permanence, of belonging somewhere, had always been something she'd struggled to hold.

But as she looked around the room, the books that had found their place on his shelves, the throw blanket she had folded on the couch, the way she knew exactly where he kept the extra tea bags, she realised something.

She already belonged here.

Instead of answering right away, she leaned forward, resting her forehead against his.

"Okay," she said, her voice steady.

Simon pulled back just enough to see her expression, and when she saw his smile, slow and sure, like everything about him, something inside her eased.

"Okay?" he repeated.

Ayanna nodded. "Yeah. Let's do it."

Simon let out a slow breath, his fingers squeezing hers once before he laughed softly. "Good," he said, like there had never been a doubt in his mind.

The rest of the evening unfolded like all the ones before it, except now, there was a quiet certainty resting between them, something unspoken but understood. They played another round of their game, drank their tea, let the night settle around them in shared glances and easy conversation.

The decision had been made long before tonight. It had been made in the mornings when she found herself reaching for a mug in his kitchen without thinking, in the afternoons spent stretched out on his couch with a book, in the way she had stopped needing an invitation to be here.

Chapter Sixteen

As Ayanna curled into the couch, Simon shifting beside her to make space, she let herself breathe in the feeling of it. A home that wasn't just a place, but a feeling.

And for the first time in her life, she let herself embrace it.

Chapter Seventeen

SIMON

There were things he knew without needing to be told.

Like the way she never turned her back to the door, even in her own home. How she flinched when someone touched her shoulder from behind. How her laugh, when it came, felt like stumbling across music in a place where silence had lived too long. Beautiful. Fragile. Rare.

He didn't ask questions she'd have to lie to answer. Didn't press her for memories she kept padlocked behind her eyes. He learned her rhythms instead, when to give space, when to stay close without saying a word. He left the bathroom light on at night. He moved quietly. He stayed.

And slowly, something shifted.

She was falling too.

He could feel it in the way she softened when she thought he wasn't looking. How her voice was gentler when she said his name, even during arguments. She let herself linger now,

Chapter Seventeen

over breakfast, over eye contact, over moments that once would've made her bolt.

There was no grand confession. No "I love you" whispered in the dark. But he felt it all the same, in the way she curled toward him in her sleep. In the way she trusted him with her worst moods and didn't apologise for having them. In how she reached for his hand under the table when she got overwhelmed, like a lifeline she hadn't meant to grab but couldn't let go of.

It wasn't easy. God, no.

She made it hard.

She second-guessed kindness like it came with a bill at the end. She argued for no reason, then got mad when he didn't argue back. She could be moody, defensive, sharp-tongued. And when things got too calm, too safe, she stirred the pot just to see if he'd still be there after it boiled over.

She'd push him away with one hand and cling to his jumper with the other. Call him too soft, too patient, like it was an insult. Like she didn't know what to do with someone who didn't flinch when she was at her worst.

Like maybe she wanted to believe he was too good to be true, just so she wouldn't have to risk trusting him.

Once, she told him not to come round anymore. Said she needed space. Said it like a dare. He didn't fight it. Just texted her later: *I'm here when you want me.* She replied at 2a.m. with one word: *Sorry.* When he showed up the next morning with her favourite crisps and didn't mention the night before, she let him kiss her forehead and didn't flinch.

That was the thing. Even at her most difficult, she didn't scare him off. She expected him to leave. And each time he didn't, she looked a little more terrified. And a little more hopeful.

But she wasn't just the hard parts. Not even close.

She was warm, when she let herself be. Kind in a quiet, practical way. The kind of kindness that didn't ask to be noticed. She made him soup when he was sick, even though she hated cooking and burned her wrist lifting the pot because she refused to ask for help. She sat beside him on the sofa while he dozed off, pretending to watch something on her phone but really just being there.

She made him laugh more than anyone he'd ever met. Not just because she was funny, though she was, wickedly so, but because she could make even the darkest parts of life seem absurd. He'd be ranting about something stupid, traffic, politics, the bin men missing the collection again, and she'd tilt her head, raise an eyebrow, and say something so dry it took him a second to realise it was a joke. Then he'd be doubled over, tears in his eyes, and she'd just smirk like she hadn't planned it at all.

She listened when he talked. Really listened. Asked questions. Remembered things. She knew which song reminded him of his dad, even though he'd only mentioned it once. She remembered the date of the anniversary he never spoke about. She noticed the way he rubbed his knee when it hurt and started keeping a hot water bottle in the airing cupboard, "just in case."

She was clever, sharper than she let on. And loyal in a way that felt almost dangerous. She'd go to war for the people she loved, even if she didn't know how to say she loved them yet. She'd turn up with snacks when his car broke down. Stay up with him when he couldn't sleep. Sit in total silence beside him when he didn't know how to say what was wrong.

He was falling, sure. But not into fantasy. Not into some flawless version of her.

He was falling for the woman who got anxious in supermarkets and impatient in traffic. Who left half-finished books stacked on the floor like landmines and made tea she never drank. Who never remembered to charge her phone but always remembered what time his shift finished.

He was falling for the way she looked when she was annoyed but trying not to smile. For the way she held her breath during sad parts of movies, like if she breathed, the characters would suffer more. For the way she never let herself cry alone, not because she needed comfort, but because she didn't want anyone to see her break.

She let him in slowly, like someone testing the water after a burn. And he was patient with it. Because he'd rather have her real than perfect. He'd rather have the hard days, the silences, the stubbornness, if it meant he got the small moments, too. The way she lit up when she forgot to be afraid. The way she rested her head on his shoulder and exhaled like she finally believed she could.

He saw it in her eyes, love, or something close. The way she looked at him like she didn't understand why he hadn't run yet. The way she reached for him without thinking, like he'd become part of her instinct.

And he wouldn't rush her. Wouldn't corner her into naming something she was still learning how to hold.

Because sometimes love didn't arrive like thunder.
Sometimes it crept in on quiet feet, sat beside you in silence, and waited for you to notice.

So no, they hadn't said it yet.

But love was in the room with them. Sitting between takeout boxes and unsaid things. Making itself at home in the silence.

And he could wait a little longer for the words.

Because sometimes the truest things weren't spoken.

They were just… known.

Chapter Eighteen

AGE 23

Ayanna's life began to find a rhythm she had never dared imagine possible. Each day no longer felt like a mere endurance test, but rather a slow unfolding of moments, calm and measured. She shared a modest flat with Simon, where sunlight filtered gently through half-open curtains, and bookshelves crowded every available corner, evidence of the quiet life she was slowly cultivating.

Mornings had become something she anticipated, rather than dreaded. Ayanna and Simon developed their own gentle routine: his meticulous brewing of coffee, her careful selection of journals and books to accompany the first hours of the day. The bitter tang of freshly ground coffee beans and the soft whispers of turning pages formed a comforting backdrop to their mornings, where contentment settled in small, steady doses.

Her journals grew numerous, lining shelves and stacking carefully beside her desk. Each notebook contained words that had once burned through her in unmanageable torrents.

Now, those same words felt manageable, something tangible she could control and understand. Writing had always been a form of survival, a desperate attempt to contain the hurt that seeped from her past, but it had slowly evolved into something softer. Now, each entry was a conscious act of healing, of making peace with memories that once tore her apart. Through the ink and paper, she reclaimed control, translating chaos into narrative, pain into poetry.

Books became not just an escape, but a guide. Ayanna learned from fictional heroines and quiet memoirs alike, seeing reflections of her own journey in pages written by strangers. Literature taught her that she was neither unique nor broken beyond repair, that healing was achievable, however messy the process. She spent entire afternoons lost in narratives, their stories imprinting upon her own, teaching her patience, compassion, and strength. Each volume she placed lovingly back on the shelf left behind a small piece of wisdom that built slowly within her, like layers of a careful sculpture.

Her relationship with alcohol had been complicated, a coping mechanism for the ache she carried. But gradually, something shifted within her. She found herself content with a single glass of red wine, savoured slowly over dinner, the warmth pleasant but no longer necessary to dull the edges of her thoughts. There was no abrupt ending or dramatic pledge of abstinence—just a subtle yet profound shift in perspective. Ayanna learned to hold a glass not because she needed to forget, but because she enjoyed the simple act of sipping, tasting, and being present.

Simon's presence, quiet yet unwavering, grounded her as she navigated this new, steadier path. His patience and his quiet companionship were fundamental parts of her growth. In his silent acceptance, she felt secure enough to examine her wounds, to confront the truths she'd spent years running from.

Ayanna began to recognise the peace in ordinary things: the softness of rain tapping lightly against the windowpane, the comfortable silence of evenings spent reading side by side, the taste of simple meals shared without hurry or urgency. Each seemingly mundane moment twisting itself into a new peace that Ayanna carefully guarded and cherished.

This new Ayanna was still imperfect, still scarred, but she carried those scars with quiet dignity rather than shame. She was no longer driven by desperation but by curiosity and kindness toward herself. She was becoming, slowly and steadily, the woman she once doubted she could ever be—one who embraced quiet joys, faced past pain without flinching, and gently, courageously continued to heal.

She had finally committed to studying for a degree and her decision to focus on English literature had surprised no one. She was halfway through a module that delved into the Romantic poets, Wordsworth, Coleridge, Byron, and found herself gravitating toward the bleak beauty hidden in their verses.

Online lectures played in her earbuds, the familiar voices of professors discussing symbolism, meter, and the intricacies of narrative form. It was both exhilarating and lonely, studying a subject she loved without the bustle of a real campus. No hallways packed with chatting classmates, no coffee breaks at the student union. Just her, the glow of the screen, and messages in the discussion forum. She studied online from her makeshift office in the corner of their lounge. She'd never gained GCSE's or A-Levels, and she found that this course hadn't required these things, and for once she felt like she could truly achieve something that was taken from her a long time ago.

Despite the loneliness, she found moments of pride. She wrote discussion posts on time, sometimes passionately. She completed research assignments that explored how certain 19th-century novels tackled social oppression. Her professors praised her clarity of thought, her knack for dissecting texts with empathy and nuance. That small dose of validation often carried her through the day. If she couldn't forge a lasting bond with another person, at least she could connect with literature on a deeper level.

While the coursework challenged her, each passed exam felt like a triumphant step away from the chaos that had dominated her childhood and teen years. Simon was her constant encourager, when finals or essays threatened to overwhelm her, his gentle insistence that she could do it stoked the embers of her confidence. At night, she would balance her books on the kitchen table while he tested her on key literary concepts, the two of them giggling whenever he butchered a difficult title or an author's name.

Their everyday life glowed with contentment: shared grocery trips turned into impromptu cooking sessions, where they discovered new recipes and teased one another about the right amount of spice. Evenings found them sprawled on the sofa, trading chapters from favourite novels. Ayanna discovered that simple domestic routines, things once foreign and daunting, could be healing acts of togetherness.

In her final term, she stood at a podium on graduation day, diploma in hand. No longer the uncertain girl who doubted every step, Ayanna beamed at the applause mingling with her own heartbeat. Completing her degree was more than an academic milestone; it was proof that she could rewrite the narrative that had once tried to define her.

As her final project, Ayanna drafted short stories inspired by the trials and triumphs she had navigated. Though fictionalised, they brimmed with the emotional truths of her life. In weaving words, she found a sense of power, of ownership over everything that had once rendered her silent. Readers, fellow students, friends, and even professors, encouraged her to keep writing, sensing the raw honesty sparking in her pages.

By the time she turned twenty-three, Ayanna had made her choice: she would be an author. In the sunny living room she now shared with Simon, she hunched over her laptop each day, pouring gratitude and pain alike into newly forming chapters.

The cursor blinked on the screen, a silent, steady metronome marking the passage of time as Ayanna sat at her desk, unmoving.

She had started this session with confidence, telling herself that today would be different, that today, finally, she would break through the invisible wall that kept her from putting real words onto the page. Now, an hour later, all she had was a half-formed paragraph about a woman standing in the rain, waiting for someone who wasn't coming.

Ayanna sighed, rubbing the back of her neck as she leaned back in her chair. The desk in front of her was a battlefield of abandoned ideas, scribbled notes, printed articles on writing techniques, a battered notebook filled with snippets of dialogue that all sounded hollow when she read them back. She glanced at her laptop screen again. The woman in the rain stared back at her, frozen in time, waiting for something Ayanna didn't know how to give her.

Across the room, Simon was stretched out on the couch, phone in one hand, a half-empty cup of coffee on the table beside him. The glow from the desk lamp softened the edges of the room, "What if I start with this idea?" she asked, her voice laced with frustration as she turned to face Simon.

Chapter Eighteen

He looked up from his phone, his expression open but indecipherable. "Which one?"

She gestured vaguely at the mess of papers. "I don't know. Maybe the one about the girl running a flower shop who falls in love with the closed-off, brooding guy next door?"

Simon set his phone down and thought for a second before answering. "It could work. What's stopping you from just going with it?"

Ayanna groaned, slumping forward until her forehead touched the desk. "Because it's *boring*."

Simon chuckled. "Then write something else."

She lifted her head just enough to glare at him. "Oh, wow, great advice. Should I also try just *being successful* while I'm at it?"

He smirked, unfazed. "I'm just saying, you don't have to *force* yourself to write a story you don't care about."

"That's the problem, though," she said, sitting up again and pushing her chair away from the desk. "I *do* care about writing. I want to write something that feels right. But every time I try, it just," She waved her hands in frustration. ", dies in my brain before it even makes it onto the page."

Simon studied her for a moment. "Maybe you're putting too much pressure on yourself."

She huffed, crossing her arms. "Maybe I *need* to. If I don't, I'm never going to finish anything."

She turned back to the screen, where the lonely woman in the rain still stood, waiting for Ayanna to figure out what happened next. But no matter how long she stared at it, nothing came.

"I keep trying to write this scene, and all I can think is that it's something I've read a hundred times before," she admitted. "Like, what's even the *point* of writing if everything's already been done better by someone else?"

Simon reached for his coffee and took a sip, considering her words. "Because it hasn't been done by *you*."

She rolled her eyes. "That sounds like something a writing professor would say before handing back an assignment with a C on it."

Chapter Eighteen

He chuckled, but there was an understanding behind his amusement. "I get it. You don't want to just write, you want to write something that actually *means* something."

"Exactly," she said, slumping back in her chair. "But I don't even know what that *is*. I have all these characters, all these ideas, but none of them feel like *mine*. I keep thinking maybe I should try writing romance, because I love romance novels, but every time I start, it feels... empty. Like I'm just going through the motions."

Simon nodded slowly. "So maybe romance isn't your thing. Or maybe you just haven't found the *right* story yet."

Ayanna groaned again, dragging her hands down her face. "That's the problem. *What is the right story?*"

Simon leaned back into the couch, watching her with an amused expression. "I don't think you're going to figure that out by beating yourself up about it."

She made a noise of frustration and spun back toward her desk. The cursor still blinked at her, patient and unbothered, as if it had all the time in the world.

Ayanna, on the other hand, felt like she was running out of it.

She had told herself that this year would be different. That she would finally *finish* something instead of abandoning every idea that didn't feel perfect from the start. But now she was beginning to wonder if she had romanticised the idea of writing. That she's got it all wrong.

Her fingers hovered over the keyboard, but no words came.

Simon watched her struggle for a moment before speaking again. "Why don't you take a break?"

She gave him a flat look. "A break from *what*? Sitting here and accomplishing nothing?"

He grinned. "Exactly."

She let out a small, defeated laugh despite herself. "You're annoying."

"And yet, you love me."

Ayanna sighed and looked back at her screen one last time before closing the laptop with a decisive *click*. The woman in the rain would have to wait.

Chapter Eighteen

She turned in her chair, stretching her arms above her head before resting them in her lap. "Fine. What should we do instead?"

Simon sat up, rubbing his chin in mock contemplation. "How about a board game? You can take out all your frustration on me in a structured, rule-based environment."

She raised an eyebrow. "You *do* realize that I will absolutely destroy you, right?"

Simon smirked. "I'm counting on it."

Ayanna rolled her eyes but stood up anyway, stepping away from the desk and into the space where life existed outside of the endless battle with a blank page. Maybe she would figure out her story tomorrow. Maybe not.

Ayanna glanced at the clock and sighed, closing her laptop with a decisive snap. She and Simon had promised to visit Granny weeks ago, but between her writing deadlines and his long shifts, the plan kept getting pushed back. In truth, Ayanna felt a sting of guilt; she knew Granny missed her and had been eager to meet Simon in person, not just through shared phone calls and Ayanna's glowing stories. Now, with the car keys jingling in Simon's hand, there were no more excuses, today was the day that Granny's curious questions, warm embraces, and genuine acceptance would finally gather them all under the same roof.

Ayanna rested her forehead against the cool glass of the car window, watching the world blur past in muted streaks of colour. The hum of the engine filled the silence between them, broken only by the rhythmic tapping of her fingers against the dashboard. Simon's hands were firm on the wheel, his expression unreadable as he focused on the road ahead.

She turned slightly, taking in the set of his jaw, the way his fingers flexed around the leather steering wheel. "You're nervous," she observed, a teasing lilt to her voice.

His lips pressed together in something between a grimace and a smile. "I don't know what you're talking about."

Ayanna let out a short laugh, shifting in her seat so she could look at him properly. "You do this thing where you adjust your grip every few seconds when you're trying to act casual."

Simon exhaled, a slow, measured breath. "I just want to make a good impression."

Chapter Eighteen

"She already likes you," Ayanna assured him, stretching out her legs as much as the passenger seat allowed. "Granny loves anyone who brings biscuits and doesn't talk through the news."

"I don't have biscuits," he pointed out.

Ayanna gasped in mock horror. "Well, that's it then. She'll take one look at you and send you right back out the door."

Finally, Simon cracked a smile, shaking his head. "Great. Do you have an emergency biscuit stash, or should I just turn the car around now?"

Ayanna grinned, reaching into her bag and pulling out a small paper bag. She held it up like an offering. "Shortbread. You're saved."

He chuckled, shaking his head. She turned back toward the window, a comfortable warmth settling in her chest. The roads here were familiar, winding through streets she had walked as a child, past corner shops and small parks where she'd played.

"Tell me more about her," Simon said after a moment. "I mean, I know the basics. But what was she like when you were little?"

Ayanna's lips curled into a soft smile. "She was my favourite person. Still is, really." She traced the hem of her sleeve absentmindedly. "When I was little, we used to sit on the dining chairs in her kitchen, the tall ones with the carved wooden backs. The pattern had these little gaps in the swirls, and we'd peek through them at the wallpaper on the opposite wall. We called it 'our secret garden.'"

Simon glanced at her, interest flickering across his features. "What was on the wallpaper?"

"Flowers," Ayanna said, her voice quieter now. "Big, sprawling daffodils and sunflowers with ivy curling between them. She used to tell me that if I looked for long enough, I'd see the petals moving, like they were growing right before my eyes."

Simon was silent for a moment, taking it in. "That's really sweet," he finally said.

Ayanna nodded, her fingers still playing with the fabric of her sweater. "She made everything feel… special. Even the

Chapter Eighteen

smallest things. She'd give names to the birds that landed on the windowsill. Tell me stories about how the teapot had belonged to some old friend, even if she just bought it last week. She made the world feel full of magic."

Simon's voice was softer now, reflective. "Sounds like she was a big part of your childhood."

"She was the best part," Ayanna admitted. Simon must have noticed the shift in her expression because his tone changed, lighter, playful. "So, does she have some kind of test for potential suitors?"

Ayanna snorted, rolling her eyes. "She's not that bad. Just expects you to be polite, listen to her stories, and pretend to be interested in antique clocks for at least ten minutes."

Simon let out an exaggerated groan. "Antique clocks? That's going to be rough."

"Oh, absolutely. She'll quiz you on the history of grandfather clocks by the end of the visit."

He shook his head, amused. "You should have warned me sooner. I could have studied."

Ayanna smirked. "I like to keep you on your toes."

Simon let out a small laugh, but Ayanna caught the way his grip tightened ever so slightly on the wheel again. He was still nervous.

She reached across the console, resting a hand lightly on his arm. "She's going to love you."

He didn't answer right away, but after a few beats, he nodded. "I hope so."

Ayanna withdrew her hand, resting it in her lap as the houses grew more spaced out, yards larger, gardens more vibrant. The familiar curve of the road leading to her grandmother's house came into view, and her heart gave a small, unexpected lurch.

It had been too long since she'd visited properly. Phone calls were frequent, but there was always some excuse, some reason why she hadn't made the trip in person. Too busy, too tired, too caught up in life.

She frowned slightly. Granny was eighty now. Time wasn't something she could take for granted.

"Almost there," she said, shaking off the unease creeping into her mind.

Chapter Eighteen

Simon sat a little straighter, clearing his throat. "Any lastminute advice?"

Ayanna considered. "Don't sit in her chair. And if she asks if you want tea, just say yes. Even if you don't."

"Noted."

They pulled up outside the small house, its familiar stone exterior dappled in sunlight, the front garden still meticulously maintained despite Granny's slowing steps.

Simon turned off the engine, exhaling as he stared out the windshield.

Ayanna tilted her head slightly. "You're not about to run, are you?"

He shot her a dry look. "Tempting. But I don't want to waste the shortbread."

She grinned, unbuckling her seatbelt. "Then let's do this." Simon hesitated for half a second longer before nodding.

"Alright."

As they stepped out of the car, Ayanna let her fingers trail briefly along the weathered gate before pushing it open. She knocked lightly on the door, and there she was.

Granny stood in the doorway, silver hair tucked under a knitted shawl, eyes bright with recognition. Her smile was immediate, arms already spreading wide.

"Ayanna, my love," she said warmly, pulling her into a hug that smelled of old books and chamomile.

Ayanna melted into it, wrapping her arms around her tightly. "Hi, Granny."

When they pulled apart, Granny turned her attention to Simon, her sharp eyes scanning him with a curiosity that made him shift just slightly on his feet.

"And you must be Simon," she said, offering her hand.

Simon shook it, firm but respectful. "It's really nice to finally meet you, Mrs. Sander."

Granny let out a short laugh. "None of that formal nonsense. Granny is just fine."

Simon nodded, smiling. "Alright. Granny."

Ayanna watched as something in Granny's face softened, approval settling in her expression. She looped her arm through Simon's and led him inside without another word.

Chapter Eighteen

Ayanna followed, a warmth blooming in her chest, her heartbeat settling into an easy rhythm at the familiarity of it all. The house hadn't changed much, same soft floral wallpaper, same polished wooden floors that creaked in certain places if you stepped just right. Granny's chair, the one no one else dared to claim, sat by the window, a knitted blanket draped over the armrest.

Simon hesitated in the doorway, eyes sweeping over the room before Granny reached out and tugged him forward with surprising strength for her small frame.

"No need to hover, dear. I don't bite," she said, her voice laced with quiet amusement.

Simon offered a small smile as he stepped inside. "I just didn't want to break any rules I don't know about yet."

Granny let out a soft laugh, patting his arm. "Smart man. But don't worry, I only have one rule, and that's making sure you're comfortable enough to come back."

Ayanna watched as Simon visibly relaxed, some of the tension leaving his shoulders as Granny shuffled toward the kitchen. "Tea, of course," she said over her shoulder, already reaching for the well-worn kettle on the stove. "And I assume Ayanna hasn't let you escape without a bribe, did she bring biscuits?"

Simon chuckled, holding up the paper bag of shortbread. "Came prepared."

Granny turned, an approving glint in her eye. "Oh, I like you already."

Ayanna rolled her eyes affectionately, helping herself to a seat at the dining table. "I told you she'd love you."

In that moment, as it always did when Granny was near, Ayanna's self-doubt seemed to wash away. This house was a time capsule of bad memories. Some of Ayanna's worst moments had happened right here. But Granny made it all fade away. Just for a moment

Granny must have noticed her drifting thoughts because she reached over, giving Ayanna's hand a light squeeze.
"You doing alright, love?"
Ayanna nodded, squeezing back. "Yeah."

Granny studied her for a moment, but then she let it go, turning back to Simon. "So, tell me about yourself. What's this young man's story?"

Chapter Eighteen

Simon sat back slightly, considering. "Not nearly as exciting as yours, I promise."

"Well, that's no good. We'll have to work on that."

Ayanna smiled behind her tea cup as Simon launched into a condensed version of his life, his love for books, the odd jobs he worked through university, how he once tried to train his dog to deliver the mail but ended up with letters that had been partially eaten. Granny laughed at that, a full, hearty sound that filled the small space with warmth.

The conversation flowed easily after that, shifting from childhood memories to favourite foods to embarrassing stories. Granny delighted in sharing every awkward story she could recall, much to Ayanna's exaggerated dismay.

"You two are trouble together," Ayanna muttered as Simon and Granny exchanged another conspiratorial glance.

"Oh, don't worry, love," Granny said, patting her hand. "I'll always be on your side."

The words, simple as they were, struck something deep. Ayanna looked down at her tea, swallowing past the lump in her throat.

Outside, the sun had begun to dip lower, casting golden light through the lace curtains. Time always moved too fast here.

"Stay for dinner?" Granny said, as if sensing the inevitability of their departure.

Ayanna smiled, already nodding. "Of course."

Simon glanced at her, a question in his eyes, but she just squeezed his knee beneath the table.

They had nowhere better to be.

Later, after dishes were cleared and the air smelled faintly of roasted chicken and warm bread, Ayanna helped Granny to her favourite chair by the window.

Simon lingered near the bookshelf, taking in the titles, while Ayanna leaned against the armrest, watching Granny's profile as she stared outside.

"You should visit more," Granny said softly. "it's been years".

Ayanna looked down, guilt creeping in. "I know."

Granny reached up, tucking a stray curl behind Ayanna's ear. "Life gets busy. I understand that. But don't let time slip away from you."

Ayanna nodded, throat tight.

Granny patted her cheek, then turned her focus back outside. "Go keep your boy company," she smiled. "He's a good one."

Ayanna exhaled, standing to join Simon at the bookshelf.

As the evening stretched on, Granny dozed in her chair, the steady rise and fall of her breath the only sound in the quiet house.

Ayanna reached for Simon's hand, lacing their fingers together as they stood in the soft glow of the lamp.

"She really likes you," she whispered.

Simon squeezed gently. "*I* really like *her*."

Ayanna let out a slow breath, leaning her head against his shoulder.

Some Girls Drown

Chapter Nineteen
AGE 24

Ayanna's fingers clamped around her phone so tightly that her knuckles whitened. The words her mother had just spoken seemed to hover in the air between them, refusing to settle into reality. Granny was gone. Just like that. No warning, no chance to say goodbye, no final moment to memorise the lines of her face or the sound of her laugh. Just gone, as if eighty years of life could simply evaporate without ceremony.

"Ayanna? Are you there?" Her mother's voice crackled through the speaker, distant and broken.

The words repeated in her head like a cruel, unrelenting echo. She was gone. The silence that followed was unnatural, thick, pressing against her chest with unbearable force. It made her stomach twist, made the world around her dissolve into nothing but the sound of her mother's breath, shaky, uneven, proof that neither of them knew how to exist in that moment.

She tried to respond, but no words came. Her lips parted, but her throat closed around any sound she might have made.

The sob that eventually broke free from her throat wasn't just grief, it was regret, it was disbelief, it was the realisation that no matter how hard she tried to rewind, there would never be another Sunday morning at Granny's kitchen table, another knowing look exchanged over steaming mugs of tea, another hand wrapped around hers in the way that always made the world feel safe.

"Ayanna," her mother whispered, her voice breaking, "Say something, please."

Ayanna sucked in a sharp breath, but it hitched in her throat, burning like a scream she couldn't let out. "I, " she started, but the words tangled. "I wasn't there."

Her mother made a soft sound of anguish. "Neither was I."

That only made it worse. It wasn't supposed to be that way. Granny wasn't supposed to slip away quietly while

Chapter Nineteen

Ayanna was too busy with work, with life, with anything that seemed important at that time but now meant absolutely nothing.

"I didn't call her last week," she said, her voice strangled.

"I kept meaning to, I, "

"She knew, love." The words held little comfort. "She understood."

But Ayanna didn't. She didn't understand how the woman who was her foundation, her softest place to land, could just... not be there anymore. She didn't understand how she could wake up in a world where Granny's laughter didn't exist, where her stories remained forever unfinished, where the peculiar scent of rose water and cinnamon that always clung to her skin was nothing more than a memory.

She gripped the phone like it was the only thing keeping her tethered to reality, but her mind was already somewhere else. She was eight years old, curled in Granny's lap, listening to a story told in that gentle, melodic tone that was her lullaby for years. The scent of fresh bread filled the kitchen, and

Granny's fingers worked through her hair, weaving tiny braids while she spoke of places Ayanna had never seen but felt she knew intimately through those stories.

She was twelve, standing on a chair to help knead dough, with Granny laughing when flour ended up in her hair. "You're wearing more than you're using, child," she had said, her eyes crinkling at the corners in that way that made Ayanna feel completely seen, completely loved.

She was sixteen, heartbroken over her first love, crying into Granny's cardigan as soft, wrinkled hands rubbed slow, soothing circles over her back. "This pain has a purpose," Granny had whispered. "It's teaching you what you need and what you deserve. And you, my darling girl, deserve the whole world."

And then she was twenty-our, staring at the cold, impersonal walls of her apartment, with nothing left of those moments except the gaping hole they left behind.

Her mother exhaled shakily, her own grief pressing through the phone. "I didn't call sooner because I didn't know how to tell you. I didn't want to say it out loud.
Saying it made it real."

It was already real. Too real. Ayanna squeezed her eyes shut as hot tears spilled down her cheeks, streaking her skin with something deeper than sadness. It was loss in its purest form, raw, unyielding, absolute.

"I can't do this," she admitted, her voice barely above a whisper.

But she had to. The reality of it settled in her bones, heavy and cold. There were arrangements to be made, a funeral to attend, a life to honour. And she needed to be there, needed to say goodbye in whatever inadequate way remained possible.

"You don't have to do it alone," her mother said, her voice cracking. "Come home. Please."

That word, home... *Granny* was home. The one place in the world where Ayanna never felt unwanted, never felt like she had to earn love. Without her, what was left? The house itself? The family that had never truly embraced her? The memories that now cut like shards of glass with every breath?

Ayanna sat on the edge of the bed, her hands trembling in her lap, her chest hollow and aching. Granny was gone.

And Ayanna never felt so lost.

"Mum?" Ayanna finally managed, her voice small and cracked.

Her mother's answer arrived on a sob, broken. "Yes?"

"I need you." The admission cost her, broke something inside her that she'd kept carefully guarded for years. "Please."

"I need you too," her mother whispered. "Please come home."

In that instant, all the distance, all the hesitations between them gave way. They were just two women fractured by sorrow, yearning to heal in the only way possible: together. Though Granny was gone, the fragments of her love still pulsed through every memory, binding them in a bond that might have been battered but was never broken.

"Hold on," Ayanna whispered, clinging to the phone as if it was the last solid thing in her world. "I'm on my way." As she hung up, the silence of her apartment settled around her like a shroud. She pressed her palms against her eyes, willing the tears to stop, knowing they wouldn't.

Chapter Nineteen

Not today. Maybe not for a long time.

She wanted to collapse, wanted to scream, wanted to undo time with sheer desperation alone. But she couldn't. Instead, she forced herself to move. She numbly pulled out her suitcase and threw it open on the bed, her hands moving on instinct, folding clothes that felt too ordinary for a trip that felt like the end of everything.

Each item she packed made it more real. A sweater she wore the last time she visited, when Granny made her laugh so hard she nearly choked on her tea. A scarf Granny knitted for her last Christmas, the scent of roses still clinging to the wool. She clutched it to her chest, inhaling deeply, as if she could hold on to the memory just a little longer.

But it was already fading, already slipping through her fingers like sand, impossible to grasp no matter how tightly she held on. She dragged in a shaky breath, swiping at the tears that blurred her vision.

"I was supposed to visit next month," she wept, more to herself than anyone else. She had it all planned. She would take time off her writing, spend a long weekend with

Granny, show her the notes for her new book. Granny always wanted to hear about her writing, always believed in her words even when Ayanna didn't.

And now those plans were nothing but wisps of smoke, dissolving into the heavy air of her bedroom. There would be no visit, no shared pot of tea, no gentle critique of her latest chapter. There would only be silence where Granny's voice should be.

She zipped the suitcase shut, the reality of it hitting her like a freight train, there would be no more stories, no more Sunday lunches, no more love-filled lectures about taking care of herself. Granny was her world. And then that world crumbled to dust.

She gathered the last of her things with mechanical motions, her purse, her keys, her phone charger. The necessities for a journey she never wanted to take. And as she shut the apartment door behind her, she felt the finality of it all. A chapter closed. A heart broken. A grandmother gone.

Ayanna walked to her car with leaden steps, the world around her dulled and distant, as if viewed through clouded glass. The suitcase weighed heavy in her hand, filled with clothes for a funeral instead of a family gathering. This wasn't how it was supposed to be. But grief, she was learning, never arrived as expected. It came in waves, in whispers, in phone calls that changed everything.

She was going home. But home, without Granny, was just a place. And Ayanna wasn't sure she remembered how to exist in that place anymore.

Chapter Twenty

In the days following her tearful arrival at her mother's doorstep and leading up to the funeral, time became nothing more than a subdued routine of shared grief and silent preparations. Despite wanting desperately to be by her side, Simon was forced to remain behind when his own mother's health took a sudden turn; specialist appointments and around-the-clock care demanded his presence at home. Though Ayanna understood, the quiet ache of his absence deepened her already overwhelming sense of loss.

The glass of water her mother placed before her each morning remained untouched, food tasted stale, and sleep came in fitful bursts punctuated by dreams of Granny's voice calling her name. The world outside continued its indifferent rotation while Ayanna remained trapped in a moment she couldn't escape, the moment when everything changed with a phone call.

Each hour dragged like lead, heavy and poisonous. She helped her mother sort through old photographs for the service, their fingers brushing occasionally over images frozen in time: Granny as a young woman with a laughing

Chapter Twenty

mouth and defiant eyes; Granny in her garden, hands deep in soil, face tilted toward the sun; Granny holding baby Ayanna, her expression a mixture of fierce protection and boundless love.

"She kept every single one of your letters," her mother said softly, sliding a ribbon-tied bundle across the kitchen table. "Even the ones from when you were too busy to call."

Ayanna's fingers trembled as she untied the faded blue ribbon. Her own handwriting stared back at her, evolving from the large, looping script of adolescence to the more contained penmanship of adulthood. Granny had preserved them all, these shards of Ayanna's life, these pieces of herself she had sent home when she couldn't return in person.

"I didn't know," she whispered, touching the paper reverently.

Her mother's smile was sad. "She read them until the creases wore thin."

The knowledge sat heavy in Ayanna's chest, both a comfort and a knife. Granny had cherished her words, had held onto them through the years. And now Ayanna would never write her another letter, never receive another response in that careful, elegant script.

Each night, she called Simon, his voice through the phone a tether to a different life. He listened as she talked about Granny, about memories unearthed with each box they opened, each drawer they cleared.

"I wish I could be there," he said, his voice rough with exhaustion. "Mum's doctors are concerned about this new medication. I need to monitor her reaction for at least another week."

"I know," Ayanna assured him, though loneliness carved a hollow space beneath her ribs. "Your mum needs you. I understand."

And she did understand. That was the thing about Simon, his devotion to his family was part of who he was, part of why she loved him. But understanding didn't stop the selfish part of her heart that wished he could hold her through this, that wished she didn't have to face her family alone.

"I'll be thinking of you," he promised, and she could hear the sincerity in his voice, could picture the worried crease between his brows. "Call me anytime, day or night."

Chapter Twenty

She promised she would, though they both knew the truth, there were some burdens that couldn't be shared, some griefs that couldn't be eased with a phone call.

Days melted into each other in the run-up to the funeral, a blur of phone calls and awkward condolences. Ayanna drifted through them in a haze, trying her best to be present for the tasks at hand while inwardly grappling with the finality of it all. Though she'd promised to share more of her feelings with her mother, some nights Ayanna still found herself awake at ungodly hours, clinging to quiet tears she couldn't bring herself to explain.

When the morning of the funeral finally came, a strange calm settled over the house. There were no more arrangements to be made, no more decisions to agonize over, just the reality that today would be goodbye. Ayanna dressed in silence, each button fastened, and shoe tied with a gravity that felt new, and found her mother waiting by the door.

"Ready?" her mother asked, though there was no real need for the question.

Ayanna gave a small nod. She had barely slept, hadn't eaten.

The idea of food made her stomach twist, made her feel as though she would choke on the sheer grief sitting in her throat.

The car ride was quiet. Not a peaceful quiet, a loaded one. Ayanna kept her eyes fixed on the road ahead, counting the lines painted onto the asphalt, the rows of houses they passed, the flickering streetlights that still burned in the early morning gloom, anything to keep her mind from sinking too deep into the reality pressing against her ribs.

Her mother didn't try to fill the silence. Perhaps she understood that there were no words that could smooth over what was lost. Perhaps she was just as afraid to speak.

When they turned onto the long stretch leading into town, Ayanna's chest tightened. She knew the moment they crossed into familiar territory. The houses took on an aged quality, the buildings stood just as they had for decades, only the paint a little duller, the windows a little more weathered.

They drove past Green's Grocery, where Granny would take her for penny sweets when she was small, her weathered hand warm around Ayanna's as they picked out treats. Past the library where Granny first introduced her to the worlds

Chapter Twenty

hidden inside books, her voice dropping to a theatrical whisper as she explained the magic of borrowing stories.

Each landmark was a needle to Ayanna's heart, each memory a reminder of the absence now etched into her life. She pressed her fingertips against the cool glass of the window, as if she could reach through time itself, back to when these places were filled with Granny's presence rather than her absence.

Her mother gripped the steering wheel a little tighter as the funeral home came into view. The car park was full, with cars packed in tight. She wasn't ready for this.

Not the funeral. Not the family. Not the memories waiting for her.

The Brooks Funeral Home stood solemn and dignified against the pale morning sky, its brick exterior and white columns suggesting a permanence that mocked the very impermanence of life it witnessed daily. Ayanna had been there only once before for a great-aunt she barely knew at twelve. But this time was different. This time, the person inside those walls was someone who had shaped her very soul.

Her mother turned off the engine, exhaling slowly. She glanced at Ayanna, something uncertain in her expression, but didn't speak.

Ayanna's throat was dry. Her pulse was too loud. She could feel it in her fingertips, in her temples, in the hollow of her throat, this persistent reminder that she was alive while Granny was not.

"Are you okay?" her mother asked, the question cautious, as though she knew the answer before it left her lips.

Ayanna swallowed hard. "No."

Her mother's hand twitched on her lap as if she wanted to reach out but thought better of it. "I know this is hard, but we'll get through it."

Get through it. As if grief was something to endure until it passed, as if there would come a day when Granny's absence wasn't a physical ache in her chest. As if they could simply move on, return to their separate lives, continue as though nothing fundamental had shifted.

She looked out the window, at the people filtering into the building, at the dark coats and bowed heads. She thought of Granny, who had lived with such vibrancy, with such

Chapter Twenty

insistent joy. Granny, who would have hated the gloomy faces, the whispered platitudes, the performative sorrow of distant relatives who hadn't bothered to visit when she was alive.

Ayanna let out a slow breath. She reached for the door handle; her movements deliberate despite the tremor in her fingers.

"I wish Simon could have come for you," her mother said suddenly, her voice small in the confined space of the car.

Ayanna paused, her hand still on the door handle. "He wanted to be here."

Her mother nodded, a quick, jerky movement. "I know. I just thought... it might be easier for you. Having someone who wasn't part of all this."

The admission surprised Ayanna. It was the closest her mother had ever come to acknowledging the fractured nature of their family, the way it had never been a source of comfort or safety for Ayanna.

"It might have been," she agreed softly. "But he has his own family to care for."

Her mother's eyes dropped to her hands, twisted in her lap. "Yes, of course." She hesitated, then added, "You have that with him, don't you? What you never had with us."

The words hung between them, fragile and painful in their truth. Ayanna didn't deny it. Couldn't deny it. With Simon, she had found what she'd always craved, unconditional acceptance, a love that didn't require her to be smaller, quieter, less herself.

"I do," she said simply.

Her mother nodded again, blinking rapidly. "Good. That's good." She drew in a shaky breath. "I'm glad you have that, at least."

Without another word, she opened her door and stepped out into the cold. The moment Ayanna walked through the funeral home doors, it hit her.

Everywhere she looked, Ayanna saw only reminders of why they had gathered: the solemn faces, the black attire, the tissue-clutched hands. Light filtered through stained glass windows, casting coloured shadows across the room like a grotesque parody of celebration.

Chapter Twenty

The wood-panelled walls seemed to lean inward, the ceiling pressing down, making the space feel smaller with each breath she took. The funeral director, a thin man with careful movements and practiced sympathy, ushered them toward the guest book, Ayanna signed her name mechanically, the pen feeling foreign in her hand. Her signature looked wrong somehow, too bold, too permanent on a page that documented loss. She handed the pen to her mother, their fingers brushing briefly. The small contact sent an electric current through Ayanna's arm, grounding her momentarily in the surreal haze of the day.

Voices spoke in calm tones, people offered condolences, exchanging soft words that did nothing to fill the empty space Granny left behind. Each "I'm sorry for your loss" and "She's in a better place now" scraped against Ayanna's raw nerves like sandpaper. She nodded thanks, accepted embraces from people whose names she barely remembered, whose faces had faded from her memory years ago.

There were neighbours who had known Granny for decades, church friends who had prayed with her every Sunday, the mailman who had always taken time to chat with her about her garden. All these people who had been part of Granny's life in ways that Ayanna, with her distance and her absence, had not.

The guilt of it pressed against her sternum, made her breath shallow and quick. She should have visited more. Should have called more. Should have been there for those ordinary moments that now seemed precious beyond measure.

Her mother led the way, moving toward the front where the casket lay and where the closest family members gathered. Ayanna followed a few steps behind, her legs feeling wooden, her body moving on instinct rather than will.

The casket was closed, draped with a blanket of white roses and pink carnations, Granny's favourites. A large photograph stood on an easel beside it: Granny in her garden, her face tilted toward the sun, her smile wide and genuine. It had been taken three years ago, during Ayanna's last extended visit. She remembered taking that photo, remembered the way Granny had laughed and told her not to waste film on "an old woman's wrinkles."

Ayanna's feet faltered; her heart thudded hard against her ribs. She couldn't do it. Couldn't sit in the front, couldn't let them see her grief, couldn't let them watch her break.

Chapter Twenty

Couldn't look at that casket and know that Granny was inside, still and silent in a way she had never been in life.

"I need to sit in the back," she whispered, her voice barely audible.

Her mother turned, hesitation flickering across her face, but she didn't argue. Perhaps she understood Ayanna's need for distance, for privacy in her sorrow. Or perhaps she was simply too worn down by her own grief to insist.

Ayanna slipped into the last row, her hands clasped tightly in her lap, staring straight ahead. The hard wooden pew pressed uncomfortably against her spine, but the discomfort was almost welcome, a physical sensation to focus on instead of the emotional storm raging inside her.

She thought she was prepared for this. She wasn't.

The walls pressed closer. The conversations around her grew louder, distorted, like waves crashing in her ears. A cold sweat broke out across her skin, dampening her brow, the back of her neck.

She needed to get out. She couldn't breathe. Couldn't stay in this room with him. Couldn't bear the thought of him seeing her, of his eyes finding hers across the crowded room, of the smile that might curve his lips, that knowing smile that had sat in her dreams for years.

She rose to her feet, slipping away as quietly as she could, her movements quick, desperate. No one stopped her. No one even noticed. They were too absorbed in their own grief, their own memories, their own reason for being there.

The relief of not being seen, of escaping without confrontation, almost made her knees buckle. But she didn't stop moving. She pushed forward, past the cars, past the people lingering near the entrance, past everything that tethered her to that place, to that moment.

The cold air hit her lungs like a physical blow, but she welcomed it. Gulped it down in greedy breaths as she stumbled away from the building, away from him, away from the twisted reality where Barney was allowed to mourn the woman who had been Ayanna's safe harbour.

She made it halfway across the parking lot before her legs gave out. She sank onto a low stone wall that bordered a small garden, her body trembling violently, her breath coming in short, painful gasps.

Chapter Twenty

This wasn't happening. Couldn't be happening. But the evidence of her senses wouldn't be denied, the cold stone beneath her palms, the distant voices from the funeral home, the fact that Barney was inside while she was out here, exiled by her own horror and revulsion.

The unfairness of it crashed over her in waves. Tears streamed down her face, hot against her cold skin. She didn't bother to wipe them away. What did it matter now? Who was left to care if she broke apart, if she smashed into a thousand pieces on this cold perch outside her grandmother's funeral?

Ayanna wrapped her arms around herself, trying to hold the broken pieces together, trying to find the strength to stand, to walk away, to survive this day that had already taken more from her than she had to give.

She had to get through this. For Granny. But right now, all she could do was breathe, one painful inhale after another.

In the quiet expanse of the funeral home's gardens, the late morning light cast a sombre glow over meticulously arranged flower beds and weathered stone paths. Ayanna wandered aimlessly, unable to make herself return to the funeral. The air was cool and filled with the smells of damp earth and wilting roses, mingling with the faint, sweet aroma of freshly cut lilies. Each step up the gravel path crunched loudly in the stillness, punctuating the deep, internal rhythm of her grief. As she settled onto a moss-covered bench, the textures of the stone and the gentle caress of the cool breeze against her skin offered a bittersweet comfort, a quiet reminder of nature's steady, unchanging presence.

Here, away from the claustrophobic formality of the funeral service, away from Barney's invasive presence, Ayanna felt she could breathe again. The sky stretched above her, pale blue with wisps of cloud, indifferent to the human sorrow below. A small brown bird hopped along a nearby branch, its movements quick and purposeful, its existence untouched by the currents of loss that pulled at Ayanna's heart.

She traced her fingers along the rough grain of the wooden bench, feeling each ridge and hollow. Granny had taught her that, to pay attention to details, to ground herself in the physical world when emotions threatened to overwhelm her. "Touch something real," she would say. "Remember that you're here, now, and that's all you need to be."

Chapter Twenty

But being here now, without Granny, felt impossible. Like trying to navigate without a compass, like trying to read in the dark.

In that hidden moment, away from prying eyes and the prattle of hollow condolences, Ayanna allowed herself to break. Her tears, unbidden and relentless, traced hot, salty paths down her cheeks. Each sob carried the weight of years of abandoned hope and aching isolation, reverberating in the silence around her.

After what felt like an eternity in that solitude, she sensed a soft approach, a familiar, comforting presence. She didn't need to look up to know who it was; something in the rhythm of the footsteps, in the quality of the silence that followed, told her.

Her mother appeared at the edge of the garden; her eyes filled with sorrow yet understanding. She didn't speak, didn't offer platitudes or questions or demands. She simply stood there, giving Ayanna the space to invite her in or send her away.

Ayanna met her mother's eyes, seeing in it a reflection of her own pain. For once, there was no pretence between them. Without a word, her mother reached out and wrapped a loving arm around Ayanna's shoulders, her embrace warm and reassuring. The contact, unexpected yet desperately needed, loosened something in Ayanna's chest. She leaned into her mother's side, allowing herself to accept the comfort offered, allowing herself to be held in a way she hadn't been since childhood.

They sat like that for several minutes, the silence between them not empty but full, full of shared memories, of mutual grief, of the complicated love that existed despite everything that had come before.

"Granny would have hated all this formality," her mother said finally, a smile ghosting across her lips. "Remember how she used to say funerals were just an excuse for people to wear uncomfortable shoes and eat mediocre sandwiches?"

Ayanna laughed; the sound surprised out of her. "And that if anyone cried at hers, she'd come back to haunt them."

The shared memory was a relief, a momentary respite from the crushing loss. It didn't erase the pain, didn't make Granny's absence less real, but it reminded Ayanna that grief could coexist with joy, which remembering could be an act of love rather than only of sorrow.

Chapter Twenty

Together, they slowly rose from the bench and began the quiet walk back toward the car, the sound of their footsteps mingling with the gentle susurration of the trees. Ayanna's legs felt weak, her body drained from the emotional exertion of the day, but her mother's arm remained around her, steady and supporting.

As they approached the car park, the funeral home loomed behind them. People were beginning to leave, filtering out in small groups, their voices low.

They reached the car just as the sun dipped below the horizon, casting the world in shades of purple and grey. The air had grown cold, carrying the sharp edge of approaching night. Ayanna shivered, pulling her coat tighter around her.

Chapter Twenty-One

By the time she arrived at the wake, the whispers had already started.

"She left the funeral early."

"I wasn't surprised. She was never here when Granny was alive, either." Ayanna heard every word. She kept her back straight, her hands clenched at her sides, refusing to let them see how much it hurt. Because that was the thing about grief. It wasn't just about loss, it was about the way people *saw* your loss. And them?

They didn't see hers.

They didn't see the nights she spent curled up with

Granny, listening to her stories. They didn't see the way Granny always made her feel safe. They didn't see the love that existed between them, even with the distance. All they saw was the years she stayed away. All they saw was the girl who left and never looked back.

Granny's house looked exactly the same and completely different all at once. The familiar blue curtains still hung in the windows, the collection of wind chimes still tinkled from the porch, the rose bushes still lined the garden path, but the absence of Granny's presence made it all feel like a movie set, a careful recreation of a home rather than the home itself.

Inside, the rooms were filled with people balancing plates of food, clutching glasses of wine, exchanging stories with laughter that seemed inappropriate given the occasion. The dining table that had hosted countless Sunday dinners was now covered with casseroles and cakes brought by neighbours and friends, each dish a well-intentioned but inadequate substitute for what was really needed; Granny herself, standing in the kitchen, wooden spoon in hand, shooing everyone away from her stove.

Ayanna moved through the rooms like a ghost, her mother had disappeared into the kitchen, busy with the practical tasks of hosting, refilling platters, directing the flow of guests, maintaining the illusion that this gathering was a celebration of Granny's life rather than a painful reminder of her absence.

The whispers followed her.

"...hardly ever visited..."

"...too busy with her own life..."

"...broke her grandmother's heart..." Each one was a needle, precise and sharp, finding the most sensitive places in her already wounded heart.

They didn't know. *Couldn't* know; the phone calls that lasted for hours, the letters, the way Granny had encouraged her to build her own life, to find her own path, to not be limited by the narrow confines of this place and this family. The way Granny had been proud of her independence, her determination, her refusal to conform to expectations that were never meant for her. But explaining would be useless. These people had already written their version of the story, with Ayanna cast as the ungrateful granddaughter, the one who abandoned her family for the allure of the city, the one who returned only when it was too late.

A hand landed on her arm, light but firm. Ayanna turned, her jaw tightening as she met the familiar face of Aunty

Chapter Twenty-One

Clara, with her perfectly coiffed hair and her lips permanently pursed in disapproval.

"We haven't seen you in so long," the woman said, her voice laced with something Ayanna couldn't place. Not genuine concern, certainly. Perhaps curiosity. Perhaps judgment. Perhaps both.

"I've been busy," Ayanna replied, her tone clipped. Aunty Clara hummed, a slow nod following. "Shame it took this to bring you back."

Ayanna's teeth clenched. The words were carefully chosen, perfectly designed to wound while maintaining the facade of propriety. A specialty of the family, cruelty disguised as concern; judgment wrapped in a thin veneer of care.

"I spoke to Granny every week," Ayanna replied. She shouldn't have to defend her relationship. Shouldn't have to explain the depth of love that existed between them. But the alternative was to let this woman, this family, rewrite history with their silent compliance. "Phone calls aren't the same as being here," Aunty Clara countered, her smile not reaching her eyes. "She missed you terribly, you know." The implication hung in the air between them: that

Ayanna had failed Granny, that her absence was a betrayal, that she had chosen selfishness over family obligation.

"Granny understood why I left," Ayanna said, struggling to keep her voice steady. "She encouraged it, actually." Aunty Clara eyebrows lifted slightly, disbelief evident in the gesture. "Well, she was always too soft with you." She patted Ayanna's arm, the touch condescending rather than comforting. "I suppose she felt guilty, given everything that happened."

The reference was deliberate, a poisoned arrow aimed at the most vulnerable part of Ayanna's heart. *Given everything that happened.* The way the family talked about it, or didn't talk about it. The way they had closed ranks. The way they had made Ayanna feel like the problem, the troublemaker, the one who had disrupted the family peace with her inconvenient truth.

"Don't," Ayanna said, the word sharp enough to cut.

"Don't pretend to know what Granny felt."

Aunty Claras expression hardened, the mask of sympathy slipping to reveal the coldness beneath. "I think *I* knew her better than *you* did."

Chapter Twenty-One

The cruelty of it, the sheer audacity, left Ayanna momentarily speechless. This woman, who had stood by while Ayanna was hurt, who had chosen silence over protection, who had valued family reputation over a child's safety, dared to claim ownership of Granny's memory.

"Excuse me," Ayanna muttered. She didn't wait for a response, didn't give her aunt the satisfaction of seeing the tears that threatened to spill. She moved away, weaving through the crowd of mourners, seeking escape from the suffocating press of judgment and expectation.

She found refuge in Granny's bedroom, the one room that seemed untouched by the invasion of well-wishers and distant relatives. The familiar quilt still lay folded at the foot of the bed, the collection of porcelain birds still lined the windowsill, the framed photographs still watched over the room from their perch on the dresser.

Ayanna sank onto the edge of the bed, running her fingers over the intricate pattern of the quilt. Granny had made it herself, had taught Ayanna the stitches when she was just a girl, their heads bent together over squares of fabric on long winter afternoons. She looked around taking in the quiet order of the room, Granny's legacy still intact, still waiting.

There were things no one here would say aloud. Things Ayanna couldn't bear to let go unspoken. She didn't want to scream. She wanted to write. To trace it all out, word by word, until the silence lost its grip.

A knock at the door interrupted her reverie. Her mother stood in the doorway, a plate of food in her hands, concern etched in the lines around her eyes.

"I thought you might be hungry," she said, offering the plate like a peace offering. Ayanna shook her head. The thought of food made her stomach twist. "I can't stay here," she said quietly.

Her mother didn't look surprised. She set the plate down on the bedside table and sat beside Ayanna, the mattress dipping slightly under their combined weight. "I know." She sighed.

They sat in silence for a moment, the subdued sounds of the wake filtering through the closed door, conversations rising and falling, occasional laughter, the clink of glasses and silverware.

Chapter Twenty-One

"They don't understand," her mother said finally. "They didn't see what she meant to you. What you meant to her." It was the most her mother had ever acknowledged, the closest she had ever come to admitting the truth of Ayanna's childhood, of the isolation, of the way Granny had been her only real advocate, her only safe harbour in the storm of family dysfunction.

"I don't belong here," Ayanna said. It wasn't a new realisation, but stating it aloud felt like a final admission, a closing of a door that had been ajar for too long.

Her mother didn't contradict her. Didn't offer platitudes about family always being family, about blood being thicker than water. Perhaps she knew it would be a lie. Perhaps she had finally grown tired of the lies herself.

"Where will you go?" she asked instead.

"Home," Ayanna said simply, *to Simon*. To the life she had built for herself, brick by brick, choice by choice. To the one person left who loved her without conditions, who accepted her without reservations, who had never asked her to be smaller or quieter or less herself. Her mother nodded, her eyes filled with a complicated mixture of understanding and sadness.

"She would have wanted that for you," she said softly.

"She always did."

And that, Ayanna knew, was the truth. Granny had never wanted her to stay trapped in the web of family expectation and obligation, had never wanted her to sacrifice her own happiness for the comfort of people who hadn't earned her loyalty. Had never wanted anything for her but freedom, and joy, and the courage to live on her own terms. Ayanna stood; a decision made. She would say her goodbyes, not to the people gathered in the house, eating casseroles and exchanging stories that painted a picture of Granny that barely resembled the woman Ayanna had known. She would say goodbye to Granny, in her own way, in her own time. She pressed a hand gently to the quilt, eyes lingering on the worn stitching.

"I'm sorry I wasn't here," she whispered. "But you knew, didn't you? You always knew why."

There was no answer, of course. Just the quiet weight of memory.

Chapter Twenty-One

"I'll carry you with me," Ayanna whispered into the room "I promise."

Her steps were purposeful, carrying her toward the front door with a determined calm. But just as the cool air from outside brushed her cheeks, an unsettling presence in the room caught her attention...

Barney.

Older now; greying at the temples slower to stand, but unmistakable. He sat at the far end of the room, legs crossed, gesturing as he spoke to Arthur. That casual, comfortable smile. Ayanna's heart felt like it had stopped.

She had known he'd be here; she had prepared herself., told herself it was just a few hours, that she could be civil, quiet, *invisible* if she had to. She'd done it before, but this was the first time she had seen his face in almost two decades. The first time she'd had to see what he looked like as an adult; as someone who had grown older while she stayed frozen in the version of herself he had broken.

She turned away sharply. Her breath caught in her throat.

Alice had seated herself across the room, spine straight, hands folded neatly in her lap as if she didn't quite know where she was supposed to be. She didn't look up, her eyes stayed on the plate in front of her like it held all the answers. Ayanna's chest tightened.
Someone pored a glass of wine. Glasses clinked.

And then she heard a voice speak out "It's nice, isn't it?" said someone in the corner of the room. "Having everyone back together. It almost feels like the old days." Ayanna froze.

The old days. The words echoed, loud in her ears. Another voice chimed in: "Granny would've been proud. Look at us, all here, stronger than ever."

Stronger than ever. Ayanna blinked. Her vision blurred, not with tears but with heat. *Stronger?* Was that what this was? A triumph? A *reunion?*

Her pulse roared in her ears. Her fingers clenched until her knuckles ached. Across the room, someone laughed, then Barney laughed too.

Chapter Twenty-One

She stepped forwards into the room silent and defiant. The air shifted, the warmth dissolving in an instant. Alice's eyes didn't move from her plate, but her fingers had stilled, hovering just above her fork; the muscles in her jaw pulsed, tight, restrained, like something inside her was bracing for impact.

Ayanna's voice was quiet as she broke the fresh and awkward silence, "Stronger?" She turned to face the group, eyes scanning from face to face. Celia. Arthur. Henry. Cousins she hadn't hugged in years. Her mother. Barney. Her voice rose, calm but shaking.
"Stronger than what, exactly?" The room stilled. "Stronger than the silence?" she asked. "Stronger than the weight of secrets you all buried and called history?" Arthur stood, smile faltering.

"Ayanna, now's not the time, dear…"

She cut him off. "Isn't it? Because I've spent years wondering when the time would come. When someone…*anyone*…would say something."

A hush settled, thick and uncomfortable. She turned slowly, until she was looking straight at Barney. His expression had changed; the smile was gone, he didn't look away, he didn't move. He stared right back at her.

And in that moment, her body betrayed her. She remembered her small hands; the closed doors, the breath she had held, the sound of footsteps, the certainty that she had done something wrong, something shameful. The coldness crept in beneath skin.

"I was eight," she said, louder now, turning her eyes towards the family that sat in silence around her. "Eight years old when it started. And I told you something was wrong, I told you I didn't feel safe, and what did you say?" No one answered. "You said I was sensitive! That I was confused! That I didn't understand!" Her voice was rising with every beat. "I understood, I understood everything! I understood that no one was going to help me. I understood that family meant keeping quiet. That love had conditions. That safety was something *other* people had." Her voice cracked. Barney stood slowly. "Ayanna, please…" Ayanna held up a hand defiantly.

"No!" The word firm and sharp "You don't get to speak first. Not now, not after all this time." The silence deepened, even the children had stopped whispering. Across the room, Alice's shoulders trembled, but still she didn't speak. Ayanna looked at her, willing her to stand up, to do *something*. But Alice just stared at her lap, her lips pressed together, unmoving. Ayanna looked back at Barney. And something inside her began to burn.

Barney's hands hung awkwardly at his sides. His face had lost its colour. And still he did not look away. Ayanna stepped forward, her voice trembled. "You've been allowed to forget," she said. "To age, to move forward, to be welcomed at weddings and Christmas dinners. But I stayed eight years old for years. I stayed in that hallway, I stayed *frozen*." Barney's brow pinched.

"I'm not here to defend myself," he said softly. "I know I can't. I'm not going to pretend I didn't know; I knew. I was old enough to understand it was wrong." His voice cracked. "I think about it all the time. That look on your face, you pulled away and I didn't stop. And then… I told myself we could… that we'd both forget. But I didn't… *couldn't*… I never forgot."

Ayanna stared at him. The words pierced something in her chest, but they didn't heal.

"I used to wonder if you laughed about it after," she whispered. "If you thought it was nothing. It would've been easier, somehow, if you had. But this…this guilt you carry…it doesn't undo the years."

He nodded slowly. "I know."

"I screamed into pillows so no one would hear. I cried during class, and no one asked why. I sat through birthdays where everyone hugged you like nothing had happened." Her voice grew stronger. "And I waited for someone to say it; to name it, to ask me if I was okay and no one did." Henry shifted uncomfortably in his seat. "I couldn't sleep in silence," Ayanna continued. "Because silence reminded me of you. And when I finally told the truth… it was you who broke me." She gestured around the room. "It was you," she said. "but it was them who left me to bleed."

Arthur stood, voice thin. "We didn't know how to handle it. We were shocked…"

Chapter Twenty-One

"Don't," Ayanna snapped. "You weren't *shocked*. You were *inconvenienced*." His mouth opened then closed... No reply. "You looked at my pain and asked me to keep it to myself. You said it would ruin the family, that it would 'tear us apart.' So instead, I tore myself apart. Quietly. So you could stay whole."

Still Alice said nothing. Ayanna's voice dropped. "Do you know what it's like to cry in the next room from your mother and realise she's not coming to help?" Alice flinched, her hands gripped the arms of her chair, her eyes brimmed but still, she didn't speak. "I wasn't dramatic," Ayanna seethed "I wasn't confused, I wasn't a liar, I was a child! I was *scared*. And no one protected me."

"I *am* sorry," Barney choked. "I live with it *every day*. You don't have to forgive me, I don't know if I deserve that. But I need to say it. I need you to know."

Ayanna's voice dropped to a whisper. "I believe you." Barney looked up, startled. "I believe you're sorry," she continued. "But I don't know what to do with that. I don't know how to let it in; I don't know how to forgive someone who shaped the worst parts of me."

Alice inhaled sharply. Ayanna turned to her. Her voice shook. "I needed you to see *me*. Not him, I needed your voice, your arms. I needed you to say, 'It's true. I believe her.' But you didn't. You never said it again".

Alices body trembled as she stood herself up. She didn't speak right away. She seemed to start a sentence, once… twice. When she finally found her words, her voice cracked:

"I heard you," she said quietly. "I… I didn't know what to do. I didn't want to believe it. Not you, not… not him." She paused, blinking rapidly, as if trying to hold herself steady. "I thought you were confused. I told myself you must've misunderstood. Because the alternative…" Her voice broke and she looked away. "The alternative was worse." She took a breath. "I failed you. I failed you so badly." The room fell to complete silence; not even the radiator dared hum. Alice's voice shook. "I told myself it couldn't be true, that you were confused, that Barney…he was *family*, just a boy. It was easier to imagine you'd misunderstood than to face what it meant if you hadn't." Ayanna swallowed hard. Her mouth was dry. She couldn't speak. "I failed you," Alice said. "In the worst way a mother can fail. I didn't put my arms around you. I didn't protect you. I told you to be quiet when I should've been screaming on your behalf." Her eyes filled, spilling over. But still, she didn't waver. "I thought I was keeping the peace," she continued. "But I was protecting them, not you." She turned to the room, her voice rising. "All of you ...all of us sat in silence. We all knew something wasn't right. We looked away, whispered behind closed doors and called that loyalty. But it wasn't loyalty, it was cowardice."

Henry's jaw clenched. Arthur shifted in his seat, eyes flicking toward each other as if waiting for someone else to interrupt. Alice's voice cracked. "We stood by, watching her slip beneath the surface, and *none of us* reached out to save her." Ayanna's breath caught, her legs felt weak as Alice turned back to her. "I see it now. I see *you*, not as a problem to solve, not as a child too full of feeling. I see you as the girl who tried to survive .. you've been so strong Ayanna." Ayanna couldn't hold it in any longer. Tears poured down over her cheeks.

"Mum..." she whispered.

Alice stepped closer. "I know." Ayanna fell into her mother's arms. There was no apology big enough, no sentence that could stitch shut the wound, but in that moment, something shifted. Something opened; It wasn't magic, it didn't fix everything. But it was real.

They stood in silence for a moment, just breathing, just existing, the rest of the room had blurred and for once, it didn't matter. Then Ayanna pulled away, slowly. Her eyes were clear; she looked at her mother, at Barney, at everyone as she spoke.

"I'm going to write it all down," she said. "Every truth. Every silence. Every time I was told to stay quiet for the sake of your comfort." Barney looked up at her, his eyes were red. But he nodded.

"I'm going to write about this family," she said clearly. "About what it means to grow up surrounded by people who are supposed to love you but won't protect you; about what it does to a girl to carry that kind of betrayal inside her."

Her mother squeezed her hand. "Tell the truth."

Chapter Twenty-One

"I will." She looked around once more. The room was still, no interruptions, no polite deflections. Just the weight of what had been spoken.

Ayanna stepped toward the door pausing only once, placing her hand on the frame. Knowing she would never be back in Granny's house again, taking in the feel of the wood beneath her fingers, and she realised it. *This was the story,* not the versions whispered behind her back, not the silence she had swallowed. *This.* She felt it like electricity in her chest, like clarity blooming. This wasn't about vengeance, it was about *freedom.* This moment of standing in front of the people who made her small and choosing to be loud anyway. She would write it, she would name them, she would never again pretend it hadn't happened. And in doing so, she would become whole. Without looking back, Ayanna opened the door and walked into the night.

"She always had a flair for drama," someone muttered near the back. A quiet scoff. A clink of glass.
But Ayanna didn't flinch. She was already gone.

In the threshold, she paused and looked back at the family. They appeared smaller somehow, reduced by the truth she had finally spoken aloud. The dining room, which had felt like a prison moments before, now seemed merely a room, one she was finally free to leave.

Outside, the rain had started to fall, washing the world clean, it fell in relentless sheets, turning the front walkway into a miniature river that carried away dead leaves and broken promises alike. Ayanna stood beneath the porch overhang, one foot on the wet concrete, the other still on dry ground. Beside her, her mother's hand found hers, their fingers intertwining with an urgency that spoke of newfound alliance and ancient regret.

Water drummed against the roof, creating a percussive backdrop to Ayanna's thundering heart. Each droplet caught the pale-yellow glow of the porch light, transforming momentarily into tiny, fragile stars before shattering against the pavement. The world beyond the shelter of the overhang was a grey blur, boundaries dissolved by the downpour, streets, houses, and hedges all melting into a single watercolour smudge.

Chapter Twenty-One

"The car's just there," Alice said, her voice nearly lost beneath the storm's percussion. She nodded toward their sedan, parked no more than twenty feet away but seeming miles distant through the watery veil. "We'll have to make a run for it."

Ayanna tightened her grip on her mother's hand. The pressure of those familiar fingers against her palm felt different now, no longer the tentative touch that had failed to protect her for so many years, but something firmer, more determined. She turned to study her mother's profile.

Alice's face was a map of complicated emotions. Her eyes, red-rimmed and swollen, held a distant, hollow quality that suggested she was seeing not just the present moment but all the moments that had led to it, every silence she had maintained, every confrontation she had avoided, every compromise that had slowly eroded her daughter's trust. The fine lines around her mouth seemed deeper tonight, carved by years of words swallowed and truths deferred. Her hair, usually meticulously styled, had come loose from its clip, thin strands clinging to her damp cheeks like delicate fracture lines in porcelain.

"Mum," Ayanna began, then faltered. What could she possibly say? *Thank you for finally defending me? Where was this courage when I needed it most? I love you? I'm still angry?* All were true, all insufficient.

Alice met her eyes, her expression raw with a vulnerability Ayanna had rarely witnessed. "I know," she whispered. "I know it's too little, too late. But it's what I can offer now."

The admission hung between them, honest in its inadequacy. Ayanna felt a complicated ache in her chest, grief for what could have been, cautious hope for what might still be possible.

A fresh gust of wind drove the rain sideways, spattering their ankles with cold droplets. In the distance, thunder rolled across the sky like furniture being moved in heaven's attic. The waiting car was a dark shape in the gloom, its engine idling with a low, constant rumble that reminded Ayanna of a patient animal.

This moment at the threshold felt marred with significance, poised between the house that had never been a true home and the uncertain journey ahead. Ayanna had stood at similar crossroads before the day she'd left for college, determined never to return; the morning after her first book was accepted for publication; the afternoon she'd decided to attend Granny's funeral despite knowing the rest of the family would be there. Each time, she had crossed over alone.

But now her mother's hand was clasped in hers, trembling slightly but undeniably present.

The scent of rain-soaked earth rose around them, primordial and cleansing. It mingled with the lingering traces of her mother's perfume, the same fragrance Alice had worn throughout Ayanna's childhood. That familiar scent unlocked a flood of memories: her mother brushing her hair with gentle strokes while humming off-key lullabies; midnight games of Risk on the bedroom floor when neither could sleep; the press of cool lips against her forehead during a childhood fever.

These tender recollections had always existed alongside the painful ones, her mother's averted gaze when Henry made cutting remarks about Ayanna's heritage.

Alice's nervous laughter covering the silence after Clara's backhanded compliments; the way she would squeeze

Ayanna's hand under the dinner table, a silent apology for the protection she wasn't providing.

"I remember," Ayanna said abruptly, "when I was eight, and I had that nightmare about drowning."

Alice looked at her, surprise momentarily replacing the sorrow in her eyes.

"You came to my room," Ayanna continued, "and you sat with me until morning. You counted my freckles to distract me, said each one was a kiss from the sun, a reminder I was special."

A tear slipped down Alice's cheek, indistinguishable from the raindrops already there. "Two hundred and fiftyseven," she whispered. "You had two hundred and fiftyseven freckles then."

"You remember."

"I remember everything, Ayanna. The good and the bad. Every time I stood up for you and every time I didn't. Especially the times I didn't." Her voice cracked on the final words.

Chapter Twenty-One

Thunder rumbled again, closer now, and the rain intensified as if responding to their shared pain. Water pooled around their shoes, seeping through the thin leather to chill their toes.

"We may not have been able to fix the past, sweetheart," Alice said after a long pause, each word measured and careful, "but every new drop of rain washes away a fraction of the pain. We have to keep moving forward, even if it means enduring a little more of this storm."

She attempted a smile, a fragile, hopeful thing that trembled at the edges but held. The gesture was so nakedly sincere, so stripped of pretence, that Ayanna felt something move inside her chest, like a door long rusted shut beginning to crack open.

"I wish it were that simple, Mom," she replied quietly, her voice barely audible above the rain's persistent rhythm. "Every drop reminds me of what I lost... and what I should have had."

The words weren't an accusation, merely a statement of truth. Alice nodded, accepting them without defence or qualification.

"I can't promise I'll always be brave enough," she said. "I've spent too many years being afraid to believe I can change completely overnight. But I can promise to try. To listen when you speak. To stand beside you, not behind you or in front of you."

A car passed on the street, its headlights briefly illuminating them in a wash of yellow light before disappearing around a corner. In that fleeting brightness, Ayanna saw her mother clearly, not as the figure of disappointment who had populated her resentful thoughts for so long, nor as the idealised protector she had longed for as a child, but as a woman who had made grievous mistakes and was now, finally, facing them.

Ayanna took a deep breath, tasting rain and possibility on her tongue. "I'm still angry," she admitted.

"You have every right to be."

"And hurt."

"Yes."

"And I don't know if I can forgive everything. Not yet."

Chapter Twenty-One

Alice nodded. "I wouldn't expect you to."

The simple acknowledgment of her feelings felt like a gift. Not a solution to all that had passed between them, but perhaps a beginning.

"Ready?" Alice asked, nodding toward the car.

Ayanna squeezed her hand once more. "As I'll ever be."

They stepped into the downpour together. Cold rain instantly plastered Ayanna's dress to her skin and sent rivulets streaming down her neck, but there was something cleansing in the sensation.

Their shoes splashed through puddles, synchronised in their hurried rhythm. By the time they reached the car, both were soaked, their carefully styled funeral attire transformed into dripping, clinging fabric. Alice's mascara had run, leaving faint charcoal trails down her cheeks. Raindrops clung to Ayanna's eyelashes, splintering her vision into diamond-bright fragments.

As they slid into the car's interior, the shelter from the rain created a cocoon of relative quiet. The soft patter of water against the roof formed a gentler percussion than the open downpour. Their breath fogged the windows, creating a barrier between their small, damp world and the storm outside.

Neither spoke immediately. Instead, they sat in shared silence, the engine's low purr a counterpoint to their uneven breathing. Ayanna watched a raindrop trace a meandering path down the passenger window, absorbing smaller droplets as it travelled. When it reached the bottom edge, it hung suspended for a moment before falling away.

Alice reached across the console and touched Ayanna's arm, a light pressure, questioning rather than assuming. Ayanna didn't pull away. It wasn't forgiveness, not entirely, but it was something. A possibility. A door not fully open but no longer locked.

Outside, the storm continued its relentless assault, but within the car, a different kind of weather was taking shape, uncertain, changeable, but containing the potential for clearing skies.

Chapter Twenty-One

The car moved through the storm like a submarine steering through murky depths, headlights barely penetrating the rain's thick curtain. Inside the sealed cabin, Ayanna pressed her forehead against the cool glass of the passenger window, watching rivulets race each other down the pane, some pushing forward with steady determination, others faltering and merging into stronger streams. Her reflection stared back at her, a fractured self slowly reassembling into something new and unfamiliar.

"If they won't listen, I'll tell the world, "She whispered, her breath forming a small cloud on the window. She traced a single letter in the condensation, A for Ayanna, for anger, for aftermath, before it dissolved back into transparency.

Alice kept her eyes on the road, hands positioned precisely at ten and two on the steering wheel. The windshield wipers worked furiously against the deluge, their rhythmic swoosh-thump providing a metronomic backdrop to Ayanna's chaotic thoughts. Left-right, past-future, hurtheal. The binary swing of possibility.

The interior lights of the dashboard cast a blue-green glow across her mother's face, hollowing her cheeks and deepening the shadows beneath her eyes. In that spectral illumination, Alice looked simultaneously younger and older than her years, a ghost of the mother Ayanna had needed and the woman she was only now beginning to become.

Each thunderclap in the distance sent vibrations through the metal frame of the car that Ayanna could feel in her bones, resonant reminders that some forces couldn't be contained or denied, only weathered and respected.

Her hands lay palm-up in her lap, still holding the phantom sensation of her mother's grip from earlier. The memory of that connection collided with older recollections of hands that had held hers too loosely, fingers that had slipped away when trouble approached.

Ayanna closed her eyes, letting the motion of the car and the storm's ambient noise wash over her. Behind her eyelids, memories flickered like an old film reel: her mother teaching her to braid her hair, those pale fingers moving with uncertainty through her dark curls; Alice sneaking into her room with cookies when Henry had sent her to bed without dinner for "talking back"; the

Chapter Twenty-One

Christmas morning when a brand-new laptop appeared beside her bed, not under the tree where the family's gifts were displayed, but private, a secret encouragement of her writing.

These gentler images had always existed alongside the harsher ones, complicating her feelings toward her mother. She remembered the careful pressure of Alice's hand against her back as they entered family gatherings, a silent encouragement to stand tall; the conspiratorial winks across dinner tables when someone said something particularly absurd; the dog-eared copy of Toni Morrison's "The Bluest Eye" that had appeared mysteriously on her nightstand the day after Clara had questioned why Ayanna would want to "read books about race all the time."

Small rebellions, private resistances, never enough, but not nothing either.

The car slowed for a red light, and Ayanna opened her eyes to see they were passing the town library, its stone facade gleaming wet in the darkness. How many afternoons had she spent there as a teenager, hiding among the stacks, finding in books the understanding and validation her family denied her? It was between those quiet shelves that she had first discovered the power of seeing her own experiences reflected in another's words, the startling recognition that she wasn't alone, that others had navigated similar waters and left maps for those who followed.

The light changed, and they accelerated through the intersection. Water sprayed from beneath their tires, a momentary rooster tail of rebellion.

"I used to dream about drowning," Ayanna said, her voice rough with emotion. "Not just that night when I was eight. For years afterward. I'd be underwater, screaming, but no sound would come out. And everyone would be standing on the shore, watching, not moving to help." Alice's knuckles whitened on the steering wheel. "I'm sorry," she said, the words inadequate but sincere.

"In the dream, I'd always look to you first," Ayanna continued, watching her mother's profile for reaction. "You'd be there among them, your mouth open like you wanted to shout something, but nothing ever came out."

Chapter Twenty-One

A tear slid down Alice's cheek, caught briefly in the passing glow of a streetlight before disappearing into shadow. "And now?" she asked. "Do you still have that dream?"

Ayanna considered the question. "Not as often. Now I sometimes dream I'm swimming. Not drowning, just... moving through the water. Sometimes alone, sometimes not."

They lapsed into silence again, but it was a different quality of quiet than before, less strained, more contemplative. Outside, the storm continued unabated, water sluicing across the windshield faster than the wipers could clear it. Through the wet glass, the town's familiar landmarks were transformed into impressionistic smudges of light and darkness.

Each location triggered a fresh cascade of memories, not all painful, but all part of the complicated memories of half-truths and unacknowledged realities that had defined her childhood. The town itself seemed to be weeping, rain washing down its facades like tears of long-denied recognition.

As they approached the edge of town, the storm began to slacken slightly, violent downpour giving way to steady rain. Ayanna found herself thinking of Granny's last conversation with her, two weeks before the end.

"You were always the strong one," the old woman had said, her paper-thin hand resting on Ayanna's wrist. "The truthful one. Don't let them silence you, girl. Some stories need telling, no matter how much it hurts."

At the time, Ayanna had assumed it was the medication talking, or perhaps the confusion. Now she wondered if Granny had seen more clearly than any of them, had recognised the festering wound at the heart of the family and understood that healing could only begin with honest acknowledgment.

"I spent so many years being careful," Ayanna said, breaking the silence again. "Measuring every word, every reaction. Making myself smaller, quieter, less threatening to their idea of what I should be."

"I know," Alice replied softly. "I watched it happen. Helped it happen."

"Today felt different," Ayanna continued. "Like something broke open inside me, not just anger, but some kind of certainty. I don't need their approval or understanding anymore. I don't need them to acknowledge what they did for it to be real."

Her heartbeat quickened as the realisation crystallised. The confrontation at Granny's hadn't given her the validation she'd once craved from her family, but it had freed her from needing it. The truth existed independent of their acknowledgment. Her experiences were real, valid, and deserving of voice, whether or not the family ever admitted their role in them.

The windshield wipers swept back and forth with hypnotic regularity, clearing the glass only for new sheets of rain to obscure it seconds later. Clear, blur, clear, blur, like the oscillation between clarity and confusion that had defined so much of her life. But each sweep revealed a bit more of the road ahead, just as each confrontation with her past brought her closer to understanding her path forward.

She thought of her laptop waiting at home, the halffinished manuscript she'd been struggling with for months. It wasn't working because she'd been writing around the truth, skirting the centre of each story out of lingering fear, fear of exposing herself. Of letting her own secrets out through lovelorn flower girls or women in the rain."

"I'm going to write it all down," she said, more to herself than to her mother. "Everything. Everything they did. I'm so tired of them hiding. I'll tell the story.
The real story, with real names and real consequences."

Alice glanced at her, then back at the road. "They'll fight you."

"Let them." Ayanna's voice was steady, her resolve firming with each word. "Let them show the world who they really are. I'm done protecting their reputations at the expense of my truth."

The rage filled words hung in the car like a declaration of independence. Ayanna felt something different, not the molten rage from earlier, but something cooler and more sustainable. Purpose. Determination. The kind of anger that didn't consume but rather fuelled steady, deliberate action.

Chapter Twenty-One

Outside, the storm was gradually subsiding, the spaces between thunderclaps growing longer, the rain less violent against the windows. Through gaps in the clouds, faint stars were becoming visible, distant points of light in the vast darkness. The transformation wasn't dramatic, just a slow easing, a gradual shift from chaos to calm.

Ayanna felt a similar transition happening within her. The raw, explosive pain of the confrontation was settling into something more measured but no less powerful a resolved clarity about what needed to happen next. She would tell her story, not just as an act of defiance against those who had hurt her, but as an offering to others who might recognise their own struggles in hers.

The wipers continued their steady rhythm, each sweep revealing a clearer view of the road ahead. The headlights cut through remaining mist, illuminating not just the immediate path but glinting off distant reflectors that marked the way forward for miles to come.

"Tell me what you need from me," Alice said after a long silence.

Ayanna considered the question. "Just this," she finally answered. "Be present. Be honest. Don't try to protect me from the truth or them from consequences."

Her mother nodded; her profile solemn in the intermittent light of passing streetlamps. "I can do that."

The simple commitment felt more valuable than any elaborate promise. It acknowledged both limitations and possibilities, suggesting not perfection but genuine effort.

As they turned onto the familiar street that led to her mother's home, Ayanna felt the tension in her shoulders begin to ease. The confrontation at Granny's had not provided the neat resolution that stories promised, no climactic moment of universal understanding, no tearful group reconciliation. Instead, it had given her something ultimately more valuable: the freedom to stop waiting for acknowledgment and instead create her own.

The storm was now little more than a gentle rain, drops tapping against the car roof with diminished urgency. Ahead, their porch light glowed warm and steady through the mist, a beacon marking not the end of the journey but

Chapter Twenty-One

a waypoint, a place to rest and gather strength before continuing onward.

Ayanna's fingers itched with the phantom sensation of keys beneath them, words waiting to be written, truths demanding to be told. For the first time in longer than she could remember, the prospect of facing her past on the page didn't fill her with dread but with a quiet, insistent energy, the kind that sustained rather than consumed.

"We're home," Alice said as the car pulled into the driveway.

Ayanna nodded, the word resonating in a new way. Home, not a place defined by others' expectations or limitations, but a space she was finally able to believe in, with Alice. A starting point for the story she was now ready to tell.

Chapter Twenty-Two

The small desk lamp cast a halo of yellow light across Ayanna's workspace, illuminating the scattered notes, dogeared reference books, and the determined set of her shoulders as her fingers moved across the keyboard. Outside the circle of light, the room faded into comfortable darkness, the boundaries of their small home office misting into shadow. Each keystroke carried purpose, adding words to the growing document on her screen, a narrative only she could tell.

Ayanna Bell paused, her dark eyes scanning the paragraph she'd just completed. The cursor blinked expectantly, a metronome keeping time with her thoughts. Three hours had passed since she'd first sat down, yet the world beyond her manuscript had ceased to exist. Only here, in the careful construction of sentences, could she properly examine the remains of memory that demanded to be preserved.

Today's section dealt with belonging, or rather, its absence. The words flowed from some deep reservoir within her, describing the peculiar loneliness of being the only Black

Chapter Twenty-Two

child in a household where differences were acknowledged through silence rather than conversation. Her mother had provided material comfort but had never quite managed to give her the language for her experience. Writing offered her that language now, precise and unflinching.

A soft creak from the floorboards in the hallway barely registered in her consciousness. The apartment settled and shifted around her, a living entity with its own vocabulary of sounds that she had learned to interpret without thought. This particular creak belonged to Simon; his careful tread recognisable even when she was lost in concentration.

The door hinges whispered as Simon entered the room. He moved with deliberate quietness, his feet making almost no sound against the hardwood floor. In his hands, he balanced a ceramic mug, the blue one with the chip on its handle that she preferred for its perfect size and weight.

"Thought you might need this," he said, his voice pitched low enough not to disturb the atmosphere of concentration she had cultivated.

The tea sent tendrils of steam into the air, Simon placed it carefully on the cork coaster beside her laptop, positioning it just far enough from her elbow to avoid disaster but close enough to be within easy reach. This small geography of placement spoke of years of companionship, of learning each other's habits until they became instinct.

Ayanna's fingers hovered above the keyboard, momentarily still. The transition from the world she created with words to the physical presence of Simon required a gentle adjustment. She didn't look up immediately, needing a moment to bookmark her place in her thoughts.

Simon knelt beside her chair, not speaking further. He understood the sacred space of creation she inhabited. His hand found her shoulder, the pressure exactly right, not demanding attention but offering support. His palm radiated warmth through the thin fabric of her sweater, a tangible reminder of connection.

His eyes, deep brown and patient, took in the tension in her posture without judgment. The slight furrow between her brows. The way her lower lip bore the faint indentation of teeth, a sign she'd been chewing it in concentration. His thumb moved in a small circle against the knot forming at the base of her neck, but he didn't linger long enough to pull her fully from her work.

"Thank you," Ayanna said, the words more breath than voice. She offered a half-smile, the corner of her mouth lifting slightly, and a single nod, a language of abbreviation they had developed over time. In that brief acknowledgment lived appreciation for more than just the tea: for his understanding of her need for space, for his presence that demanded nothing, for his recognition of when to approach and when to recede.

The moment passed between them like a current, quick but charged with meaning. Simon rose, pressing a light kiss to the crown of her head before stepping back. Ayanna's fingers returned to the keyboard, finding their rhythm again as she slipped back into the narrative.

The sound of typing filled the room once more, a percussive score to her thoughts. The keys made different sounds depending on the force behind them, lighter taps for descriptive passages, firmer strikes for dialogue or moments of emotional clarity. Tonight, her typing had an intensity that Simon recognised as breakthrough rather than frustration.

She reached for the tea without looking, her hand finding it unerringly. The first sip parted her lips with a small sigh of appreciation. The warmth travelled down her throat, a counterpoint to the coolness of the evening air coming through the partially open window. She set the mug down and continued typing, the brief interruption seamlessly integrated into her workflow.

Simon moved to the small loveseat in the corner of the office, settling into his usual spot. He picked up the book he'd left there the night before, opening to the marked page. The soft rustle of turning pages joined the symphony of small sounds, the hum of the laptop, the distant traffic outside their third-floor apartment, the occasional clink of the mug against the coaster as Ayanna took another sip.

When she paused to reference one of her notebooks,

Simon looked up from his reading, attuned to the change in rhythm. He watched as she flipped through pages filled with her distinctive handwriting, slanted and compact, economical with space but generous with observation. Her finger traced a line of text, and he noticed the chipped polish on her nail, midnight blue with tiny flecks of silver like a miniature night sky. She had painted them three days ago, sitting cross-legged on their bed while he read aloud from a poetry collection they'd discovered at a used bookstore.

These were the details Simon collected and treasured: Ayanna in moments of ordinary existence, the quiet rituals that structured their days together. He returned to his book when she resumed typing, careful not to distract her with his gaze.

An hour passed in this manner, the space between them comfortable with the knowledge that proximity didn't require interaction. Simon refilled her tea once without comment, the fresh mug appearing at her elbow like a magic trick. Ayanna acknowledged it with a touch to his wrist as he set it down, a brief press of fingers that conveyed gratitude.

Outside, night had fully settled over the city. The window reflected their domestic tableau, Ayanna illuminated by the desk lamp, Simon a softer presence in the background. They created a picture of shared solitude, each engaged in separate pursuits but anchored by mutual awareness.

When Ayanna finally stretched, arching her back and rolling her shoulders, Simon closed his book. The movement signalled a transition, a coming up for air after deep immersion. She saved her document, the decisive click of the trackpad punctuating the completion of her work session.

"Good place to stop?" Simon asked, his voice still hushed despite the break in her concentration.

Ayanna nodded, running a hand through her hair. "I found the thread I was looking for," she said. "Sometimes I think these stories have always existed somewhere, just waiting for me to find the right words to shape them."

Simon smiled, understanding this was neither metaphor nor mysticism but her writer's way of processing the complex task of translating memory into narrative. "The words found you too," he said simply.

She turned toward him fully for the first time that evening, her eyes meeting his with fresh awareness. The half-smile from earlier bloomed into something more complete, tired but satisfied. In that moment of connection, the separate spheres they had occupied merged again into shared space, the transition as natural as breathing.

The room held them in its familiar embrace, witness to this daily ritual of work and companionship, of focus and care. The lamp continued to cast its circle of light, now illuminating not just Ayanna's workspace but the path between them as they prepared to leave the office and rejoin the wider world of their home.

Chapter Twenty-Two

The digital clock on Ayanna's laptop read 9:37 PM when Simon decided enough was enough. He approached her desk with the gentle determination of someone who knew exactly how far to push. His fingers found her shoulders, applying just enough pressure to remind her body that it existed beyond the rectangular frame of her computer screen. The tension beneath his touch spoke of hours spent hunched over words, of a mind so consumed by narrative that it forgot the needs of its physical vessel.

"Time to resurface," Simon said, his voice a thread pulling her toward the present. "The manuscript will still be there tomorrow."

Ayanna's resistance manifested as a small noise, not quite agreement but not outright refusal. She saved her document, a ritual that preceded any departure from her work, and closed the laptop with deliberate slowness. The snap of the computer shutting echoed her reluctance.

"Twenty minutes," she countered, turning to face him.

"Just enough to clear my head."

Simon's smile held no triumph, only understanding. "Twenty minutes becomes an hour once we're there." He knew her patterns: how initial resistance gave way to relaxation once removed from the gravitational pull of her writing.

"And you'll regret none of it," he added, already retrieving her jacket from the hook by the door. It was the soft denim one with patches on the elbows that she preferred for evenings out, comfortable yet put together, like armour that didn't announce itself as such.

Ayanna rose, stretching arms above her head to release the stiffness that had settled into her spine. Her body unfurled slowly, joints cracking in protest after hours of stillness. Simon watched with patience, recognising the transition she needed to make from creator to participant in the wider world.

"Where are we going?" she asked, though they both knew the answer.

"The Anchor," Simon replied, holding her jacket open.

"Tuesday means Maya's behind the bar."

Ayanna slipped her arms into the sleeves, a small smile forming at the mention of their favourite bartender. Maya mixed drinks with the precision of a chemist and

Chapter Twenty-Two

remembered their preferences without prompting, a small courtesy that made the world feel less anonymous.

They left the apartment without further discussion, the hallway light flickering as it always did on the third floor. Simon's hand rested lightly against the small of Ayanna's back as they descended the stairs, not guiding but accompanying. Outside, the November air carried a warning of winter, sharp enough to flush their cheeks but not severe enough to rush their pace.

The walk to The Rusty Anchor took exactly seven minutes, a fact they had timed during their first year in the neighbourhood. They moved in comfortable silence, their steps finding synchronicity without effort. Street lamps cast their shadows long and then short, a rhythm of light and dark marking their progress through the familiar blocks.

The Rusty Anchor announced itself with a neon sign where half the letters sputtered between brightness and darkness, giving the impression of a message in some maritime code. The façade was misleadingly unremarkable. Brick weathered to a soft uncertainty of colour, a door that required just the right amount of shoulder pressure to open. Ayanna applied this pressure now, the familiar resistance giving way to the interior world they sought.

Inside, The Rusty Anchor revealed its true character. The ceiling hung low, discoloured by decades of conversations rising as smoke once did. Booths lined the perimeter,

their leather worn to a suppleness that came only from countless bodies sliding across their surface. Mismatched light fixtures, salvaged ship lanterns, art deco sconces, and at least one repurposed chandelier missing half its crystals, created islands of illumination throughout the space.

The bar itself stretched across the back wall, solid oak polished by countless forearms and elbows to a deep, honeyed glow. Behind it stood Maya, her silver-streaked hair pulled back in a precise knot, her hands moving with practiced efficiency as she mixed two drinks simultaneously. She acknowledged their entrance with a raised eyebrow and the slightest nod, her version of a warm greeting.

The usual Tuesday crowd populated the space, a collection of regulars each claiming their territories. An elderly man in a cardigan the colour of forgotten pennies occupied his eternal corner stool. A group of graduate students from the nearby university huddled around a table cluttered with journals and half-empty glasses, their academic debates punctuated by bursts of laughter. Two women played a desultory game of darts, more interested in their conversation than their scores.

Simon guided Ayanna toward their preferred booth in the back corner, where the acoustics created a pocket of relative quiet and the worn cushions had moulded themselves to their particular contours over time. They slid into opposite sides by habit, though in this booth the distance between them remained intimate, their knees meeting comfortably beneath the scarred wooden table.

"The usual?" Maya called from behind the bar, already reaching for bottles.

Simon raised two fingers in confirmation, and they watched as she began their ritual drinks. Maya's movements had the fluid precision of muscle memory, muddling fresh mint and berries in the bottom of heavy glasses, measuring spirits without glancing at the pour, adding just the right amount of ice crushed fine enough to melt slowly rather than water down the flavours too quickly.

The bar's ambient sounds formed a familiar backdrop to their evening, the soft clatter of glasses against wood, truncated conversations from neighbouring tables, the low throb of jazz from the ancient jukebox in the corner. Someone had selected a John Coltrane piece that seemed to speak directly to the mood of the room, both melancholy and warm.

Maya approached their table with two cocktails balanced expertly in one hand. "One Blackberry Bourbon Smash and one Mint-Infused Gin Sonata," she announced, setting the drinks before them with a flourish that suggested she took pride in her creations despite her studied casualness. Ayanna's bourbon glowed amber in the low light, while Simon's gin cocktail caught the overhead lamp in its pale green depths.

"You're looking tired," Maya observed, directing her comment to Ayanna with the directness of long acquaintance. "Writing or worrying?"

"Both," Ayanna admitted, wrapping her fingers around the cool glass. "But mostly writing."

Maya nodded, satisfied with the answer. "Good. The world needs your words more than your worries." With that pronouncement, she returned to the bar, leaving them to their private sphere.

Chapter Twenty-Two

Simon lifted his glass in a small toast. "To taking breaks." "To necessary interruptions," Ayanna countered, a smile playing at the corners of her mouth as she clinked her glass against his.

The first sip travelled through her with welcome warmth, the bourbon's smoky sweetness complemented by the tart burst of blackberry. She felt her shoulders loosen, the mental demands of her manuscript receding like tide from shore. Simon watched the change come over her, the subtle relaxation of the muscles around her eyes, the way her posture softened from rigid focus to present awareness.

"Tell me about your day," she said, leaning forward on her elbows, her fingers absently tracing the rim of her glass. The invitation was genuine, Simon's observations always offered a perspective that refreshed her own thinking.

He took another sip before beginning, organising his thoughts. "I swung by the community centre to help out again today," he said, his voice pitched just loud enough to reach her above the bar's ambient noise but no further. "They asked me to sit in on the youth program that's like last time. The one I told you was like pulling teeth for the first month."

Ayanna nodded, recalling how anxious he'd been that first time he went and never expecting he'd end up there nearly every week since, slowly becoming an accidental counsellor without even realising it, a development that she found both funny and undeniably endearing.

"There's this one kid, the one who always keeps his hood up," Simon said, voice quieter than usual. "He actually talked today, just three sentences, maybe, if that. He mentioned how he used to help his grandfather in the garden when he was little and said he still remembers how beat-up the old man's hands looked. Cracked skin, knuckles scarred from decades of work… but somehow they were still gentle and soft enough to handle the tiniest seedlings."

A faint smile crept onto Simon's face. "It wasn't anything fancy. But the way he noticed those details, things most of us wouldn't even think about, it really took me by surprise. How he described the veins on the back of his hands, the way his knuckles had swollen but remained nimble… it was like listening to poetry disguised as ordinary speech."

Ayanna's smile deepened, recognising the particular joy Simon took in witnessing these moments of unexpected beauty in his work. While he never shared identifying details

Chapter Twenty-Two

about his clients, he often described these small revelations, the human connections that reminded him why he'd chosen his path.

"What did the others do?" she asked, taking another sip of her drink.

"That's the part that gave me hope," Simon said, leaning closer. "They listened. Really listened. No eye-rolling, no side conversations. When he finished, there was this perfect silence, and then one of the girls started talking about her uncle teaching her to fix a carburettor." He shook his head slightly, still marvelling at the moment. "They found common ground in being taught something by someone who saw them as worthy of knowledge."

Ayanna reached across the table to touch his hand briefly, a silent acknowledgment of the significance. She understood the value Simon placed on these breakthroughs, how carefully he tended the fragile connections forming in his groups.

The conversation flowed from there into other aspects of their day, a difficult call Simon had with a supervisor, Ayanna's breakthrough with a particularly challenging section of her manuscript, a funny exchange Simon had witnessed in the coffee shop near his office. Throughout, Ayanna's hands remained in motion, tracing the condensation on her glass, tapping gently against the table to emphasise a point, briefly touching Simon's fingers when his words resonated with particular clarity.

Around them, the bar's rhythms continued; Maya mixing drinks with theatrical flair for a newly arrived couple, the dartboard erupting in good-natured argument over a questionable score, the jukebox transitioning to Ella Fitzgerald's smoky vocals. But these elements receded to background as Ayanna and Simon created their own personal space through attention and response.

"Remember when we first came here?" Simon asked, his eyes catching on the chipped corner of their table where someone had carved initials long ago.

Ayanna smiled, memory washing over her features. "You spilled an entire beer trying to seem casual after I said I was considering dating you."

"In my defence, you announced it as if you were considering buying a slightly suspicious used car," Simon countered, his expression warm with amusement.

Chapter Twenty-Two

"I was conducting a risk assessment," she said playfully, her fingers finding his across the table. "Turns out you were worth the investment."

They shared a look then, one of those exchanges that contained years of private history, jokes only they understood, challenges weathered together. In the dimness of the bar, with conversations flowing around them and the clink of glasses marking time, they held this moment of connection. Their fingers intertwined on the tabletop, neither pulling away even as Maya approached with a second round they hadn't ordered but somehow knew they would want.

The evening stretched beyond Ayanna's initial twenty-minute limit, just as Simon had predicted. But as they sat together in their familiar booth, sharing observations and silences with equal comfort, neither one thought to check the time.

They returned to their apartment just after midnight, the night air having painted their cheeks with matching flushes that had nothing to do with the cocktails they'd shared. Simon locked the door behind them, the familiar click of the deadbolt sliding home marking the transition from public to private space. In the darkness of their entryway, Ayanna reached for him first, her fingertips finding the line of his jaw with practiced precision. The day's roles, writer, therapist, public selves, dissolved in that touch, leaving only the essential connection that hummed between them.

They moved through the apartment without switching on lights, familiar enough with its geography to navigate by the ambient glow of streetlamps filtering through partially drawn blinds. The hallway to their bedroom was a tunnel of shadow and suggestion, their footfalls muffled by the runner Ayanna had found at an estate sale months ago. Simon's hand found the small of her back, the slight pressure guiding though she needed no direction.

Their bedroom welcomed them with its particular quality of silence, a room that held memories in the fibres of the curtains, in the dips of the mattress, in the personal geography they had mapped together over years. The streetlight outside their window cast rectangular patterns through the sheer curtains, painting silver-blue geometry across the rumpled bedding they had left that morning. The light caught the edges of familiar objects, the spines of books on nightstands, the curve of a water glass, the glint of Ayanna's silver earrings in the ceramic dish on the dresser. Simon closed the door behind them, not for privacy, they lived alone, but from habit, a symbolic containment of the

Chapter Twenty-Two

space where they were most vulnerable with each other. Ayanna stood by the edge of the bed, her silhouette outlined by diffused light, curves and angles transformed into something both known and mysterious. She turned to face him, and in the illumination, her eyes held both question and answer.

"Come here," she said, her voice lower than usual, textured with intention.

Simon crossed the distance between them, his movements unhurried yet purposeful. His hands found her shoulders first, thumbs tracing the delicate architecture of her collarbones through the soft fabric of her shirt. The touch was gentle but deliberate, a continuation of the massage he had briefly offered hours earlier when she hunched over her keyboard.

Ayanna's eyes closed briefly at the contact, her body responding to the familiar pattern of his fingertips. This was a language they had developed over time, where to press, how firmly, when to release. Simon's hands moved with the confidence of someone who had studied the map of another's body until it became intuition rather than conscious thought.

"You're still carrying tension here," he murmured, fingers finding the knot at the base of her neck that never fully released. The pressure of his touch increased slightly, working at the persistent tightness with patient insistence.

Ayanna leaned into his hands, allowing herself to be supported. "It's where I store all the words I haven't written yet," she replied, her attempt at lightness betrayed by the small sound of relief that escaped her as his fingers found exactly the right spot.

They stood like this for long moments, her body gradually yielding under his attentions. The massage transitioned imperceptibly into something else, his hands sliding down her arms, then to her waist, drawing her closer until the space between them disappeared. Her arms encircled his neck, fingers threading into the hair at the nape of his neck where it curled slightly against his collar.

Their kiss began soft, exploratory despite years of familiarity. Each time held the potential for rediscovery, for noticing something new in the well-known geography of each other's mouths. Simon tasted of the mint from his last cocktail, while Ayanna carried the lingering sweetness of blackberry on her tongue. The combination created something new between them, ephemeral and particular to this night.

They moved toward the bed in slow increments, unwilling to break contact long enough for efficiency. Clothing yielded to careful hands, buttons released one by one, zippers lowered with deliberate slowness, fabric sliding against skin with whispered friction. There was no rush in their movements, no desperate fumbling. The gradual revelation of skin was its own form of conversation, punctuated by small sounds of appreciation and recognition.

When they finally lay together on the bed, the sheets cool against newly exposed skin, Simon propped himself on one elbow to look down at Ayanna. The streetlight caught the planes of her face, illuminating the soft curve of her cheek, the fullness of her lower lip, the slight furrow that remained between her brows even in moments of pleasure. His free hand traced these features as if memorising them through touch, his fingertips gentle against her temple, her cheekbone, the corner of her mouth.

"You're still thinking about your manuscript," he observed, no accusation in his tone, just understanding.

Ayanna's smile was lopsided, caught between apology and confirmation. "Not entirely," she admitted. "But it's always there, humming in the background."

"Then we'll just have to make it recede for a while," Simon replied, lowering his mouth to the hollow of her throat where her pulse beat visibly against the delicate skin.

His lips travelled a careful path across her body, attentive to the map of responses they had charted together over time. He knew which touches made her breath catch, which caresses caused the small muscles in her abdomen to tense in anticipation. His hands on her back and shoulders worked double purpose, continuing to release the physical tension of her day while building a different kind of tension altogether.

Ayanna was not a passive recipient of these attentions. Her hands moved with equal purpose across Simon's body, finding the sensitive spot along his ribs, the particular pressure that made his breathing shift when applied to his lower back. They had learned each other through years of experimentation and observation, creating a shared vocabulary of desire specific to their bodies.

When he finally moved above her, their bodies aligned with practiced ease, she reached up to cradle his face between her palms. In that moment of deepest physical connection, they maintained eye contact, a level of vulnerability that had taken time to achieve. The streetlight caught the sheen of moisture on his lower lip, the intensity of focus in his eyes.

Their movements found rhythm without conscious thought, bodies remembering the particular cadence that built pleasure between them. The sounds they made were quiet, soft exhalations, half-articulated words, the occasional gasp when sensation intensified beyond expectation. The bed frame creaked gently beneath them, adding its voice to the symphony of their intimacy.

Ayanna's hands moved to Simon's shoulders, fingers pressing into muscle as the tension within her built toward release. Her eyes closed briefly as sensation overtook thought, her body arching slightly beneath him. Simon watched the subtle changes in her expression, the parting of lips, the flutter of eyelids, the moment when the persistent furrow between her brows finally smoothed completely. There was power in this witnessing, this privileged observation of another person's most unguarded moment.

His own release followed, the culmination of gradually building pressure and emotion. The breath left his lungs in a long, shuddering exhalation. He lowered his forehead to rest against hers, their breathing synchronising in the aftermath. For several heartbeats, they remained connected, neither willing to break the circuit of warmth and intimacy they had created.

Eventually, Simon shifted to lie beside her, one arm still draped across her waist, his fingers tracing idle patterns on the curve of her hip. The room felt different now; charged with shared breath and mingled scent, the air between them warm and heavy with satisfaction. Outside, a car passed, its headlights briefly painting the ceiling with moving patterns before returning the room to its silver blue glow.

Ayanna turned her head to look at him, her expression soft with the particular vulnerability that followed physical release. "Thank you for taking me away from the desk," she said, her voice slightly husky.

Simon smiled, pressing a kiss to her shoulder. "Thank you for letting me," he replied, understanding that her willingness to be drawn away from work was its own form of gift.

They lay in comfortable silence, bodies cooling, breathing slowing. Simon's eyes grew heavy, the day's accumulated fatigue washing over him now that tension had been

Chapter Twenty-Two

released. Ayanna stroked his hair as his breathing deepened toward sleep, her touch gentle against his scalp. She watched as his features relaxed completely, the line between his brows smoothing out, his mouth slightly open in the absolute trust of deep sleep.

She remained awake, listening to the rhythm of his breathing, feeling the occasional twitch of his fingers against her skin as dreams began to form in his sleeping mind. When she was certain he wouldn't wake, she carefully extracted herself from his embrace, replacing her warmth with a pillow that he instinctively pulled closer.

The digital clock on the nightstand read 1:47 AM as she retrieved her laptop from the desk across the room and settled at the small table near the window. The screen's glow illuminated her face with blue-white light, creating a bubble of illumination in the darkness. Her fingers hovered above the keyboard for a moment before beginning to type, the words flowing with renewed clarity after the evening's respite.

The hours passed unmarked as Ayanna wrote, translating experience and memory into narrative. The room grew colder as night deepened toward morning, but she barely noticed, wrapped in the cocoon of creation. Occasionally, she glanced at Simon's sleeping form, drawing comfort from his presence even in unconsciousness.

Dawn arrived with subtle persistence, the quality of light changing from artificial silver to the warmer gold of early morning. Birds began their conversations in the tree outside their window, their chirping a counterpoint to the steady click of keys beneath Ayanna's fingers. Simon stirred as the room brightened, his body responding to the cycle of light even before consciousness fully returned.

His eyes opened to the familiar sight of an empty space beside him and the equally familiar sound of typing. He turned his head to see Ayanna silhouetted against the growing morning light, her shoulders hunched slightly over the keyboard, her hair falling in loose coils around her face. The scene mirrored where they had begun the previous evening, the cycle completing itself with perfect symmetry.

Simon rose without speaking, pulling on a pair of sweatpants from the drawer. He padded softly to the kitchen, movements automatic in the routine they had established over years. The kettle filled with water, set to boil. The canister of tea opened, leaves measured precisely into the

Chapter Twenty-Two

infuser. Honey added to the bottom of the mug, her morning preference different from her evening choice.

When he returned to the bedroom, Ayanna was still typing, absorbed in the world she created on the page. Simon approached quietly, setting the steaming mug beside her laptop with the same care he had shown the night before. The scent of black tea with hints of bergamot rose between them, a sensory bookmark for this particular time of day.

Ayanna's fingers paused on the keys as she registered his presence. She looked up, her eyes slightly unfocused as they adjusted from screen to person. The transition took a moment, the return journey from the landscape of her creation to the physical reality of their bedroom.

"You had been busy all through the night," Simon whispered, his hand settling briefly on her shoulder.

There was no reproach in his tone, only recognition and acceptance of her process. He understood that her need to write was not a rejection of rest or of him, but a fundamental expression of herself.

Ayanna reached up to cover his hand with her own, a silent acknowledgment of his understanding. Her eyes held gratitude for more than just the tea, for the space he gave her to create, for his recognition of her rhythms, for his willingness to orbit her focus without demanding to be its centre.

The morning light strengthened, illuminating them both as they stood in this moment of quiet connection. On the screen, words continued to accumulate, the story taking shape one character at a time. Beside the laptop, steam rose from the tea in a translucent column, temporary sculpture marking the passage of time. And between them, the understanding continued to build, sentence by sentence, gesture by gesture, day by day.

Chapter Twenty-Three
AGE 25

Ayanna's fingers trembled slightly from too much caffeine and too little sleep. The soft glow of the laptop screen illuminated her face in the dim office, casting shadows that accentuated the hollows beneath her cheekbones. Scattered around her desk lay the physical remnants of her journey, dog-eared reference books, spiral notebooks filled with cramped handwriting, and yellow sticky notes adorned with questions she had finally answered within the pages of her manuscript.

The desk beneath her elbows had witnessed countless hours of her labour, its surface bearing coffee rings chronicling her progress. A half-empty mug sat precariously close to a stack of scrawled upon papers, the drink inside long gone cold. Outside the window, dusk was settling over the city, but Ayanna had barely noticed the transition from afternoon to evening, lost as she was in the final revisions of her work. She squinted at the screen, reading the same paragraph for the third time. The words, her words, seemed to swim before her eyes, familiar yet strangely alien. Two years of writing had culminated in this document, this digital collection of her thoughts, her experiences, her truth. Her hands felt heavy as she reached to adjust the screen brightness, the joints in her fingers stiff from hours of typing.

The door opened with a gentle creak, but Ayanna didn't look up. She knew it was Simon by the rhythm of his footsteps, by the subtle shift in the air of the room when he entered. A familiar scent of tea drifted toward her as he approached. Ayanna blinked twice, pulling her focus from the screen to the tray Simon carried. Two ceramic mugs steamed in the cool air, and beside them sat a small plate of shortbread cookies, the kind his mother sent every month.

"You're a mind reader," she said, her voice rough from disuse. She hadn't spoken aloud in hours, perhaps since lunch, when Simon had poked his head in to remind her to eat the sandwich he'd left in the refrigerator.

Simon placed the tray carefully on the corner of the desk, manoeuvring around stacks of paper with practiced ease. "Not mind reading. Just the wisdom that comes from watching you dive headfirst into the final stretch of every project since we met." His smile was gentle, teasing but without an edge. "How does it feel? Being this close to the finish line?"

Chapter Twenty-Three

Ayanna turned back to the screen, scrolling slowly through the pages she had completed. The manuscript represented more than just months of work; it contained pieces of herself that she had never before shared publicly. Her experiences as a Black child in a white family, the isolation, the bullying, the abuse, the gradual awakening to her own identity, all of it laid bare in carefully chosen words.

"Terrifying," she admitted, her free hand unconsciously moving to touch the screen as if to reassure herself of the reality of what she had created. "Like I've peeled back my skin and invited people to look at what's underneath." Simon nodded, his eyes warm with understanding. "That's what makes it powerful, Ayanna. You've turned your experience into something that can reach others who feel just as isolated."

His words hung in the air between them, a simple truth that she had clung to during the difficult passages of writing. The cursor blinked steadily at the end of a paragraph where she had been working, marking the spot where she would resume.

Outside, a siren wailed in the distance, rising and falling like a lonely cry before fading. Ayanna reached for a cookie, the simple act of eating something sweet a small rebellion against the seriousness of the moment. Crumbs fell onto the keyboard, and she brushed them away with a small laugh. "My final edit is getting crumbs in the works," she said, the hint of a smile softening her features.

Simon returned her smile, reaching for a cookie of his own. "I think every great work of literature has had its share of crumbs. Probably coffee stains too." The lightness of the exchange broke some invisible tension, and Ayanna felt her shoulders drop further from where they had been nearly touching her ears. She saved the document again, a writer's superstition she had never been able to shake, and closed the laptop.

"Tea break," she announced, picking up her mug and leaning back in the chair. "Official tea break." Simon's eyes crinkled at the corners, his relief visible but tactfully understated. He reached out to tuck a strand of hair behind her ear, his touch lingering against her cheek. "Proud of you," he said simply. Ayanna turned her face into his palm, eyes closing briefly at the contact. When she opened them again, they shared a look of understanding that transcended the need for further words. The manuscript was nearly complete and tomorrow would bring a new phase of their journey together, but for

Chapter Twenty-Three

now, there was this moment, this quiet triumph shared in the warm circle of lamplight as the city hummed beyond their windows.

The night air hit Ayanna's face like a gentle slap, a welcome shock after hours enclosed in her office. She inhaled deeply, tasting the city's peculiar blend of exhaust, restaurant vents, and the faint sweetness of blooming street trees. Beside her, Simon buttoned his jacket against the unexpected chill, his shoulder brushing hers in a gesture that was partly accidental, partly instinctive. The manuscript was complete, not published, not bound, but complete, and that reality hummed between them like an electrical current as they walked the three streets to The Midnight Sonata.

"You've been quiet since we left," Simon observed, his voice low enough to be heard only by her. "Are you okay? Second thoughts about celebrating?"

Ayanna shook her head, the motion loosening a coil of hair that had been tucked behind her ear. "Not second thoughts. Maybe... aftershocks? I keep feeling like I've forgotten something critical, like when you leave for holiday and can't shake the sense that the oven is still on." Simon's laugh was soft. "The writer's version of phantom limb syndrome. The book has been part of you for so long that its completion feels like a loss."

"Sometimes I forget why I love you, and then you say something like that," Ayanna said, slipping her arm through his as they approached the entrance to the lounge. The Midnight Sonata occupied the ground floor of a prewar building, its façade distinguished by a discreet brass plaque rather than garish signage. Simon held the heavy door open, and warmth spilled out onto the sidewalk. Inside, the transformation from city street to sanctuary was immediate and complete. Amber lighting cast from artfully arranged fixtures gave the space a permanent golden-hour glow. The wooden floors, polished to a honeyed sheen by decades of foot traffic, reflected the light upward, creating the illusion that the entire room was suffused with a gentle radiance.
A host greeted them with quiet efficiency, leading them through the main space where conversations flowed quietly like a stream over smooth stones. The walls were lined with dark wood panels and framed black-and-white photographs of musicians, their faces captured in moments of pure absorption. The scent of cedar and citrus hung in the air, undercut by the faint sweetness of spilled spirits.

"Your usual booth is available," the host said, gesturing toward a window alcove partially secluded from the main floor. Ayanna felt a small swell of pleasure at the recognition; they had been coming here since they discovered the place during their second year of dating, when they could barely afford the cocktails but desperately needed somewhere that wasn't their cramped first apartment keeping it for special occasions and celebrations.

Simon thanked the host with a nod as they slid into the curved booth. The table between them gleamed, its surface bearing only the faintest traces of rings from hundreds of drinks set upon it over the years. Simon placed his hand flat on the cool surface, the gesture unconsciously proprietary, before passing a leather-bound menu across to Ayanna. "What does a newly-completed author drink?" he asked, his eyes crinkling at the corners.

Ayanna studied the menu, though she had nearly memorised its contents over the years. "Something I'll regret tomorrow morning," she decided, a smile tugging at the corner of her mouth. "The Hemingway Daiquiri, I think. Strong enough to acknowledge accomplishment, tart enough to remind me that the hard part is just beginning."

Simon nodded approvingly. "Literary and metaphorical. Perfect." He caught the eye of a passing server and placed their order: the daiquiri for Ayanna and a Black Manhattan for himself.

The lounge had filled steadily since their arrival, the ambient noise level rising with each new patron. A trio of musicians had taken their places on the small stage in the corner, piano, bass, and saxophone. They began to play without announcement, the notes of a standard rising organically from their instruments to weave through the conversations around them.

Ayanna leaned back against the booth's curved cushion, feeling the tension of the day begin to dissolve. The familiar surroundings wrapped around her like a well-worn sweater, comfortable in its constancy. Simon watched her with quiet attention, noting the subtle transformation as her shoulders lowered and the line between her brows softened.

"You're staring," she said without opening her eyes.

"Admiring," Simon corrected. "There's a difference."

Their drinks arrived, presented with understated flourish. Ayanna's daiquiri was pale and frothy in its coupe glass, while Simon's Manhattan gleamed darkly in a tumbler, a single large ice cube clinking against the sides as the server

Chapter Twenty-Three

set it down. A small dish of salted almonds appeared alongside the drinks, a courtesy from the bartender who knew their preferences.

Simon lifted his glass, waiting for Ayanna to meet his eyes before speaking. "To completion," he said simply. "And to whatever comes next."

The crystal made a delicate sound as they touched glasses. Ayanna took a sip, the sharp citrus cutting through the rum's warmth on her tongue. The first swallow of alcohol after a long day of work sent a pleasant heat spreading through her chest, loosening something that had been wound tight for too long.

"So," Simon said, setting his glass carefully on a small napkin, "tell me about the ending. You've been so secretive about it." Ayanna traced the rim of her glass with one finger, gathering her thoughts. The ending had been the most difficult part to write, requiring multiple attempts before she felt it struck the right balance.

"You'll have to wait and read it," she said laughingly, leaning forward. Her voice took on the animated quality that emerged whenever she discussed her work, a passionate intensity that transformed her features. A server passed by their table, depositing fresh napkins without interrupting the flow of their conversation. The saxophone player launched into a solo, the notes climbing and falling with emotive precision.

"I'm worried it's too raw," Ayanna admitted, dropping her voice slightly. Simon reached for an almond, popping it into his mouth before continuing. "The strength of your writing has always been your honesty. People will respond to that."

The music had shifted again, the trio now playing something with a gentle swing rhythm. Couples had begun to occupy the small dance floor, moving together with varying degrees of skill.

"Do you remember," Simon began, his eyes following the dancers, "when we came here after your first assignment? Back when you were studying literature?"

Ayanna smiled, the memory surfacing easily. "We couldn't afford the drinks then. We ordered one each and nursed them all night."

"You wore that blue dress with the torn hem that you kept fixing with safety pins," Simon continued, his voice warm with nostalgia. "And you were so nervous about the feedback that you checked your email seventeen times between rounds."

"Fifteen, at most," Ayanna protested, laughing. "And you weren't much better. You kept asking the staff if they had a good Wi-Fi signal."

Simon grinned, acknowledging the truth of her recollection. "And now look at you. A completed manuscript. All that work finally paying off." "And still nervous," Ayanna added, but the admission carried none of the heaviness it might have earlier. "Just in new ways." The server returned, offering them a second round. They both declined, preferring to extend the pleasant buzz of the first drinks rather than push toward intoxication. Instead, they ordered sparkling water with lime, a tradition they'd established years ago, always end the evening clear-headed enough to enjoy the walk home. As the night deepened around them, the lounge grew quieter, patrons gradually departing until only the most dedicated remained. The trio played with increasing intimacy, as if performing for close friends rather than customers. Simon and Ayanna's conversation meandered from the manuscript to future plans, to friends they needed to reconnect with, to the possibility of a brief getaway once the book was released.

The bill arrived, tucked discreetly into a leather folder. Simon reached for it automatically, but Ayanna's hand covered his. "This one's mine," she said firmly. "For all the cups of tea and backrubs and listening to me read the same paragraph sixteen different ways."

Simon inclined his head in acceptance, watching as she slipped her card into the folder. Their fingers brushed as she passed it back to him to hand to the server, a casual contact that still carried a charge after years together. As they prepared to leave, gathering coats and exchanging quiet nods with the staff, Ayanna felt a sense of completion that had nothing to do with manuscripts or publishing. It was the feeling of being fully seen and understood, of sharing both accomplishments and uncertainties with someone who valued both equally. They slid out of the booth together, Simon extending his hand to help her to her feet though she needed no assistance. Their fingers intertwined naturally as they navigated between tables toward the exit. At the door, they paused to button coats against the night air, now considerably cooler than when they had arrived. "Ready?" Simon asked, the question encompassing more than just their departure from the lounge.

Ayanna nodded, squeezing his hand once before they stepped out into the night, leaving the warm amber light behind them but carrying its glow within.

The next afternoon sunlight spilled through the gauzy curtains of Alice's kitchen, painting golden rectangles across the dining table. The light caught the rim of a blue willow plate, traced the edge of a sterling silver fork, and warmed the petals of wild daisies and black-eyed Susans arranged haphazardly in a hand-thrown clay vase. Ayanna adjusted her position slightly, shifting the manuscript on her lap so that it remained hidden beneath the table, not yet ready to be presented. Across from her, her mother poured tea from a floral pot that didn't match any of the cups on the table, a collection of orphaned china Alice had accumulated over decades of car boot sales. "You take lemon now, don't you?" Alice asked, her hand hovering over a small dish of thin yellow slice, an effort to prove she was paying attention. "Yes, please" Ayanna replied, watching as her mother's slender fingers delicately deposited a lemon slice into her cup.
The kitchen was neat but lived-in, filled with evidence of Alice's solitary life since Ayanna had left. Cookbooks lined a

small shelf above the counter, their spines cracked, and pages marked with post-it notes. A single breakfast dish dried in the rack by the sink. The refrigerator bore magnets from places Alice had visited, small acts of independence after decades of life under the watchful scrutiny of her family. Simon stood in the doorway between the kitchen and the living room, a half-empty glass of water in his hand. He'd positioned himself there with deliberate casualness, present but giving the women space for their growing relationship. His eyes met Ayanna's briefly, a silent checking that she answered with a happy nod.

"The garden is coming along beautifully," Ayanna offered, nodding toward the window where they could see raised beds contained neat rows of vegetables. Her mother had taken up gardening after the fallout after Granny's funeral, another reclamation of space and time.

"The tomatoes are nearly ready," Alice replied, a hint of pride warming her voice. She paused, her fork tapping lightly against her plate in a nervous rhythm. "And the writing? You mentioned on the phone that you'd finished?"

Ayanna felt the weight of the manuscript on her lap, its pages held together with a large binder clip. She'd had it professionally printed and bound that morning, wanting this copy to feel substantial, real. "I have," she said, her voice steady despite the fluttering in her stomach. "It's done."

Alice's eyes brightened, though her expression remained carefully measured. "That's wonderful, sweetheart. How long did it take in the end?"

"Almost a year," Simon answered from the doorway, his voice carrying a note of gentle pride. "Though she's been living it much longer than that."

The comment hung in the air, its implications understood by everyone in the room.

Alice's looked momentarily to her plate, where she'd been pushing around a piece of quiche without eating it. When she looked up again, a new resolve had settled in her features. "I'm so proud of you," she said quietly.

Ayanna nodded, feeling Simon's attentive presence like a steady hand at her back. "Thank you."

A small, genuine smile crossed Alice's face, softening the fine lines around her eyes. She reached across the table, her fingers lightly tapping Ayanna's wrist where it rested beside her teacup. "You know, one day I might be counting tiny feet alongside those freckles," she said, deliberately changing the subject to safer ground. The non sequitur, her mother's habitual retreat to talk of potential grandchildren whenever emotional waters deepened, would once have frustrated Ayanna. Today, she recognised it as her mother's attempt to express continuity, to project their relationship forward beyond the reckoning that the memoir represented. She allowed herself a brief, genuine smile in return.

"One day, perhaps," she acknowledged, neither shutting down the possibility nor making promises. "But today, I have something else to share with you."

With deliberate movements, Ayanna lifted the manuscript from her lap and placed it on the table between them. Alice's breath caught audibly. For a long moment, no one spoke. The refrigerator hummed in the background, and somewhere in the distance, a lawn mower started with a distant growl.

"This is it?" Alice finally asked, her voice barely above a whisper. "The whole thing?"

Ayanna nodded. "The complete manuscript." From the doorway, Simon watched as Alice hesitantly extended her hand toward the stack of paper, her fingers stopping just short of touching it. The gesture reminded him of someone approaching an altar, filled with reverence and trepidation.

Chapter Twenty-Three

"May I?" Alice asked, looking up at her daughter with eyes that held equal parts fear and longing.

"Of course," Ayanna said softly. "It's why I brought it."

"There will be difficult parts," Ayanna said gently, watching her mother's face. "Things that might be painful to read. But I've tried to be honest without being cruel, and to understand rather than simply accuse." She paused, then added, "I learned that from you, too, in recent years."

Alice looked up, surprise momentarily displacing the complex emotions on her face. "From me?"

Ayanna nodded. "You've shown remarkable courage since Granny died, facing truths about everything that would have been so much easier to deny. Watching you rebuild your life has been... Amazing."

A flush of colour rose in Alice's cheeks, pleasure and embarrassment mingling visibly. Her hand moved across the table, not stopping until her fingers gently squeezed Ayanna's. The gesture conveyed what words might have complicated, acknowledgment, gratitude, a willingness to face whatever the pages contained.

The clock on the wall ticked steadily, marking the passage of this pivotal moment. Outside, clouds shifted, momentarily dimming the sunlight before it returned in full force, illuminating the tableau at the table with renewed clarity. Simon moved then, stepping fully into the kitchen with a deliberate lightness. "Should I put on some more tea?" he asked, his voice gentle but matter of fact, offering a practical next step to carry them forward.

"That would be lovely," Alice replied, withdrawing her hand from Ayanna's but maintaining the connection through her gaze. "The beans are in the cupboard, I got that Ethiopian blend you mentioned liking." The small gesture, remembering Simon's preference, showed the gentle regard and care Alice had been steadily building in recent years, attempting to repair what had once been broken through inattention.

Ayanna watched as Simon moved comfortably around her mother's kitchen, opening cabinets with the familiarity of someone who had visited often. His ease in this space was relatively new, developed over the past two years as Ayanna and her mother had cautiously rebuilt their relationship. Initially, he had been a buffer between them, his presence making difficult conversations possible by diluting their intensity. Gradually, he had become a welcome part of their reconfigured family dynamic. "I'd like to read it while you're here," Alice asked, her hand resting lightly on the manuscript's cover. "Not all of it today, of course, but perhaps a chapter? So, we can talk about it?"

The request surprised Ayanna. She had expected her mother might want privacy for her first encounter with the text, time to process her reactions away from witnessing eyes. This desire to share the experience, to invite conversation rather than retreat from it, represented a significant departure from old patterns.

"I'd like that," Ayanna replied, warmth spreading through her chest at this unexpected gift. "Perhaps after coffee?"

Alice nodded, a smile transforming her face in a way that momentarily revealed the younger woman she had been before life and motherhood had reshaped her. The coffee maker began to bubble and hiss under Simon's attention, releasing a rich aroma that mingled with the scent of the wildflowers on the table.

The three of them moved together in choreography, clearing lunch dishes from the table to make space for the ritual of tea, coffee and reading. Ayanna collected the plates, stacking them carefully before carrying them to the sink. Simon retrieved cream from the refrigerator, pouring it into a small pitcher that matched none of the other dishes. Alice folded napkins, her movements precise and deliberate, a habit from decades of maintaining perfect order in her household.

"I've been thinking," Alice said as she arranged cookies on a plate, her voice carefully casual, "about taking a writing class at the college. Just a beginner's course. Nothing fancy."

Ayanna looked up from rinsing plates, catching Simon's eye over her mother's head. His raised eyebrows mirrored her own surprise. "That sounds wonderful, Mum. Any particular reason?"

Alice shrugged lightly, though the gesture couldn't disguise the significance of her words. "Reading your emails these past months, hearing you talk about your process... it made me realise I've never really expressed myself that way. I have stories too, you know. Different ones, but still mine."

The simple statement hung in the air, a revelation that shifted something fundamental between mother and daughter. Ayanna felt a constriction in her throat, an emotion too complex to name rising like a tide. "I think that's a brilliant idea," Simon said, filling the silence as he poured coffee into mismatched cups. "Writing has a way of clarifying things, even if no one else ever reads it."

"Exactly," Alice agreed, seeming relieved at his understanding. She carried the plate of cookies to the table, setting it beside the manuscript that waited like a bridge between past and future. "Besides, it might help me understand your work better, Ayanna. To try it myself."

Ayanna dried her hands on a dish towel, taking a moment to compose herself before turning. "I'd be happy to help you find the right class," she offered, her voice steady despite the unexpected compassion she felt. "Or recommend books to start with."

As they settled back around the table, the manuscript remained at its centre, no longer an object of trepidation but a point of connection. Simon poured coffee into Alice's cup first, then Ayanna's, finally his own, the domestic ritual underscoring the normalcy of this extraordinary moment.

Alice opened the manuscript again, this time turning past the dedication to the first page of the introduction. "Would you read it?" she asked Ayanna, pushing the pages gently across the table. "I'd like to hear it in your voice first."

Ayanna glanced at Simon, who had taken a seat beside her, his presence solid and reassuring. He nodded slightly, an encouragement that required no words. Clearing her throat, Ayanna began to read, her voice gathering strength with each sentence. The words she had laboured over for months flowed into the sunlit kitchen, transforming the familiar space into something new, a place where truth could be spoken and heard, where past and present could converse without drowning each other out, where three people could begin to write a different story together.

Outside, the afternoon light began its slow shift toward evening, but inside, time seemed suspended in a moment of possibility, not an ending, but a beginning disguised as one.

A note from the Author

The truth is a malleable thing. This book was born from real fragments, shards of memory, yet it also bears the imprint of imagination, the longing for a resolution I never found in life. Some events described here happened precisely as I've told them; others I only wish had been part of my story.

I never confronted the whole of my family with the righteous fury I imagined. I didn't have the courage, or maybe I was worn down from years of fractures in the place we all called "home." But I did confront one of them. And that, finally, changed something.

Some of the people in this book are drawn directly from life. Their words, their acts, and their choices, those remain embedded in my memory, even if some of the details have become lost under time's relentless current. Barney did too, but his shape shifted over time. The pain he caused didn't end with the act, it lived on in the silence, the unspoken years, the absence of any apology. But when I finally found the strength to speak to him many years later as an adult with my own children, he didn't deny it, deflect it, or excuse it. He listened. He owned it. His eventual apology was not performative, not easy. It was slow, careful, and steeped in a kind of sorrow that felt sincere. That doesn't undo what happened; but it was the first time someone who hurt me truly saw the damage and said, *"I did that. I was wrong. I'm sorry."* I never expected to hear those words. I'm still not sure what to do with them. But they mattered.

Arthur, too, shaped my childhood in ways that left their mark. The version of him in these pages is written through the eyes of a child who needed someone to intervene and didn't get that. But in the years since, Arthur has shown up in ways I didn't expect. He's been there for my mother during her hardest times. He's stepped in quietly, supportively, as an adult when others stayed absent. That doesn't erase the past. But it adds dimension, and I believe it's only fair to say so.

If you are reading this and see yourself reflected in these pages; please understand this wasn't written in cruelty or as an act of revenge. It came from a place of silence that lasted too long. The child in this story remembers what she needed. The adult who wrote it remembers who eventually showed up. Both versions are true.

I also want to clarify: some characters were invented out of necessity. They fill the spaces where truth offered only a dead end. Where I needed kindness, or a guiding light, I wrote someone new into existence. Where life was grey, I painted in colour. Perhaps it's a form of self-preservation, an attempt to weave warmth into the cold places still lodged in my heart.

And then there's Simon; the anchor who held me steady through storms I never thought I could weather. Let me be blunt: he was no fairy-tale knight in shining armour. I never wanted that, and frankly, the idea of being "rescued" is just awful to me. I wasn't looking for someone to fight all my battles for me. What Simon did was much more valuable: he taught me how to heal myself. He never minimised the damage or told me to simply "move on." Instead, he gave me space to fall apart and helped me gather the pieces, carefully and patiently, until I began to see that I was worth saving. In the times I wavered or felt unworthy, he offered gentle reminders that my scars did not define me; they were simply one chapter in a much longer book. Step by step, he showed me that it's possible to stand up again without losing the softer parts of who you are.

Looking back, I'm aware of how many stories I left untold or only hinted at in passing. I can't change everything that happened. I can't force forgiveness or rewrite my own history of silence. But by committing these pages to the world, I've found a measure of solace, an affirmation that even in the grip of heartbreak, there can be growth, and that even if "family" fails in its promises, we can forge new bonds that are as strong as blood.

So, yes, this is based on a true story, and in many ways it's also a wishful fairytale I pulled together for my own heart. Fiction and reality co-exist here, often inseparably, and I don't regret that mixture. Sometimes, telling the absolute truth is too bleak. Sometimes, we need the space to dream of what could have been, especially if it helps us imagine what still might be.

In the end, the greatest truth in these pages is that no single person, no matter how brave or broken, needs to walk alone. While Simon was never my "knight" (and I would never have let him be), he travelled beside me. He kept my secret terrors at bay, not with grand gestures but with everyday reassurance, cups of tea, small words of comfort, a hand always reaching out when I stumbled. And that small, unwavering truth has become the touchstone for this entire journey: we are all worthy of healing, love, and hope, even if we can't slay every dragon that lurks in our past.

Printed in Dunstable, United Kingdom